MURDER SUICIDE

MURDER

SUICIDE

KEITH ABLOW

ST. MARTIN'S PRESS ☙ NEW YORK

www.stmartins.com

Book design by Jonathan Bennett

Library of Congress Cataloging-in-Publication Data

Ablow, Keith R.
    Murder suicide / Keith Ablow.—1st ed.
      p. cm.
    ISBN 0-312-32389-1
    EAN 978-0312-32389-9
    1. Clevenger, Frank (Fictitious character)—Fiction. 2. Millionaires—Crimes against—Fiction. 3. Inventors—Crimes against—Fiction.
4. Forensic psychiatrists—Fiction. 5. Massachusetts—Fiction.
6. Epileptics—Fiction. I. Title.

PS3551.B58M87 2004
813'.54—dc22

                                      2004045057

First Edition: July 2004

10 9 8 7 6 5 4 3 2 1

For Karen Ablow

ACKNOWLEDGMENTS

I am tremendously grateful to my editor, Charles Spicer, my agent, Beth Vesel, and my publishers, Sally Richardson and Matthew Shear, who care so deeply about their work—and mine. No writer stands in better company.

Early reads by Christopher Keane, Jeanette and Allan Ablow, Paul Abruzzi, Stephen Bennett, Charles "Red" Donovan, Julian and Jeanne Geiger, Michael Homler, Rock Positano, and attorney Anthony Traini were invaluable.

My friend, collaborator, and co-therapist, the irrepressible gentleman genius J. Christopher Burch, was there every step of the way.

Finally, I thank my wife, Deborah, daughter, Devin, and son, Cole, for constant reminders of how magical and moving life stories can be.

But when the self speaks to the self, who is speaking?—
the entombed soul, the spirit driven in, in, in to the central
catacomb; the self that took the veil and left the world—
a coward perhaps, yet somehow beautiful, as it flits with
its lantern restlessly up and down the dark corridors.

—Virginia Woolf, "An Unwritten Novel"

MURDER SUICIDE

PROLOGUE

The shadow of night still clung to a frosty Boston morning, the silence broken only by the crisp, clean sounds of the slide on a Glock handgun being pulled back, a 9mm slug popping up out of the magazine, clicking into the chamber.

John Snow, fifty, M.I.T. professor, genius inventor, stood in an alleyway between the Blake and Ellison towers of the Massachusetts General Hospital, just off Francis Street. He was scheduled for experimental neurosurgery one hour later, surgery that would radically alter his entire life.

He looked down at the gun aimed at his chest. His pulse raced with fear, but it was fear once-removed, like that of a witness to another man's shooting. He wondered whether that was because he had already said good-bye to the people he loved—or had once loved.

"You can't do this," he said, his voice trembling, his words wafting off the buildings.

Silence, again. A freezing drizzle starting to fall. The gun shaking slightly.

"If you ever want to be more than what you are, you have to be able to reinvent yourself."

The gun steadied.

He heard footsteps in the distance. He glanced down the alleyway, the faintest hope lifting his heavy heart.

The barrel of the gun touched his chest, just below his sternum.

He closed his gloved fist around it.

The barrel pressed harder against him.

The footsteps were coming closer.

"You can't hold onto the past," he managed, through clenched teeth.

The trigger of the gun started to move.

He sunk to his knees and peered up into the darkness, speechless now, his mind finding what comfort it could in the words that had sustained him during his medical odyssey, words from the Bhagavad Gita, the holy Hindu text that had inspired Thoreau and Ghandi:

Death is certain for anyone born, and birth is certain for the dead; since the cycle is inevitable, you have no cause to grieve.

The gun moved a few inches off his chest.

He managed a tight smile.

The trigger started moving, again.

He felt the pain before he heard the blast, pain beyond anything and everything he had ever known or imagined, a bolt of lightning exploding through him, searing into his chest, his arms and legs and groin and head, so that he could barely see and certainly could not feel his blood as it soaked his shirt and hands, spilling through his fingers, onto the pavement. It was pain that obliterated anything in its path, so that after a moment it seemed too great for his body to contain, then too great for his mind to contain. And then it was as though it did not even belong to him. And then it did not exist at all. He was free of it, and of all his suffering, and of everyone—just as he had intended to be.

ONE

Paramedics rushed John Snow into the Mass General emergency room at 4:45 A.M., unconscious, with shallow respirations. They had radioed ahead, reporting Snow as the victim of a self-inflicted gunshot wound to the chest. Snow's neurosurgeon, J. T. "Jet" Heller, thirty-nine, was one of the six doctors and five nurses who responded to the code red.

A medical intern named Peter Stratton had heard the gunshot on his way home from a night on call and dialed 911 from his cell phone. Police responded and found Snow collapsed in the alleyway in a pool of blood. His arms and legs were tucked close to his chest, fetal position. A black leather travel bag and a Glock 9mm handgun lay on the pavement beside him.

Snow was stabilized in the field, but his EKG flatlined as he crossed the threshold into the E.R. The team shocked his heart back into rhythm three times, but his pulse never lingered longer than several seconds.

It was Heller who took the heroic steps, starting with a pericardiocentesis. Heart muscle is surrounded by a tough, membranous sac called the pericardium, stretched around it like a latex glove. But a bleed (a pericardial effusion) can occur between the muscle and the membrane, causing the pericardium to swell like a water balloon, putting pressure on the heart and preventing it from

3

pumping. So when Snow's heart would respond to nothing else, Heller inserted a six-inch hypodermic needle under Snow's sternum and drove it down toward the heart at a thirty degree angle, aiming to pierce the pericardium, siphon off any pooled blood and free the left ventricle to do its job. He tried seven times, but each time he pulled back on the syringe, he got nothing but air.

Snow's EKG had been flat line for over a minute.

"Should we call it?" a nurse asked.

Heller swept his long, blond hair back off his face. He stared down at Snow. "Get me a syringe filled with epi," he said.

Epinephrine was a cardiac stimulant sometimes administered intravenously to patients in cardiac arrest. No one moved to get it. They knew J. T. Heller had something much more invasive than an I.V. in mind, and they knew it was futile. Whether the bullet had ripped a hole in Snow's heart or transected his aorta, the wound had been fatal.

"He's gone, Jet," Aaron Kaplan, another of the doctors, said. "I know he's your patient, but . . ."

"Get me the epi," Heller said, his sapphire blue eyes still fixed on Snow.

The team exchanged glances.

Heller pushed his way past the others to the code cart, rifled through the supplies, came up with a syringe full of epinephrine. He walked back beside Snow, squirted a bit of the epi into the air, then thrust the needle under Snow's sternum and emptied the 10cc directly into his left ventricle. He glared up at the monitor. "Beat, goddamn you!" He kept staring five, ten, twenty seconds. But there was only that flat line, that terrible hum.

Then Heller took the ultimate step. He reached to the bedside tray, picked up a scalpel and, with no hesitation, cut a six-inch transverse incision below Snow's sternum, reached into Snow's chest, grabbed hold of his heart and began open cardiac massage, rhythmically squeezing and letting go of the thick, muscular cardiac walls, trying to manually throw the heart back into gear.

"For Christ's sake, Jet," another doctor whispered, "it's over."

Heller pumped even more vigorously. "Don't quit on me," he kept muttering. "Don't you quit on me." But it was no use. Every time Heller stopped squeezing, Snow's EKG drifted back to a flat line.

Heller finally took his bloody, gloved hand out of Snow's chest. And as he did, Snow began to seize, his whole body trembling like a fish out of water, his teeth chattering, his eyes rolling back in his head. The seizure lasted just half-a-minute. Then Snow lay completely still, his eyes staring blankly at the ceiling.

Heller backed away from the gurney. He was soaked with sweat and blood. He stared at Snow, shook his head, as if in a daze. "You coward," he said. "You . . ." He looked up at the others. "I'll call it." He glanced at the clock on the wall. "Time of death, 5:17 A.M."

TWO

Grace Baxter, owner of a toney Newbury Street art gallery, wife of George Reese, founder and president of the Beacon Street Bank & Trust, hugged herself to stop from shaking. Her internist had kept her on Zoloft and Ambien and a little Klonopin for about a year, but it was her very first hour of psychotherapy, and quite possibly the very first time someone had listened to her—really listened to her—for anything close to an hour. "I'm sorry to fall apart like this," she whispered. "But the medicines aren't working. I don't want to get up in the morning. I don't want to go to work. I don't want to get into bed with my husband at night. I don't want this life."

Dr. Frank Clevenger, 48, glanced out the window of his Chelsea waterfront office at the line of cars creeping over the steel skeleton of the Tobin Bridge as it arched into Boston. He wondered how many of the people inside those cars really wanted to be going where they were headed. How many of them had the luxury of ending up somewhere where they would be expressing something genuine about themselves, or at least something that didn't make them feel like frauds, playing dress-up? How many of them would be returning to homes they wanted to live in? "Are you thinking of hurting yourself, Grace?" he asked gently, looking over at her.

"I just want the pain to stop." She rocked back and forth in her seat. "And I don't want to hurt anyone ever again."

Irrational feelings of guilt were one of the hallmarks of major depression. Some patients actually came to believe they were responsible for the Holocaust or for all the suffering in the world. "Hurt them in what way?" Clevenger asked her.

She looked down. "I'm a bad person. A horrible, horrible person."

Clevenger watched tears start down her cheeks. She was thirty-eight and still exquisite, but her wavy, auburn hair, emerald green eyes and the perfect slope of her nose and cheekbones all said she had been otherworldly at twenty-six, when she had married George Reese, fourteen years her senior and already fabulously wealthy. Only now, with her physical presence just beginning to wane, was she confronting the fact that she wasn't in love with her husband or her work or her lifestyle—not the expensive cars or the private jet or the Beacon Hill townhouse or the vacation homes on Nantucket and in Aspen. She was beginning to suspect that beauty and wealth had carried her far away from her *self* and she didn't know the way back or whether there would be anything left of her if she ever made it back. "Sometimes hurting other people can't be avoided, Grace," Clevenger said. "Not if you intend to be a complete person yourself."

Baxter folded her hands on her lap. "When I married him, he let me keep my name. It was supposed to be a symbol that neither of us owned the other." Her fingers tugged at the three diamond tennis bracelets she wore on one wrist. Her thumb rubbed the face of the gold and diamond Rolex she wore on the other. "I hate these things," she said. "George gave them to me. Anniversary gifts. They might as well be handcuffs."

That comment made Clevenger wonder just how dark Grace's thoughts really were. Maybe she was floating an elegant metaphor for life in a gilded cage, but the fact that she had mentioned hurting someone and wearing handcuffs in the same minute worried him. Maybe she had something truly destructive in mind.

In the year since Clevenger had solved the Highway Killer case, catching serial killer Jonah Wrens before he could dump another decapitated body along some lonely stretch of asphalt, the gap between his forensic work and his psychotherapy practice had been closing. Not too many garden variety depressives and neurotics showed up at his door. Most of the people looking for him to heal them were struggling against the impulse to harm others.

Grace wouldn't be the first woman to feel imprisoned enough by her marriage to trade it for a jail cell. "Is there anyone you fantasize about hurting?" he asked her.

She squinted at the floor, clearly imagining something. Whatever it was made her blush. "No," she said. She looked up and smoothed imaginary wrinkles out of her skirt. "I just meant I want to be a better person. I want to learn to appreciate what I have."

That sounded like a dodge. People blush when one of their core truths is revealed. Something with roots in the soul. The name of a lover. A sexual preference. Even a deeply held personal goal. And it was looking more and more like the impulse to harm someone was part of Grace's core. That fact—more than her pat explanation that she had seen Clevenger talking about the Highway Killer on television and liked the looks of his jeans and black turtleneck and shaved head—might really explain why she had chosen to seek therapy from a forensic psychiatrist with a knack for getting inside the heads of killers.

"You can tell me," Clevenger prodded her.

"I have to go," Grace said, wiping her eyes. "I swear to you: I'm not a danger to anyone, including myself. I never have those thoughts."

That was what psychiatrists call a *contract for safety*, the words a potentially dangerous patient has to speak to avoid being involuntarily hospitalized—committed to a locked psychiatric unit. It made Clevenger wonder whether Grace knew her way around the psychiatric profession a little better than she let on. "I need to ask you quite directly: Do you have any intention of hurting your husband?"

"'Do I have . . .' That's ridiculous." She stared at him, unblinking.

He returned her stare. "Fair enough."

She stood up, ran her fingertips down the row of gold buttons on her black Chanel jacket. "I'll call and schedule something in the next few days, if you have an opening."

Clevenger kept his seat. He wanted to make it clear that the decision to avoid going deeper was Grace's, and hers alone. She would have to turn her back on him. On the truth. "We still have ten minutes," he said.

She stood there several seconds, looking uncomfortable, as though Clevenger's silence might coax her back into her seat. But then she turned abruptly and walked out.

Clevenger watched through his window as she walked briskly to her car, a big, blue BMW sedan, with smoked windows. She fumbled in her handbag, shook it violently, reached in again. She started to cry. She finally pulled out her keys, threw open the car door and disappeared inside, slamming the door behind her.

"Does she get a refund?" North Anderson asked, from the doorway to Clevenger's office.

Clevenger turned to him.

"She looked worse on her way out than on her way in."

Anderson had been Clevenger's partner at Boston Forensics for the past two years. He was a former Baltimore cop turned private investigator, a black man who looked a decade younger than his forty-four years, probably because he was addicted to weightlifting—three hours every day. There wasn't an ounce of fat left on his body. The only hints that he'd lived the tough life he had were the jagged scar over his right eye and the slight limp to his left leg, the former from a suspect wielding a knife, the latter from one with a .45. Both of them had ended up face-down on the pavement. The one with the knife went to jail. The one with the gun went to the morgue.

"She's living a lie," Clevenger said, glancing at Baxter's car pulling past the chain-link fence and gate that separated the Fitzgerald Shipyard—where Boston Forensics made its home— from the rest of Chelsea. "That hurts. More and more every day."

"The truth will set you free," Anderson said. "Unless you're guilty." He smiled the winning smile that made people like him and open up to him, as easily in Boston as they had in Baltimore. Because he liked people, with all their foibles. "We got a call from a Detective Mike Coady, out of Boston P.D."

"What's up?" Clevenger asked.

"You know that guy about to have brain surgery at Mass General?"

"Sure, scheduled for it this morning. John Snow. He was front-page in *The Globe* again."

"His surgery's been canceled."

"Why?"

"He's dead."

"Dead? From what?"

"They found him in an alleyway between a couple of buildings at the hospital. Took a 9mm slug to his chest."

"Jesus. They have the shooter?"

"Coady thinks so—Snow himself."

"He committed suicide?"

"No witnesses. The bullet came from Snow's own gun."

"So what does Coady need us for?" Clevenger asked.

"The Medical Examiner won't officially rule out murder," Anderson said. He crossed his massive arms. "Coady has a backlog of eleven open murder cases."

"So the good detective wants me to come up with a convenient psychological profile, posthumously, to fit the suicide theory," Clevenger said. He shook his head. "I'll call and tell him to live or die on the ballistics report."

Anderson shrugged. "I could poke around, see if there's any talk on the streets, just to get a flavor of the thing."

"Why waste the energy, if all Coady wants is a rubber stamp to close the case?"

"Nobody really believes we rubber-stamp anything."

"Maybe that's why he's hoping we do this time. Instant credibility." He picked up the receiver. "Got his number?"

"Sure," Anderson said. But he just stood there.

Clevenger looked at him askance. "What?"

"You know how you sometimes get a gut feeling? I mean, maybe I'm buying all the hype on this Snow guy, but he was about to travel some medical ground that's never been traveled before. He was gonna make history. Every reporter in the country was angling for an interview with the guy post-op. I'm no shrink, but I figure that kind of momentum can carry you through some pretty bad days. And he shoots himself in an alleyway, a stone's throw from the O.R.? That doesn't make a whole lot of sense."

"You don't think he killed himself."

"I think that's the answer Coady is looking for. It might be the right one. But a man took a bullet to the chest this morning, and my gut tells me to get the whole story."

"From a dead man."

"If the truth was easy to come by," Anderson said, "Coady wouldn't have called you in the first place."

THREE

Clevenger climbed into his black Ford F-150 pickup and started the drive over the Tobin Bridge to Boston. He had arranged to meet Detective Mike Coady at the morgue on Albany Street at noon. If he was going to get inside John Snow's head, he figured he might as well start with his corpse—the last page of his life story—and work backwards.

What he knew already about Snow he had learned from newspapers and television. Snow was an aeronautical engineer who had received his Ph.D. at Harvard, rising through the ranks of academia to become—at thirty-two—the youngest person to ever win a full professorship at the Massachusetts Institute of Technology's famed Lincoln Lab. A few years later he left M.I.T. to start Snow-Coroway Engineering, headquartered in Cambridge. And over the next two decades he had seen his inventions in the fields of radar technology and rocket propulsion net more than one hundred million dollars from firms like Boeing and Lockheed Martin.

But Snow's genius seemed to have come at a price. He suffered seizures, as though the combined force of knowledge and inspiration swirling through his mind sometimes surged too intensely. And these were not the subtle, absence seizures that made a person stare off into space. They were tonic-clonic, grand mal seizures that made Snow collapse, unconscious, breathing like a bellows, his

13

limbs jerking wildly, his teeth clamping shut, sometimes tearing through his tongue.

According to a *20/20* segment on Snow, he had had his first seizure at age ten while struggling to solve an equation his calculus tutor had laid before him, an equation that would have frustrated most mathematicians. When Snow snapped his pencil in two, the tutor apologized for asking too much of him. But then he noticed that Snow had scrawled the correct answer at the bottom of the page—and that his rigid limbs were beginning to shake.

His mother and father feared the worst—a brain tumor. But a neurological work-up revealed no mass. There was no bleed, no infarct. An EEG told the story: clusters of delta and theta electrical spikes shooting through his temporal lobes, sparking up toward his frontal lobes. Bolts of inspiration gone wild.

John Snow had epilepsy. And while Dilantin controlled it when he was a boy, only a combination of two medications half-controlled it by the time he finished high school. By age thirty-five, he was taking three medicines and still seizing. The more intensely he focused on what he loved—inventing—the more he suffered. It was as if his gift fueled his disease. By fifty, his regimen included four anticonvulsants. And even on that cocktail of drugs, he would collapse in fits at least a dozen times a year.

So John Snow had set out to fix his broken brain. He'd read dozens of neurology and neurosurgery textbooks, journals and research studies, interviewed neurologists and neurosurgeons around the world, scoured the Internet, all in pursuit of the answer to a single question: What parts of his brain would need to be removed to rid him of the runaway circuits responsible for his convulsions?

That was a daunting question because the brain's circuitry was wet. Trouble tended to seep through the tissue. Each nerve cell in the brain (and there were billions) was constantly leaking and absorbing charged ions as electrical current traveled down its long axon, dead-ending into a collection of membranous bubbles that held chemical messengers like serotonin and norepinephrine, bursting those bubbles, spilling the chemicals onto the next nerve cell down the line. And so on and so on. A mind-boggling electrochemical chain reaction cascading in every direction.

But not infinitely. The brain had discreet structures within it, too, like states in a country, with boundaries that were difficult to cross, even for electricity.

Snow convinced his neurologist to order him a complex combination of EEGs, PET scans, and MRIs to hunt for his pathology. Then he wrote a software program that cross-referenced the results, generating a three-dimensional computer image of his brain in which the areas that were most clearly implicated in his seizures glowed red. Those under less suspicion glowed blue. Taken together, they included parts of the brain's temporal lobe, occipital lobe, cingulate gyrus, amygdala and hippocampus—the staging grounds for the neuroterrorism that besieged him.

Next, Snow handpicked his neurosurgeon—J. T. "Jet" Heller, Chairman of the Massachusetts General Hospital Department of Neurosurgery. Just thirty-nine years old, brilliant and brash, Heller had made a name for himself successfully separating Siamese twins joined at the head. He had also become famous for elegant, nearly bloodless cryosurgery to remove aggressive glioblastoma brain tumors while sparing healthy tissue.

Heller was a maverick willing to go out on a limb for a patient and attempt what seemed impossible, even if it meant clashing with the Mass General establishment, including the Medical Ethics Committee. He'd done it for Snow, holding a press conference to protest the Ethics Committee's initial decision to block Snow's surgery on the basis that it was too aggressive and could have unforeseeable side effects—including possible damage to Snow's vision, memory and speech. It was Snow's right, Heller argued, to decide what he was willing to risk to rid himself of his illness. He threatened to resign from the medical staff if the Committee ultimately refused him permission to proceed.

Boston radio talk show hosts like Kiss 108's legendary Matty Siegel took up Snow's cause. Letters streamed into the hospital. Nationally renowned medical ethicists weighed in on his side. And, in a rare reversal, the Ethics Committee reconvened and greenlighted the procedure.

Now Snow was dead, shot through the heart less than an hour before he was scheduled to go under the knife. Maybe, Clevenger thought, Heller's commitment to get Snow his surgery had outpaced Snow's own desire for it. Snow might have been swept along in the campaign to overturn the Ethics Committee's ruling and not known how to tell Heller he had changed his mind. He could have arrived at MGH despondent, having to choose between bailing out and continuing to suffer debilitating seizures or braving surgery that might blind him or leave him mute. Maybe he couldn't live with either choice.

Clevenger parked outside the morgue and walked inside. The receptionist told him he could find Jeremiah Wolfe, the Medical Examiner, in the "cold room" where autopsies were performed. Detective Coady was with him.

Clevenger walked down the concrete-block corridor, through a set of swinging doors, into the chilly air. Jazz music played on a tinny loudspeaker. Wolfe and Coady were standing on either side of a stainless steel table where a body lay under a sheet. "Doctor Clevenger," Wolfe called out, "welcome."

Wolfe was near seventy, a wafer-thin man with round spectacles and a full head of unruly, unnaturally black hair. He had shown Clevenger more dead bodies than either man wanted to remember.

"We never seem to find a nice occasion," Clevenger said, heading over.

"Occupational hazard," Wolfe said. "Detective Coady," he said, nodding across the table at a bulldog of a man, about forty-five, with red hair and a ruddy complexion, dressed in a dark blue suit. He stood about five-foot-seven, with massive shoulders.

"Thanks for coming, Doc," Coady said.

Clevenger shook Coady's meaty hand. Then he stared down at Snow's lifeless face, all the energy that had animated his inventive mind and athletic body gone to who knows where. He looked twenty years older than the slightly unkempt, but strikingly handsome man Clevenger had seen on television days before; his eyes now seemingly focused on something very far away, empty of the obvious intelligence that had once burned through them, his skin already the gray of dried parchment, his full head of silver hair matted with blood. "He looks even worse than they usually do," Clevenger said.

"The Glock will do that," Coady said. He nodded at a bloody 9mm slug on a stainless steel tray beside the table.

"He lost nearly seventy percent of his blood volume," Wolfe said.

Maybe that explained how empty Snow looked. But Clevenger thought he sensed something else missing. There was nothing in Snow's expression that gave him the sense that he was at peace. At first, he dismissed the observation, told himself he was making more of Snow's tight lips, set jaw and searching eyes than he should, that he was probably seeing nothing more than early rigor mortis. But that didn't erase what he felt in his gut. Because even though he was a medical doctor, even though he had studied physics and epidemiology and biochemistry long before psychiatry, the scientist in him had not suffocated the poet. And he could not deny having the distinct impression that there was a piece of work to be done before John Snow could truly be laid to rest. Maybe that was what North Anderson had been feeling back at the office—that Snow's story was still unfinished.

"Are you both comfortable with the music, or you'd like something else?" Wolfe asked.

Clevenger and Coady looked at one another. Coady shrugged.

"I think we're fine," Clevenger said.

"Take note," Wolfe said, "there was a Herculean effort made on Dr. Snow's behalf in the E.R." He checked to make sure the warning had registered. Then he pulled back the sheet.

"Holy Christ," Coady said.

A hole the size of a man's fist—Jet Heller's fist—was ripped in Snow's chest. The left ventricle of his heart, swollen and blue-black from Heller pumping it, ballooned through the open wound. The anatomy was so distorted, the skin so mottled from bruising, that the pathology associated with Snow's cause of death—a bullet hole above his first rib—was almost completely obliterated.

"The doctors tried to save him by reaching through an incision they made in Dr. Snow's chest wall and pumping his heart by hand," Wolfe said. "As you can see, tissues were stretched, torn. I'm confident about the point of entry of the bullet, just above the first rib." He used a telescoping metal pointer to indicate the spot. "I'm certain it passed through the right ventricle of the heart and came to rest in the third thoracic vertebra. But to make an educated guess whether the wound was self-inflicted, I would need to know the bullet's precise angle of travel. That would give me an indication whether an assailant aimed the pistol, holding it level to the ground, or whether Dr. Snow, pointing the barrel upward, shot himself."

"So why can't you figure that out?" Coady asked. "The angle."

"Because the posture of the victim is also a variable. And I don't know that. Dr. Snow could have been standing straight up or leaning to his left, or his right. He could have been on his knees, begging for his life. Without knowing his position when he was struck, I can't extrapolate from his injuries and plot a clear trajectory for the bullet."

Coady shook his head. "You forgetting Chuck Stuart? You said 99.9 percent he shot himself. What's different this time?"

Coady was referring to the famous case of Charles Stuart. Back in 1989 Stuart had murdered his pregnant wife Carol and shot himself in the abdomen after parking their car in a tough Boston neighborhood. He later claimed a black man had car-jacked them on their way to a hospital birthing class, then opened fire on them.

"First of all, Stuart was known to be seated behind the wheel at the time of the 'assault.' The bullet was found in the seat back. Secondly, there's extensive iatrogenic damage here."

"Please watch the syllable count, Professor," Coady said. "I went to Zoo Mass." U. Mass., 4.0., Phi Beta Kappa, double major in criminal justice and sociology—but Coady never mentioned any of that. He didn't need the guys on the squad thinking he was any different than they were.

"*Iatrogenic*," Clevenger said. "Caused by hospital workers." He nodded at Snow's ballooning left ventricle. "The cardiac massage."

"Right," Coady said. "That's just beautiful. What about his glove?" he asked Wolfe. "Didn't you say there were powder burns left on it?"

"There is indeed evidence of gun powder on the leather," Wolfe said. "But, again, the pattern was disrupted by spillage of fluids in the E.R.—blood, IVs, antiseptic. I can't say whether it's more likely the powder was deposited when Dr. Snow held the gun and fired it or when someone else was pulling the trigger, and he tried to push the gun away."

"So you're telling me we got nothing," Coady said.

"We have precisely what we had when we spoke on the phone," Wolfe said. "Nothing conclusive."

Clevenger leaned to get a closer look at Snow's fingernails, glowing under the fluorescent lights. "Manicured," he said. "Clear nail polish, hardly any scratches."

"If he had a pedicure," Coady said, glancing at Snow's feet, "we'd at least know something conclusive about him."

Wolfe ignored Coady. "Was there a thought you wanted to share, Doctor?" he asked.

"Why would a man depressed enough to shoot himself have his nails manicured a day—two, at the most—before going through with it?" Clevenger asked.

Coady pursed his lips, nodded. "First year on the force I get called over to the Hancock Tower. Guy in a tux at a Christmas party threatening to take a header off the roof. Bow-tie, cufflinks. The whole nine yards. I bet his nails were shined up real nice."

"Point well taken," Clevenger said.

"I'm no psychiatrist," Coady said, "but so far as I can tell, people's behavior can be highly contradictory. A guy loves his wife so much he kills her when she says she's gonna leave him. Kills her because he can't stand the thought of not being with her. Makes no sense, right? 'Cause he ain't gonna be hanging out with her when she's in a box, and he's doin' life."

"It makes no sense, on the face of it," Clevenger said.

"On the face of it, right. But when somebody like you digs a little deeper—or a lot deeper—maybe the pieces start to fit. You can get into the killer's mind. His reality. Which is why I called you in. You do that with Snow here, I figure we'll understand why he blew himself away in that alley, polished fingernails and all. Then I can get the media off my back and move on to a case with a real victim."

"Not that you're trying to force anyone's hand," Wolfe said.

"Course not," Coady said.

At least Coady wasn't pretending to have an open mind, Clevenger thought. "You do have a favorite theory—that Snow committed suicide," he said. "Do you also have a theory why he did it?"

"Like I told the professor here," Coady said, "I don't think he had the guts to go to the O.R. He lost his nerve."

"A moment of cowardice," Clevenger said. "I've wondered about that." He nodded to himself. "But if he shot himself on impulse, how do we explain him taking a gun with him, in the first place?"

"He was licensed to carry. He must have wanted the gun with him when he got out of surgery."

"Why?"

"He was rich," Coady said. "He had a company doing business with military contractors. He . . ."

"He might have felt threatened," Wolfe said. "Not that it's my place to theorize."

"Anything's possible," Coady said, tightly.

"Did he drive himself to the hospital?" Clevenger asked.

"No," Coady said. "He's had a driver the past seventeen years. A Czech immigrant, name of Pavel Blazek. Guy says he dropped him off on the corner of Staniford Street, two blocks away from where he shot himself, about fifteen minutes before the 911 call came in."

"And Snow was married, with a family? I think I read that. His wife is a pretty-well-known architect."

"Wife, two kids; sixteen-year-old son, eighteen-year-old daughter."

"But he went to the hospital alone to have brain surgery. The Snows don't exactly sound like the Waltons."

"Listen, a case like this can generate plenty of suspects," Coady said. "A man was found dead in an alleyway. There were no witnesses. If we find out a dozen people hated his guts, half of them won't have alibis. Three, four of them might look like they're better off with him dead than alive. *But that doesn't mean they killed him.* The fact remains he was shot with his own gun."

"Did he have anything other than the gun with him when he was found?" Clevenger asked.

"A black leather bag with a laptop and some kind of notebook or journal inside. Pages and pages of chicken scrawl and drawings. Everything's being tagged for evidence back at the station."

"Can I get a look at it?"

"Whenever you like. I'll make you a copy of the journal and any files off the laptop."

"I could pick them up tomorrow morning."

"You got it," Coady said. He cleared his throat. "One thing: I know the media can't get enough of you since the Highway Killer case."

"There's no need for . . ." Wolfe started.

"I already got *The Globe, Herald*, and every network in town hounding me," Coady interrupted. "I'd like to avoid Geraldo Rivera, Larry King, et. al., crawling up my ass, if at all possible. If you have something to say, let's keep it between you and me."

"No comment, all the way," Clevenger said.

"Excellent," Coady said. "I appreciate it."

"No problem," Clevenger said. "One thing I can tell you right now: If this isn't a suicide, you could have another body on your hands very soon. Because if Dr. Snow didn't put that gun to his chest and blow a hole in it, it was somebody who didn't feel shy firing a Glock at point blank range while his victim watched. Someone filled with fury. And there's no reason to think he's any less angry right now."

"Thanks for the warning," Coady said coldly.

"Just between you and me."

FOUR

Clevenger had a few hours before his adopted son Billy Bishop, eighteen, needed to be picked up from boxing lessons at the Somerville Boxing Club. He decided to drive over to Mass General and drop in on J. T. Heller.

He parked in the Mass General garage and walked to the Wang building.

Heller's office suite was on the eighth floor, down a nondescript corridor that ended with a short run of mahogany, recessed paneling and incandescent wall sconces. Frosted, sliding glass doors etched with DEPARTMENT OF NEUROSURGERY, CHAIRMAN, J. T. HELLER, MD led to his waiting area.

Inside, half-a-dozen patients, a few of them with freshly shaven heads and scars bisecting their scalps, sat on claw-footed, tufted, leather sofas reading magazines or dozing off under at least fifty framed photographs, newspaper clippings and magazine articles chronicling their surgeon's rise to fame. There were shots of Heller with celebrities of every ilk—politicians, actors, professional athletes. Black-and-white candids showed Heller at fund-raisers and awards ceremonies with leading ladies, models and debutantes he had romanced at one time or another. One article, from *Boston* magazine, was blown up bigger than the rest and carried the headline, "Jet Heller Will Go to Hell and Back to Save Your Life."

Clevenger walked up to Heller's receptionist, a slim, black-haired woman about twenty-five who looked like she could easily make the cover of *Vogue*. She looked up at him as though she couldn't quite place him. "Are you a new patient?" she asked, in a British accent. The phone rang. She kept looking at Clevenger as she answered it. "Dr. Heller's office."

Clevenger heard another line ring. He looked down at the blinking light on the phone. Someone answered the call, put it on hold.

"I can take your name and give it to the doctor," the receptionist said. "No. I can't say precisely when he'll return your call." She wrote down *Joshua Resnek, Independent News Group,* along with a phone number. "No, I wouldn't be able to let you hold until he's free."

Clevenger knew Resnek well. He was Boston's most aggressive reporter, the one who had held Clevenger's feet to the fire when it looked like Jonah Wrens, a.k.a. The Highway Killer, might just keep leaving bodies strewn along the nation's interstates forever.

"Very good, then," the receptionist said. "Yes. Yes, of course. I'll make sure he gets it." She hung up, looked back up at Clevenger. "Which doctor referred you?"

Clevenger realized his shaven head made him blend right in with Heller's post-op patients. He lowered his voice just above a whisper. "I'm not a patient. My name is Frank Clevenger. I'm a psychiatrist working with the police on the John Snow case. I wondered if Dr. Heller might be able to fit me in for a few minutes."

"Oh, Lord. I am so sorry," she said. She extended her hand. "Sascha Monroe."

Clevenger shook it, noticing her long, slender fingers, her slim wrist and the obvious confidence in her grip.

"I didn't mean to offend you," she said. "I should have recognized you. I've seen you on television so many times."

"No offense taken."

"Dr. Snow's death has been a terrible shock."

"Did you know him very well?" Clevenger asked.

"We would talk while he was waiting for Dr. Heller. I thought we had a real rapport."

"Now, you wonder?"

"I would never have predicted him doing what he did."

Monroe obviously believed Snow had committed suicide. "It's hard to predict human behavior," Clevenger said.

"I think of myself as a pretty intuitive person—at least I did— but I missed all the signs. He must have been suffering so much inside. Beside himself, really. And I just couldn't sense it." She seemed truly disappointed in herself.

"I can tell that you cared about him," Clevenger said. "That means he could tell, too. Sometimes that's as much as you can give a person when everything's fading to black."

"Thank you," she said. "Thank you for that." She looked at Clevenger in a way that told him she meant it. "Let me check on Dr. Heller for you." She stood up and disappeared through a set of columns set into an archway in the rose-colored marble wall behind her desk.

Clevenger watched as she walked past two secretaries working in Heller's inner office, then disappeared through a set of towering, mahogany French doors.

She was back out in under fifteen seconds. "He'll see you as soon as he finishes up with this patient. Five or ten minutes, if you can wait."

"I can wait."

Heller's patient, a woman about forty, left in five minutes, but it was twenty-five minutes before Heller called for Monroe to escort Clevenger to his office. Clevenger figured Heller either needed the time to review his patient's medical record and write out a progress note or he needed it to stroke his ego, to make it clear he wasn't sitting around waiting for drop-ins.

Monroe escorted Clevenger to Heller's open door. "Dr. Clevenger to see you," she said. She turned and walked away.

Heller stood up behind his desk. "J. T. Heller," he said, starting over to Clevenger. He was at least six-foot-three, with a gleaming smile and blond hair nearly to his shoulders. His eyes were a remarkable shade of blue—dark, but luminous, like sapphires. His voice was deep, but surprisingly gentle. He looked and sounded like a sturdy, amiable Viking, in black crocodile cowboy boots. His name was embroidered in big, red script letters over the pocket of his starched, white lab coat, which hung just above his knees. He wore the coat open, showing a black crocodile belt with a big, polished silver belt buckle with a red, enameled Harvard academic crest. "Sorry to keep you waiting. Please, come in."

Clevenger shook Heller's hand. "Frank Clevenger."

"As if you need the introduction," Heller said. "Let's be honest: You're more famous than I'll ever be." He let go. "That was some cross-country ride the Highway Killer took you on."

"Yes," Clevenger said, trying to keep the image of Jonah Wrens's decapitated victims out of his mind. "It was quite a ride."

"But you got him."

"We got him," Clevenger said, "after he got seventeen people."

"When you beat cancer, you beat it, my friend," Heller said. "You're gonna lose things on the way. That's how it is in any war."

"That would be the surgical perspective," Clevenger said, forcing a smile.

"What other perspective could there be?" Heller asked, with a wide grin. "Please, sit down." He motioned toward a pair of black suede armchairs in front of his long glass-top desk.

Clevenger sat in one of the armchairs. Heller took the other one, instead of his desk chair. Was that his way of making a visitor comfortable, Clevenger wondered? Or was it his way of directing Clevenger's gaze over Heller's shoulder, to a wall covered with academic degrees from Harvard College and Harvard Medical School, membership certificates to the American Medical Association and the American Board of Neurosurgery, a Phi Beta Kappa key, a photograph of Heller and the President, the Harvard Teaching Award for 2001 and 2003, *Boston Magazine*'s Best of Boston Doctors Award for 2003 and 2004.

"I'm glad you're here, Frank," he said. "May I call you that?"

"Of course."

"And please, call me Jet."

Clevenger nodded. He glanced at Heller's desk, uncluttered to the point of obsession. The only objects on it were a black computer monitor and black keyboard, a black leather blotter with a blank sheet of letterhead centered on it, and a silver Cartier pen with a little clock built into the cap.

"Obsessive compulsive disorder," Heller said. "I have every symptom."

"I can help," Clevenger joked.

Heller shook his head. "I enjoy my pathology. It's . . . How do you guys put it? *Ego-syntonic.* I like my margins clean."

Heller was referring to removing tumors completely, leaving no cancerous cells behind. "Then I wouldn't even consider depriving you of your symptoms. Your patients obviously benefit from them."

"Maybe." Heller suddenly looked burdened. "I don't know exactly why you're here, Frank, but I'm glad you are. I need someone to help me understand what happened to John Snow." He sounded half sad, half angry. "I don't mind telling you, I'm having a bit of trouble with this."

"Say more."

"Understand, I'm no stranger to patients dying on me. You saw that woman who just left here?"

"Yes, I did."

"Forty-one years old. Three little kids. I give her five, six weeks. An outside chance at seven."

"I'm sorry to hear that. What's her diagnosis?"

"Glioblastoma." His lip curled slightly, as though mentioning the enemy was enough to spark his fury. "Ten days ago, she had a funny experience. She couldn't remember her black Lab's name. Fifteen, twenty seconds, then it came to her. But it struck her as odd. She started to worry. Her mom had the start of Alzheimer's before she turned fifty. So she goes to see her internist—Karen Grant, over at the Brigham. Karen grabs an MRI. Boom. Malignant tissue obliterating forty percent of her cortex. Inoperable. Nothing at all I can do for her."

"That's got to be tough."

"For her it is," Heller said.

"I meant, for you," Clevenger said.

"No. It isn't. See, that's what I'm getting at. When I'm not even in the game, I don't lay my heart on the line. I'm not a masochist. But with John . . ." He leaned forward slightly, raised his hands like a priest blessing a parishioner. "I could have changed John Snow's life. That's why I went to war with the Ethics Committee. I put my career on the line for him." His blue eyes blazed with intensity. "I could have pulled off a miracle today."

There was the arrogance Heller was famous for. "You could have stopped his seizures," Clevenger said, testing how easily Heller could be brought back to earth.

Heller suddenly seemed aware his hands were midair. "Just for starters," he said, laying them back on his thighs. "John's epilepsy was clearly connected to his creative genius. When he applied his mind most intensely—when he was inventing—he was at greatest risk for a seizure. I can't say why that was the case, but it was. Seizure-free, he could have done things with his mind that literally would have short-circuited it before. He seemed elated by that prospect. And, then, he goes and does this." The muscles of his jaw suddenly began churning. "I don't get it."

"What sort of man was he?" Clevenger asked.

Heller thought that over a few seconds. "Driven." He smiled. "We had that in common."

Clevenger laughed. Heller might be arrogant, but he obviously knew it, and that instantly made him more likable.

"He was a passionate man," Heller went on. "About his work, about everything in life. He hated the fact that his brain was 'broken,' 'defective'—his words, not mine. So, you tell me: Why would he quit?"

Clevenger didn't see any reason to keep Heller completely in the dark about the Snow investigation. "Why do you assume he *quit*?" he asked.

Heller shrugged. "You don't like that word. Okay. You're a psychiatrist. I respect that. I know people sometimes take their own lives because they're depressed. They lose their jobs, go bankrupt. Their marriages break up. Maybe some of them were abused or abandoned as kids. And I know John had his share of trouble in life. Things were falling apart on him." He seemed suddenly to be struggling to keep his anger in check. "So maybe you can help me understand why he would bail on me after I . . ."

"I meant," Clevenger interrupted, "why do you assume he killed himself?"

Heller looked taken aback. "As opposed to . . .

"*Being* killed."

Heller sat straight up, as though a gust of wind had blown him back against his chair. "He shot himself with his own gun."

"A gunshot from his pistol caused his death," Clevenger said. "But it's possible someone else could have been with him in the alleyway this morning."

"Someone else," Heller said, looking confused. "I never even considered . . . The police were very clear with me on the phone this morning. So were the paramedics in the E.R. They said it was suicide. A Detective Coady."

"It might be," Clevenger said. "And if Snow did kill himself, I'll try to find out why."

Heller stood up and walked to the wall of windows behind his desk, folded his arms and looked out at the Boston skyline. Several seconds passed in silence. He shook his head. "You wouldn't be here if the police were sure it was suicide," he said. "You're telling me there's a real chance my patient was murdered. He may actually have intended to go the distance with me."

Heller seemed to be viewing Snow's cause of death as a verdict on whether Snow had abandoned him. "I can't say yet," Clevenger said. "I need to find out much more about who he was—and whether someone might have wanted him dead."

"And you'll have to be thorough. You'll want to get your hands on every bit of information about him you can."

"I like my margins clean, too." Clevenger said.

"Then you need to know something." He turned around, looked at Clevenger. "John would have been risking more than his speech or his vision in the O.R. today."

"What do you mean?"

Heller seemed uncertain how much he wanted to divulge.

"Was there a significant risk of death?" Clevenger asked.

"In a manner of speaking," Heller said. He walked back to his seat, sat down. "If I tell you this, I need you to keep it between you and me. It's privileged doctor-patient information. I figure you're kind of like John's psychiatrist—postmortem. This is a curbside consult. Doc-to-doc."

"Okay," Clevenger said. "Doc-to-doc."

Heller leaned forward, planted his elbows on his thighs. "The areas of the brain involved in John's seizures," he said, "included the hippocampus, the cingulate gyrus and the amygdala. Those turn out to be the areas most intimately involved in facial recognition and the emotional components of memory—at least if you believe the animal studies coming out of UCLA and the University of Minnesota. It's preliminary work, but those structures are looking more and more like the data bank where we record who we know and how we feel about them. I think the initial findings will come out in *Neurosciences* within two or three months."

"You're saying Snow could have suffered amnesia?"

"A very severe and particular form," Heller said. "His memory for facts would have been unaffected. His intellect would have survived. His imagination may well have flourished. But he would have been alone. The surgery would very likely have turned anyone with whom he had an emotional connection into a stranger—his wife, his children, everyone."

Now Clevenger was the one leaning forward. "So he could still be an inventor, but he wouldn't remember the people close to him. A kind of interpersonal amnesia."

"Precisely," Heller said.

"And he was still willing to go through with the surgery?"

"I thought so—until this morning. Things had become . . . complicated for him. He and his business partner—Coroway—were at each other's throats over Coroway's plan to take the company public. John was dead set against it. He didn't want to be controlled by anyone, especially bean counters. And his marriage was in trouble." He paused, seemingly unsure again how much to divulge.

"I need to know," Clevenger said.

Heller looked him in the eyes. "He had a mistress. I think he saw the surgery as a chance for rebirth, a chance to escape."

"To escape . . ." Clevenger said.

"All the loose ends in his life. The messiness. Everything that was broken. He'd made preparations—a living will of sorts. He wanted to give his children their inheritances, settle up financially with his wife, move on cleanly."

"The Ethics Committee didn't have anything to say about this?" Clevenger asked. "Doesn't it amount to elective amnesia?"

"They didn't focus on it," Heller said, sitting back.

"They didn't focus on it, or you didn't tell them?"

"As I said, the data is very new," Heller deadpanned. "They didn't focus on it."

Clevenger could only begin to imagine how Snow's decision to hit the reset button on the software running his existence would have affected the people he planned to leave behind. His son. His daughter. His wife. His business partner. His lover. They would be strangers to him. Would they feel abandoned? Enraged? "Did he consider the impact on his family?" Clevenger asked. "Of him leaving them so suddenly? So completely?"

"It was his life," Heller said, a sharp edge to his voice. "That's what the Ethics Committee failed to understand—at first. John wanted two things: to be free of his seizures and free of his past. I happened to be in a position to help him achieve both. If a man owns anything, he owns his brain and his mind. Don't you agree?"

Clevenger wasn't prepared to answer that question. There was something about Heller that made you *want* to agree with him. He was extraordinarily charismatic. His personality was like a strong, cool current that would carry you right along with it if you were content to go. But Clevenger didn't know what he really thought of Heller's plan to use a scalpel to sever his patient's emotional connections to others. That felt like playing God. "It doesn't matter what I think," he said, finally. "It matters what people around him would have thought, whether one of them would have felt threatened or angry enough to do him in. Did any of his family members try to block the surgery?"

"His wife Theresa pushed for an inpatient psychiatric evaluation to assess his competency to consent to the surgery. She thought the risks were too high, that he was being irrational. But so far as I know, she was only aware of the speech and vision issues, along with a question of mild short-term memory loss. John indulged her request. He spent five days here on Axelrod six."

"Can you get me his records?" Clevenger asked.

"Leave me an address. I'll get them off to you as soon as I can," Heller said. "If he didn't lose faith, if he was actually prepared to go to surgery with me, I'd like nothing better than to see the son-ofabitch who stole John's future spend the rest of his in a cage."

"Do you think he ever told his wife—or anyone else—about the extent of the amnesia?"

"So far as I know, he was confiding in two people: me and his lawyer, Joe Balliro, Junior."

"Balliro. Snow wasn't fooling around."

"He was laying some very complicated legal groundwork," Heller said. "The living will, and so on."

"So with all the paperwork, someone could have found out. A secretary in the office. A photocopy clerk. A friend of a friend of Snow's mistress."

Heller nodded to himself. "His mistress. There's a wild card."

"How so?"

"John tried to end the relationship a few weeks before his surgery. He thought it would be easier on her. She considered the two of them soul mates. She was pushing for a real life together."

"And Snow?"

"I think he had trouble loving people."

"Why do you say that?"

"I listened to him quite a bit. He was a perfectionist. He loved ideas and ideals. Genius. Beauty. Perfect romance. Not much in the world met his expectations—not even his own brain. He was uncompromising." He paused. "He told me she didn't respond well to the breakup."

"Any idea what he meant by that?"

"She threatened to hurt herself, again. I guess she had a history of cutting her wrists, or something."

"Sounds borderline," Clevenger said, referring to borderline personality disorder, a character disorder with symptoms including intense, unstable relationships, extreme fear of abandonment and repeated threats of suicide.

"I can't speak to her diagnosis," Heller said. "What I know is that she's very beautiful, very wealthy and very troubled. She's married. Runs a gallery somewhere in town."

Clevenger was silent. His pulse started to race. He suddenly had a very bad feeling that his work on the Snow case had started even before he visited the morgue. "Did Snow mention her name?" he asked Heller.

"He called her Grace," Heller said. "I didn't know if that was her real name and I didn't push him on it." Heller noticed Clevenger wasn't looking so good. "You alright?" he asked.

"Did he happen to mention what sort of business her husband is in?" Clevenger asked. Then he just waited for his day to come full circle, like a boomerang. One, two, three seconds . . .

"I know she was very private about it. Paranoid. She said she didn't want to be overshadowed by her husband anymore. Owned by him. But I'm pretty sure she said it was banking. Yeah, definitely. She told him that much."

THE FOUR SEASONS

• ANOTHER WINTER DAY, ONE YEAR BEFORE.

Snow had just delivered the morning keynote at a conference on radar system design at the Four Seasons Hotel on Tremont Street. He walked out of the hotel. The sky was dark. A light drizzle was falling. He couldn't bear the thought of going back inside. He crossed the street and disappeared into the Public Garden.

He wasn't scheduled to present again for a few hours—a panel discussion on missile detection. If he lingered in the lobby or at a reception, he would face one engineer after another tirelessly trying to pick his brain. What they never seemed to grasp was that he couldn't share what he knew. He had been a spectacular success as a researcher at M.I.T., but had utterly failed as a teacher. How was he to teach a moment of inspiration, an epiphany? The facts in his brain were inert until a force greater than he breathed life into them, converting them into the seeds of ideas. And then those ideas grew without his consent, branching where they needed to. He was really no more than a plagiarist of the inventions born inside him.

He walked past the public skating rink, noticing the happy faces of the children and their parents as they glided over the ice. He, himself, had little time for leisure. The creative force inside him drove him seven days a week, fifty-two weeks a year. He had a wife, a son and a daughter, a gracious home, enough money to never work another day. But the force had *him*, and that trumped everything.

The Garden ended at Arlington Street. He crossed it, started down Newbury. He remembered a cafe three blocks away, figured he'd stop there, grab an espresso. But within a few minutes the sky went charcoal gray and started pouring freezing rain. And just as it did, he looked through the window of the nearest storefront and saw the most beautiful woman he had ever seen.

She was in her mid-thirties, with auburn hair and the body of a mermaid, wearing a simple black dress—and she was looking back at him through impossibly green eyes. He had the sense she had been looking at him for some time. For a split second he wondered whether she was real or another product of his imagination.

He walked inside, found himself surrounded by magnificent oil paintings hanging in splashes of light along the walls. They were scenes of Boston, including the Public Garden and Commonwealth Avenue, but the artist had made something more of them, deconstructing all harshness of line and form to create an ideal city in which people and buildings and the streets and the sky were joined by swirls of color, swept into a world far more enchanting than the sum of its parts.

His gaze traveled to the far wall, to the portrait of a naked woman standing behind lace curtains at dusk, gazing out the bow window of her brick town home onto lanterned Beacon Street.

Snow walked toward the portrait, stopped about ten feet away. He knew instantly that it was of the woman he had seen in the window. He imagined himself in the painting, behind her, hands on her shoulders, kissing her neck.

"The artist is Ron Kullaway," she said, walking up beside him. "He lives up in Maine."

Her voice combined strength and intelligence with a hint of vulnerability. "Magnificent," he said, without looking at her.

"He's becoming one of America's greats. You've seen his work before?"

"I haven't."

"I think he makes life seem worthwhile," she said. "Worth living."

He felt the back of her hand brush ever so lightly against his. Or did he? "How does he do that?" he asked.

"I think it's what he leaves out, more than what he paints."

"The structure," Snow said. "The boundaries."

"What limits us. He either doesn't see it or chooses to ignore it."

Snow finally let himself look at her. When he did, he was even more taken with her. "You never asked him? It must have taken him quite a long time to capture you." He looked back at the canvas.

She smiled.

"How much is it?"

"Two hundred thousand."

"For a glimpse of life as worth living."

"Some people never even get that." She paused. "If it's something you can walk away from, you shouldn't even consider it."

He stepped back from the painting, turned to her. "John Snow," he said, extending his hand.

"Grace Baxter," she said, taking it.

He noticed she wore a wedding band and a diamond solitaire that had to be five carats. On her wrist were three diamond tennis bracelets. All those gems said she belonged to someone, but nothing else made him feel she was taken—not her tone of voice nor the look in her eyes nor the touch of her hand. "Would you have dinner with me tonight?" he asked, letting go. "I promise to make a decision on the painting before we leave the restaurant."

She agreed to meet him at Aujourd'hui, upstairs at the Four Seasons, after his last presentation. But she arrived early. He saw her standing at the back of the room listening to his remarks, "Reducing Rotational Energy in Flight." He noticed men in the room, including his partner Collin Coroway, stealing glances at her. He wished he could be saying something more than he was, something expansive about the universe or creativity or love. But he was confined to the laws of physics.

She never looked even slightly bored.

"What do you call the work you do?" she asked him later, as he poured her a glass of wine.

"I'm an aeronautical engineer. An inventor."

"And what kinds of things, exactly, do you invent?"

"Radar systems. Missile guidance systems."

She smiled.

"Care to share the thought?"

"It's not really my place. I hardly know you."

Sitting with her, hearing her voice, smelling her perfume, made him want to tell her the absolute truth. "It doesn't feel that way," he said.

"No, it doesn't."

He felt something long frozen inside him begin to thaw. "So you can share that thought," he said.

"Okay . . ." she said. "Why do you think you focus so much energy on what can and cannot be seen? Why are you interested in radar, and how to get around it?"

"It's something I have a gift for," he answered. "It chose me. I didn't choose it."

"But *why*?" she asked. "*Why* do you have that 'gift'?"

He looked confused.

"Is there something about you, John Snow, that you don't want people to see? Or is it that you're not willing to look at yourself?"

In that instant, Snow felt something he had never felt before. He felt as though someone had connected with his truth, a truth even deeper than his genius, a truth of the heart.

"You have the answer, but you're not ready to share it," she said.

"Maybe," Snow said.

"You won't even confirm or deny that." She sipped her wine.

"Tell me more about you."

"You want me to go first. Okay. What do you want to know?"

"Do you have dinner with all your customers?"

"Oh." She ran a fingertip along the rim of her wine glass. "You want to know if you're special."

Again, Snow felt a nearly gravitational pull toward his core. "Yes," he said. "I suppose I do."

"I wouldn't be here for a commission. The last thing I need is money."

They had that in common. "What do you need?"

She shook her head. "We both have very good radar, John. And we both like flying below it."

"You're married," he said.

"I am. And you?"

He nodded.

She suddenly looked sad to him, and he was amazed at how her apparent sadness moved him. He was often at a loss when people became emotional around him, unable to fathom what they might be feeling or why, and that made him feel even more alone, even more a hostage to his mind than he usually felt. Not so with this woman. "I don't want to be invisible," he said.

She looked around the room, checking to make sure no one was looking, then slid her hand under his.

Her touch made his breathing ease, his pulse slow. He didn't know what to do or say, so he slowly pulled his hand away, reached into his suit jacket pocket and took out a check made out for two-hundred-thousand dollars to the Newbury Gallery. He placed the check beside her glass. "I'll take the painting," he said. "But this can't be the last time we see each other."

"I told you I'm not for sale."

There was a cool edge to her voice that made him panic. "I didn't mean it that way," he said. "Really. I'm not good at this." He looked into her eyes, slid his hand under hers this time. "What I meant was . . . I wouldn't want the painting to remind me that we managed to hide from one another."

She looked into his eyes, saw he meant what he had said and slipped her thumb into the palm of his hand.

They met at the Four Seasons one week later, this time in a suite overlooking the Public Garden. They had spoken by phone every day since their dinner, sometimes two or three times in a day, luxuriating in sharing more and more of each other's worlds—the art that literally surrounded Baxter at the Newbury Gallery, Snow's inventions taking form at Snow-Coroway Engineering.

Neither of them could risk a public relationship, so neither took offense that their intimacies should unfold inside the hotel.

Snow's driver, Pavel Blazek, a man he trusted implicitly, reserved the suite, charging it to his own credit card.

Snow arrived fifteen minutes before Baxter. He walked into the marble bathroom, looked at himself in the mirror. He had the skin and hair and physique of a much younger man. His forehead was broad, his jaw straight, his chin slightly cleft. He was handsome, and he knew it, but he knew it objectively, in the way he knew the properties of carbon or the laws of gravity. He had never known what to use his looks for.

Now, for the first time, he wanted to be attractive—for Grace. He was wearing a new shirt and blazer, when any of his old ones would have done for him. He had had his unruly hair trimmed. He had shaved away two days growth of beard, when he usually waited longer, until it became scratchy and distracted him from his work.

He poured himself a glass of water, reached into his pocket for two Dilantin tablets, swallowed them. In the hours he had spent on the phone with Baxter, he had made only a single, passing reference to having had seizures as a child. He withheld the fact that they had never completely stopped. He did not want her to think of him as broken.

He walked through the bedroom to a plate glass window facing the Public Garden. It was a sunny, ice-cold day. Everything looked crisp. He could see the skating rink, crowded with families. And he thought how nice it would be if he could go skating there with Grace one day.

He checked his watch. Almost 4:00 P.M. She would be there any minute. He felt half-excited, half-worried. Because he still wondered whether Baxter was real or something he had dreamed up. He had allowed himself to share more of his thoughts and feelings with her than any other human being. Was that because she was his soul mate or because he wished he were the kind of man who could have a soul mate? With his marriage on life support, had he simply conjured up a rationale for pulling the plug? Did he have the potential to be fully human or was he pretending he did?

A knock at the door. He froze, gripped by the fear that his wife had followed him, or worse, his daughter or son. But the fear was irrational; there was no way they could know where he was. Blazek would never violate his trust. At that moment, inside those four walls, he was free. He breathed deeply with that thought and headed to the door.

As an act of faith, he didn't look through the peephole before reaching out and opening the door.

Grace Baxter stood there in what he had asked her to wear—the simple black dress she had been wearing when he first saw her.

He felt his heart race. A new feeling. A feeling he liked.

She held out her hand. He took both of hers and walked backwards as she followed him into the sitting room. She looked around. "I guess this will have to do," she joked, taking in the expanse of the place, nearly a thousand square feet, with Asian wall hangings, recessed panel walls, tray ceilings, crown moldings, crystal light fixtures. She glanced through a set of French doors into the bedroom, saw the king-sized bed with its pristine, white pillows and sheets and comforter. She gently let go of his hands and walked over to the window that looked onto the Garden. Then she gracefully stepped out of her shoes and leaned against the window frame, just behind the sheer curtains.

He felt almost as though he were with her behind the lace curtains of her townhouse, when Kullaway had painted her naked. And just as he was imagining it, she reached behind her neck, unhooked her dress and let it drop to the floor. She leaned against the window frame. She was naked and perfect, her auburn hair cascading over her delicate shoulders, her back tapering to a slim waist, then arching just slightly above the parts of her he wanted to touch so badly. Her legs were toned, but not muscular. She was everything he had imagined. Perfect. He walked toward her, half thinking she would disappear when he reached out for her. But when he did, she turned around, wrapped her arms around him and kissed him. And then he felt himself losing his sense of time and place and gaining something greater, something asleep in him that was now stirring—passion for another person. He pressed against her, kissed her even more deeply.

She pulled back, breathless. "Undress for me," she said.

Snow's wife had never seen him undress, scarcely seen him naked. Their sex was something stolen from one another under the covers by night. He slowly unbuttoned his shirt, took it off, dropped it to the floor. He unfastened his belt, unbuttoned his pants, hesitated, then unzipped them. He took a step toward her.

She held up a hand. "Finish."

He felt embarrassed, and it must have shown.

"It's all right," she said. "I just want to see all of you."

He stepped out his pants, took off his socks and underwear, stood naked in front of her.

"You really don't have any idea how magnificent you are, do you?" she asked, coming to him. She kissed his neck, his ears, his chest, then sunk to her knees. "In here," she said, "we do anything we want to do."

FIVE

• 3:40 P.M.

Clevenger had to struggle to concentrate on the road as he drove out of the Mass General garage, headed to pick up Billy at the Somerville Boxing Club.

He thought back to his session with Grace that morning—her trembling, her guilt, how he had worried she might be on the verge of killing herself or someone else. He pictured her rocking back and forth in her seat, hugging herself. And he thought of what she had said: *I don't want to hurt anyone ever again.*

Was she fresh from the kill? Is that why she was falling apart? Had she just shot the man she loved through the heart, leaving herself alone in a marriage that felt like death?

Or hadn't she hurt anyone? Even if she had found out about Snow's impending amnesia, maybe she simply planned to start psychotherapy on the day he went under the knife. Maybe his decision to remake his life had inspired her to remake her own.

Clevenger grabbed his cell phone and dialed his office to see if Baxter had tried to reach him. Boston Forensics' office manager, Kim Moffett, a twenty-nine-year-old with the wisdom of an eighty-year-old, answered.

"Any calls?" Clevenger asked.

"I've been trying to get you for the past hour," she said.

He glanced at his cell, saw he had voice mail. He had turned off the ringer before dropping in on Heller. "What's up?"

"Most of it can wait. But you've gotten five calls from Grace Baxter."

"She alright?"

"She says it's no emergency, but she keeps calling. She wants an appointment for tomorrow morning. I've got you out of the office all day at MCI Concord—that competency-to-stand-trial evaluation. But I told her I'd check with you."

Clevenger was scheduled to visit the state prison at Concord to determine whether a schizophrenic man who had killed his father was sane enough to stand trial. The trial wasn't slated to begin until winter. "Tell her I'll see her at eight tomorrow morning," he said. "And call Concord and reschedule for me, if you would."

"No problem. Where are you? You're supposed to be in Somerville in fifteen minutes."

"On my way."

"North wanted me to tell you he has some information on someone named Collin Coroway."

"Is he in?"

"No, but I can get him. Hold on."

Moffett patched Anderson through.

"Frank?" Anderson said.

"Right here."

"I started checking out Snow's business partner, Coroway."

"And?"

"No one to take lightly. Former Green Beret, active duty in Vietnam, wired to the intelligence community. He's been written up a bunch of times in the industry trades that cover military contractors. It looks like Snow-Coroway Engineering runs on Snow's ingenuity and Coroway's connections. Eighty-five percent of their business is government-related. Radar systems, sonar, missile technology."

"And the two of them were arguing over whether to go public."

"They were at war over it. Classic confrontation. The guy with a head for business versus the guy with his head in the clouds. Coroway was the numbers man. Snow was the dreamer. You got to wonder just how hot the battle got."

"I'm with you," Clevenger said. The list of people who might have wanted Snow dead was already starting to grow. If Collin Coroway had learned of Snow's plan to sever the personal connection between them, potentially evolving into a direct competitor, he might have decided to end their partnership with a bullet. "He's not the only one who's got to be checked out," Clevenger said. "I just left Jet Heller's office. He let me in on a secret: Snow was having an affair—with my patient this morning, Grace Baxter."

"Who just happened to look like death," Anderson said.

"You're reading my mind."

"That's a frightening thought. You seeing her again?"

"Tomorrow, first thing. In the meantime, it would be nice to nail down where Collin Coroway was at about 5:00 A.M. today."

"Would that be stepping on Detective Coady's toes?"

"Certainly."

"Apologize for me," Anderson said. "I never learned to dance."

"Consider the apology accepted."

"I'll check in later." He hung up.

Clevenger took the Hanover Street Bridge out of Boston, got to the Somerville Boxing Club a few minutes early.

Billy was sparring in the Spartan ring that took up half the place. Exposed light bulbs burned overhead. Fifteen or twenty other teenagers were hitting heavy bags, lifting weights and skipping rope at stations surrounding the ring. The room had to be close to ninety degrees and smelled like it had absorbed the sweat of the hundreds of boxers who had trained there, some of them making Golden Gloves like Billy, one of them, Johnny Ruiz, ending up Heavyweight Champion of the World.

Clevenger walked to the far corner of the room, leaned against the cinder block wall and watched Billy throwing jabs at his opponent, a shorter boy with massive shoulders who was backing away, covering up.

"Measure him," trainer Buddy Donovan, sixty-something, with a right hook that could still snap a man's neck, called to him from the side of the ring. He was wearing a no-nonsense set of gray sweats with S.B.C. stenciled across the top. "Pick your shots." He spotted Clevenger, nodded at him.

Clevenger nodded back, then watched Billy land a stiff right to his opponent's jaw. The kid looked like he was about to fall into the ropes, but caught himself at the last moment.

No question, Billy could fight. He was strong and lightning fast, with real reach. He had worked his body until his torso looked like a suit of armor. But he had more than muscle and reflexes. He had a fighter's instincts. He could sense his opponent's strategy and adjust, sense his weaknesses and exploit them. He had studied the sport, read books on it, watched videos of the greats, again and again: Marciano. Liston. Ali. Frazier. Foreman. Leonard.

It had been Billy's idea to take up boxing, but Clevenger had encouraged him. He figured it would be a good way for Billy to release some of his anger, so it wouldn't spill out on the streets of Chelsea.

He had adopted Billy two years before, after solving the murder of Billy's infant sister on Nantucket. With Billy's history of drug abuse and assault, the police had focused on him as the lead suspect. But Clevenger had proved them wrong. By the time he finished working the case, Billy's name had been cleared, and his father had been jailed. His mother had been deemed an unfit parent.

That left Billy free, and headed for foster care, until Clevenger stepped in.

Clevenger watched Billy take a hard left to his forehead. He shook it off, started to dance. The bell rang, ending the round.

"Don't let him back you up, Nicky," Buddy Donovan called out to Billy's opponent. "You come in low, you keep coming."

Billy spotted Clevenger. "The doctor is in," he called out, walking to his corner.

"Looking good," Clevenger said.

Billy winked.

The truth was Billy looked dangerous. His long, dirty blond hair was done up in dreadlocks. A tattoo across his back read, "Let It Bleed," each green and black letter two inches high, the words inked across scars from the beatings he had taken from his father.

Parenting Billy felt like holding his hand as he walked a tightrope over the flames of his tortured past. Sometimes it seemed like he was pretty steady on his feet and making good progress. Other times it seemed like he was destined to plummet into that hell, become part of it.

The most worrisome thing was that he had no fear. It had done him no good as a child to be scared; he got beaten, anyway. And the capacity to be afraid is one of the main ingredients to being empathetic. You have to be able to let yourself suffer, in order to imagine the pain of others.

Donovan rang the bell for the next round. Billy jogged to the center of the ring. His opponent came toward him, hunched over, stalking. Billy bounced foot-to-foot. He waited until the boy was within reach, then delivered three quick left jabs that skipped off his headgear.

The boy took one step closer and fired a right that landed squarely on Billy's shoulder, knocking him sideways.

"He's stronger than you are," Donovan called out to Billy. "Keep moving."

Billy glanced at Donovan and started dancing again. But he couldn't tolerate being called weak, much less thinking of himself that way. He stopped, took a step toward his opponent and planted his feet. Just as he did, he got hit with a left hook to his nose. Blood streamed down over his lips.

"I told you to move," Donovan said. "You can't go toe-to-toe with him."

Something new came into Billy's eyes. The strategic vision, the search for an opening, was gone, replaced by something that looked like pure hatred. It was as though tasting blood had tapped something primitive and hardwired in him. He held his gloves down by his waist and took another step toward his opponent. The boy threw a straight right that would have ended the fight had it landed, but Billy leaned way back, and it brushed his chin. Then Billy descended like a storm, firing rights and lefts with the ferocity of a street fighter. Some of his punches were wild, but enough connected with the boy's shoulders, head and neck to leave him wobbly.

"Back to your corners," Donovan yelled. "We're all done." He climbed into the ring.

Clevenger started over.

Billy threw a left hook that missed and a powerful right cross that crushed into the boy's left ear.

The kid stooped to one knee.

"I said stop!" Donovan yelled, louder this time. He pushed Billy back toward the ropes. "When I tell you we're done, we're done. You got it?"

Billy rubbed his gloves into his eyes, like a little boy waking up from a dream. "Sorry," he said. He touched one glove to his nose, stared at his blood.

"Take a shower and cool off, for Christ's sake," Donovan said.

He turned and headed over to the other boy, who was back on his feet, but still shaky.

Billy looked down at Clevenger, standing by the side of the ring.

"Get dressed," Clevenger said. "I'll take you home."

Donovan walked over to Clevenger as Billy headed to the locker room. "He's got the gift, Doc. He could go pro some day, if he wants it bad enough. He's just got to learn to keep himself under control."

"Yes, he does."

"Because someone with more of an eye than Nicky would have laid him out when he started throwin' wild in there."

Donovan seemed worried about Billy's loss of control for a very different reason than he was. "He wasn't able to back off when you told him to, either," he said.

"That, I wouldn't pay much mind. These kids work up a head of steam, they can't turn it off. That comes with age and experience."

"Let's hope," Clevenger said.

"I've been at this game a long time," Donovan said. He slapped Clevenger's shoulder and walked off toward the locker room.

Clevenger started back toward the entrance, checking out the other kids sweating through their workouts. He would have liked to believe Donovan was right, that Billy was no different than they were, that the brakes on his eighteen-year-old nervous system just slipped sometimes. But Clevenger knew more about Billy than Donovan did. He knew Billy's history of violence outside the ring, the times he had left kids bleeding on the pavement, with broken jaws and concussions.

He knew something else about Billy, because he knew it about himself. When you are the target of a brutal father, that brutality leeches into your own psyche. Conservation of energy rules the mind as it does the planets. Absorbing a man's rage means literally that. You can either feel it and fight to cleanse yourself of it, or you can try to ignore it, in which case it will grow stronger and stronger, until—whether through depression or aggression—it commandeers every corner of your soul.

As Clevenger waited in the truck for Billy, his mind wandered back to Grace Baxter. He thought of calling her to make sure she planned to keep her appointment. But he worried she would keep him on the phone, and he had been trying to focus completely on Billy when they were together.

Billy came out of the place in full teenage regalia, wearing a black, Aéropostale T-shirt, baggy military style pants worn off his hips and Nike high tops, unlaced. His three silver hoop earrings were back in his left ear. His beaded, leather choker was back around his neck. He walked with a swagger that was put on, like a kid playing a tough guy in a movie.

He got in the truck, stared straight ahead. "Thanks for picking me up."

"No problem."

Clevenger backed out of his space, started down Broadway, headed for Route 99 and the back roads to Chelsea.

"I broke up with Casey," Billy said.

Billy had been with Casey Simms the past two years, a seventeen-year-old from Newburyport, an hour up 95 North. Clevenger wondered whether announcing the breakup was his way of explaining why he'd lost his cool in the ring. "I didn't see that coming," Clevenger said. "You two seemed to be getting along."

"She's getting clingy, all of a sudden. Crazy jealous."

"All of a sudden. Any idea why?"

"She's a girl," Billy said, without taking his eyes off the road.

"You okay with it? The breakup?"

"Sure."

That was about as much access to Billy's emotional life as Clevenger was getting lately. "Does breaking up with her have anything to do with you going after that kid after Donovan called the fight?"

Billy shrugged. "I didn't hear him."

Clevenger looked over at him.

"Really," he said, glancing at Clevenger. "I know what you're thinking: I was projecting my frustration with Casey onto Nick. But I'm not about to blame my behavior on that unconscious dynamic." He turned to Clevenger and smiled his most winning smile. "In other words, I should have been listening, and I take full responsibility. You good with that, Doc?"

Billy always had a way of making light of his troubles. But Clevenger couldn't take them so lightly. "If you go deaf on Donovan again, you're out of there for the summer, Champ," Clevenger said. "If you respect the sport, great. If it's an excuse for a rumble, skip it."

"Got it," Billy said, turning back and staring through the windshield again. Fifteen, twenty seconds passed in silence. "You gonna get the case of that guy in the alleyway at Mass General? Now they're saying maybe he didn't blow himself away, after all."

"Who's saying that?"

"A reporter on the radio. I caught it while I was warming up."

Clevenger had given up on trying to keep Billy in the dark about his forensic work. He didn't think it was particularly healthy for him to focus on violence, but he didn't think it was particularly healthy for him to grow up with a father keeping his occupation a secret, either. And maybe if Billy saw him working with the police, he would be more inclined to respect the law. "The Boston Police Department hired me today. They want me to help them figure out if Snow committed suicide or not."

"Cool," Billy said excitedly. "What do you think?"

"It's too early to think much of anything."

Billy nodded to himself. "The guy was supposed to get his brain operated on, right?"

"Right."

"Could he have died?"

"That's always possible with neurosurgery."

"Then no way did he off himself."

Clevenger looked over at him. "Why not?"

"Because, like they say, freedom is having nothing left to lose. You can *always* kill yourself, dude. If you think you might die anyhow, why not roll the dice? Maybe you never wake up. Or maybe you wake up and feel better—like a whole new person." He paused. "I used to wish for that. Didn't you?"

"To wake up a new person, or not to wake up?"

"Both. Either. Whatever."

Clevenger looked over at Billy, who made real eye contact with him for the first time since he'd gotten in the truck. He had a way of coming close all of a sudden. It felt good when it happened, but it didn't happen often, and it never seemed to last. "Yes," he admitted. "Either."

"And didn't you once tell me most depressed people feel the shittiest in the morning?" he asked.

"A lot of them."

"That's because when they get out of bed, they're still exactly who they were the night before. But this guy was having his *brain* cut up. Anything could have happened."

There was real simplicity and real logic in what Billy was saying. Snow had been trying to break free, to leave his life behind and begin anew. With suicide always an option, wouldn't he at least wait to see how the surgery turned out for him? As an inventor, wouldn't the chance to reinvent himself be intoxicating? "That's a very interesting way to look at it," Clevenger said. "You may be right." His gut told him to move on. He really didn't want Billy dwelling on murder or suicide. "Back to Casey," he said. "You really have no idea why she's so worried about you with other girls?"

"I've been hanging out," Billy said. "It's nothing like she thinks." He stared straight ahead again.

That was about as far as Clevenger figured he was going to get. "We can talk later," he said.

"Yeah," Billy said. "Later's good."

SIX

Billy stayed at home just long enough to grab some food—then took off to meet a few friends. That left Clevenger in the two-thousand-square-foot loft they shared, its wall of towering, arched windows framing the Chelsea night, dominated by the river of headlights flowing over the upper deck of the Tobin Bridge into Boston, steam from a nearby twenty-story smokestack billowing through its green, iron skeleton.

Beneath the bridge were two square miles of tenement houses, factories and brick row houses that had played host to wave after wave of immigrants who rolled into Chelsea like it was a second womb—enrolling their children in her schools, registering for bene-fits at the Social Security Administration on Everett Avenue, learn-ing to speak the language, getting their first jobs in her gas stations and liquor stores and warehouses—then being reborn, moving up and out to more affluent towns like Nahant, Marblehead and Swampscott.

Clevenger turned on the computer he kept on an antique pine desk facing the windows. He wanted to do his own search on John Snow, Collin Coroway and Snow-Coroway Engineering. And he wanted to find out what he could about Grace Baxter. While he waited for it to reboot, he walked to Billy's doorway and looked into his room. His weight bench and barbells sat in the middle of it.

A mattress was pushed against one wall. A couple hundred CDs and DVDs were stacked along another. Clothes spilled out of his closet. He smiled at a photograph taped to the closet door—him and Billy, the day Billy had moved in.

Most of the time, parenting a troubled teen—even one as tough as Billy—felt surprisingly good. It structured Clevenger's existence, the way being responsible for another human being can. And Clevenger's psychiatric training helped him deal with the fact that life with Billy could make him feel isolated and angry, because it reminded him of his own hellish adolescence, his own sadistic father.

The part of parenting that Clevenger was least equipped for was the fact that raising a teenager really *was* isolating. You focused a lot of your time and energy on one other person—a person who wasn't your friend, who wasn't supposed to help you through your bad days or bear your lousy moods.

Clevenger was finding out how alone you could feel in the room next to your child, even when you loved that child as much as he loved Billy. And he couldn't make the loneliness go away in the easy ways he once had.

Take women. Clevenger had had love affairs during the past two years, including an on-again, off-again relationship with Whitney McCormick, the FBI's chief forensic psychiatrist, who had worked the Jonah Wrens case with him. But he couldn't abandon himself to romance, even with her, even though she still appeared in his dreams. He couldn't pour himself into a woman and dissolve his anxieties in the haze of passion. Giving your son the very decided impression he was your main focus in life meant going to sleep and waking up by yourself. It meant managing love affairs like part-time jobs.

And then there was his on-again, off-again love affair with alcohol and drugs. He had found it less stressful to stay sober for himself, one-day-at-a-time, than to make that commitment in the name of raising a healthy child. Because a slip now and then was at least thinkable when the only person you were likely to hurt was yourself. If the pain got too intense, you knew you could turn it off, even if you had to pay for it in spades down the road. Now, with Billy's future linked to his own, with the fact that taking a drink would mean that Billy's father was a *drinker*, Clevenger could never touch the stuff. He was wedded to reality, no matter how painful that reality became.

He thought again of what John Snow had been preparing to do, his plan to free himself from his tangled neurons—and, quite possibly, from all entanglements. On the one hand, the idea was intoxicating. Snow could have lived the unfettered life of a stranger in a distant land, with no obligations to anyone, no guilt over past sins, nothing defining or limiting him. On the other hand, the question had to be asked how much Snow's freedom would have cost the people who considered him part of *their* life stories, *their realities*? With him gone, could they ever resolve the dramas in which he had been an actor, or would they be burdened by them forever? And should that be his concern? Are any of us free to the extent that we are free to move on completely?

What would it do to Billy if Clevenger were to decide that their emotional bonds—positive and negative—were null and void, that they had no future together, and not even a shared past? Would Billy be able to survive the abandonment? Would he be able to hold all the love and fear, trust and resentment that had been theirs together? Or would their sheer weight crush him?

Was Snow's plan to leave an act of self-preservation, an act of destruction, or both?

The phone rang. Clevenger walked back to his desk and answered it. "Frank Clevenger."

"Bad news," North Anderson said.

"What? Where are you?"

"The office. I just got a call from Mike Coady. The police responded to a 911 call from 214 Beacon Street. George Reese, Grace Baxter's husband."

"God, no," Clevenger said, thinking she had murdered him, or tried to. His legs felt weak. Baxter had given him a glimpse of her desperation, and he had made the wrong decision, letting her go home, instead of committing her to a locked psychiatric unit. "How bad?" he asked.

"The paramedics worked it hard, but they never had a chance. Body's been there a while, probably a couple hours."

Clevenger managed to ease himself into his desk chair before his legs gave out. "How did she kill him?"

"How did she . . ." Anderson started, then stopped. "The husband is fine, Frank."

Clevenger's mind couldn't—or wouldn't—add up the facts to come up with the awful answer. "I don't understand."

"It's Grace," Anderson said. He was silent a few seconds. "She killed herself."

Clevenger closed his eyes. He saw Baxter walking to her car at the shipyard, tears streaming down her face. He looked out into the Chelsea night. "How?" he managed.

"It's not a pretty story."

"Are they ever?"

"This one . . ."

"Just tell me."

"She went into the master bath and sliced her wrists, then her throat. Then she stumbled into bed and bled out."

"Who found her?"

"Her husband. She was supposed to meet him at the Beacon

Street Bank for a cocktail party. A fund-raiser or something. She never showed up. He came home looking for her."

"Did she leave a note?"

"Yeah. Coady didn't say what was in it."

"Can you meet me over there?" Clevenger asked. Part of his reason for wanting to go was that Grace had been his patient, if only for one session. The rest of his reason was that two lovers had died within several hours of each other. One possibility was murder-suicide—that Grace Baxter had killed John Snow, then killed herself. But there were other possibilities. He wanted to see where Grace had died, take a look at the layout of the place, whether there were signs of a struggle.

"I should tell you they also found a piece of paper on the night stand with your name and number on it, along with her appointment time for tomorrow. I guess the husband knows she was in to see you today. He's looking for someone to blame."

"He won't have to look hard for me. I'll be at 214 Beacon in fifteen minutes."

"See you there."

Clevenger left a note for Billy, then drove into Boston. He knew psychiatrists lost patients, just like other doctors did, that some psychiatric illnesses were fatal. And he knew he had heard everything the law said he needed to hear from Grace Baxter— her contract to not harm herself or anyone else. But his mind kept replaying the forty minutes or so they had spent together, kept going back to when he had asked her whether she intended to strike out at her husband. Why hadn't he dwelled on the real danger—that she would do herself in? Why hadn't he felt that risk in his gut?

He found a space on Beacon and jogged three blocks to number 214, a stately bowfront of two-hundred-year-old brick, with wide, granite steps and a pair of black, wrought iron lanterns framing a high-gloss crimson door. Two officers stood in front of the steps. Three cruisers and North Anderson's black Porsche Carrera were parked out front.

The officers recognized him and stepped aside.

As he walked up to the door, it opened. Anderson walked out, shut the door behind him.

Clevenger looked down Beacon. "I didn't see this coming."

"If you didn't, no one could have."

Clevenger looked at him. "I'm not sure."

Now Anderson looked away. "The husband is more bent out of shape than Coady let on. Maybe it's better to let them take her body to the morgue. You can learn what you need to from Wolfe."

Clevenger shook his head. "Where is she?"

"I can be our eyes here."

Clevenger started to move past him.

Anderson caught his arm. "Upstairs, in the master bedroom. Coady's there. Her husband is in the den to the right of the entryway."

Clevenger opened the door and walked into the house.

George Reese, Grace Baxter's husband, stood up from a burgundy leather armchair, cocked his head and stared at Clevenger through storm gray, bloodshot eyes. He was imperially slim, about six feet tall, and looked younger than his fifty-two years. His white, wing tip shirt was covered with blood. His jet black hair, worn oiled back, had fallen over his forehead.

Clevenger walked over to him. The palms of his hands and one of his cheeks were bloody, too. "I'm very sorry about..." he started.

Red blotches appeared on Reese's neck. "You have real nerve setting foot in my home," he said, struggling to keep his voice down.

Anderson moved to Clevenger's side.

Reese squinted at Clevenger. "She told me she called you five times today. And you never got back to her. What did you put before my wife's life?"

Clevenger smelled alcohol on Reese's breath. He glanced into the den, saw a bottle of Scotch open on the coffee table. "She called for an appointment," Clevenger said. "She got one for eight A.M. tomorrow morning." He knew that didn't sound like much of an answer.

"She didn't make it until morning," Reese seethed.

"I wish I could have done more," Clevenger said.

Reese took another step forward. Anderson started to move between them, but Clevenger signaled him to stay back.

"Five calls," Reese said. "Do most of your patients phone you half-a-dozen times in a few hours?" He spoke through clenched teeth. "Do you even know Grace's history, Dr. Clevenger? Did you bother to get her records before you saw her? Did you talk to her last psychiatrist?"

Those questions brought Clevenger back to another uncomfortable memory of his session with Grace Baxter—the way her "contract for safety" had rolled off her tongue, making him wonder how many times she had worried psychiatrists before. But he hadn't asked her.

"Three suicide attempts," Reese said. "Nine admissions to locked units."

Clevenger dropped his gaze for an instant, then made himself look Reese in the eyes, again.

"You didn't have an hour for her, maybe at the end of your busy day? You had somewhere to be?"

"I'm sorry about your wife," Clevenger said.

Reese leaned to whisper in Clevenger's ear. His breath was 80 proof. "You go on up to our bedroom and take a look at her. Go see what you've done." He stepped aside.

Clevenger walked past him, up the sweeping staircase to the second floor, with Anderson close behind. He heard Mike Coady's voice down the hall and headed toward it. He froze as he walked into the master bedroom.

Anderson put a hand on his shoulder. "She must have been stumbling around trying to get to the bed."

The comforter had been folded away from Baxter, who lay naked on bedclothes drenched with blood. The walls and carpet were speckled with it. A section of the light blue velvet drapes that hung over the windows had been pulled to the ground and lay in a blood-stained heap on the floor.

Clevenger walked to the bed along a plastic pathway rolled out by the crime scene investigators. He looked down at Baxter. Ruby lacerations crisscrossed her neck—a real hack job. Her wrists had each been cut once horizontally. She was still wearing her diamond bracelets and Rolex watch. They were covered in blood.

Coady walked to the opposite side of the bed. "Patient of yours?"

"She told me they felt like handcuffs," Clevenger said.

"Huh?"

"The bracelets," he said. "The watch."

"Pretty fancy handcuffs."

"Yes, they were."

"She got both carotids," Coady said. "The bathroom's even more of a mess."

"What did she use?"

"Carpet knife. They're renovating the third floor. Her husband says it must belong to one of the contractors."

Clevenger nodded.

"She left him a note," Coady said. He held out a plastic bag with a piece of five-by-eight stationery inside.

Clevenger took the bag. The stationery was blood-spattered, but legible.

My Love,

I cannot go on. As I fall off to sleep each night and as I leave sleep each morning I have only precious moments when I feel alive, before I wake fully to what my life has become. Imagine having only those few instants of happiness in an entire day and night, the sweetest and most fleeting illusion of freedom, and you may understand and even forgive what I have done.

I remember each of our kisses, every touch. When you entered me, I entered you. I escaped and left my pain behind. I cannot face it alone.

I was wrong to rely on you for my happiness. Your life is your own. But the idea of you leaving me darkens my horizon so completely that I cannot see any future, nor bear one more step toward it.

Please forgive me, everything.

Forever,

Grace

"Husband says they were talking about splitting up," Coady said. "He'd seen a lawyer."

Clevenger handed the bag back to him. "Is there somewhere we can talk?"

"Follow me."

Clevenger followed Coady along another length of plastic, into the bathroom. The walls were mirrored. Everywhere Clevenger turned he saw himself covered in the blood that had sprayed from Baxter's carotids. A cold sweat gripped him.

Coady used his gloved hand to close the door behind them. "Carpet knife," Coady said, pointing to the sink.

Clevenger looked into the sink, saw the carpet knife, its blade bloodstained. "She was Snow's lover," he said, without looking up.

"What are you talking about?"

"Grace Baxter and Snow. They were having an affair."

"She told you that?"

"No," Clevenger said, making eye contact with Coady. "I met with J. T. Heller today. Snow told him about it."

Coady looked like his mind was working to generate a simple solution to a complex problem. "Maybe she hears her man offed himself, gets depressed herself and . . ."

"Possible," Clevenger said. He paused. "How do you rule out the husband?"

"What?"

"The most common way women kill themselves is by overdose," Clevenger said. "Sometimes they cut their wrists. But her neck, and a single horizontal cut to each wrist? That would be one for the psychiatry journals. When someone goes for the carotids it's in response to psychosis—a delusion that the devil's blood is in your veins, that sort of thing. I didn't see any evidence of psychosis in Baxter."

"Let's be honest," Coady said. "You didn't see any of this coming."

That line landed like a kick to Clevenger's gut. It took him a few seconds to recover. "No," he said, finally. "I didn't. But that's important, too."

"Oh, I get it," Coady said. "This can't be happening because the all-seeing Frank Clevenger, M.D. missed it. We can't accept the obvious if it means you obviously fucked up."

"He is covered in her blood."

"He walked in, saw his wife of twelve years bleeding out in bed and tried to perform CPR. When we got here the body was still warm. No pulse, but still warm."

Clevenger didn't respond.

"What's his motive?" Coady asked. "Jealousy? Snow's death was all over the news today. He had to know he didn't exactly have to compete with him anymore." Hearing his own words seemed to jar him a bit.

"Agreed," Clevenger said. "Snow was out of the way."

"Oh, so now he's guilty of a double homicide. We got a banker, a pillar of the community, in a homicidal rage, killing his wife's lover in the A.M., then offing his wife in the early evening. And it's not like he walked in on them together, grabbed a gun and blew them away. No irresistible impulse here. He *planned* to off them both in the same day." He paused. "Now that would be one for the criminal science journals."

"Maybe he didn't plan very well," Clevenger said. He took a beat. "Look, I'm not saying he's necessarily involved. But his wife was cheating on him. She and her lover are dead. And he managed to get her blood all over him."

"Okay," Coady said, dismissively. "I won't officially rule him out."

"Just unofficially?"

"How about I run my own investigation? I had a single question for you: Was John Snow psychologically capable of suicide? If you want the case, that's the scope of the work. Whether or not we rule Baxter a suicide isn't your concern."

"I hear you," Clevenger said.

Coady knew he was being brushed off. "You should back off. You have a vested interest in this *not* being a suicide. Because if it is, it might also be a decent malpractice case."

"Which might be the only way to start getting the facts," Clevenger said. He turned and walked out.

SEVEN

• 8:40 P.M.

Clevenger left with Anderson. They met up again at their offices in Chelsea.

"What are you thinking?" Anderson asked, taking the seat beside Clevenger's desk—the one Grace Baxter had sat in.

"We have two people in love, or at least intimately involved, dead within hours of one another," Clevenger said. "Their affair certainly feels like the place to start. Someone couldn't stomach what they had, or couldn't stomach the fact that it was over."

"That could be Grace herself. She could be the shooter."

"Possible," Clevenger said. "But to inflict those wounds on herself, she had to be psychotic." He shook his head. "Maybe she was sicker than I could tell. She talked about feeling guilty. Maybe it was more than that. Maybe she was convinced she was evil. Maybe she believed bleeding out was the only way to purge herself of her sins."

"Could killing Snow have put her in that frame of mind?" Anderson said.

Clevenger looked back at him. "It could have." Part of the elegance of performing forensic evaluations of killers was understanding that their mental states could be dramatically affected by the act of murder itself. Killing can throw a person into something that looks a lot like mania, or even paranoid schizophrenia—sometimes

71

minutes, sometimes hours after the act. He shook his head. "She just didn't feel like someone who was losing contact with reality."

"Until we have something else, we go with your gut. If this was a murder-suicide, it's all over. Same thing if they each committed suicide. But if there's somebody out there guilty of a double homicide, we're the only ones looking for that person."

Anderson was right. The two of them were the only ones searching hard for the truth. And if that truth included a killer brazen enough to murder a high profile inventor and his high society lover, it was time to start worrying about their own safety. "We should start watching each other's back," he said.

"You got it," Anderson said.

"I think my next stop is Snow's wife, find out whether she knew about Grace Baxter. I get Snow's journal from Coady tomorrow morning. I'll take a look at it before I visit her."

"I still have Coroway to track down. And somehow we're going to have to get access to George Reese."

"Agreed."

"You realize we don't exactly have a client here," Anderson said. "You have a report on Snow's mental state to generate for Coady, but he might even pull that back if we go full throttle on a double homicide theory."

Clevenger thought about that. They were free to walk away from the case, and part of him would have liked to. There were plenty of other cases simmering in the office, not to mention how much time and energy it took to keep Billy out of trouble. But he knew that if someone had killed Grace Baxter and John Snow, that person would rest easier once he and Anderson quit. And that would keep him up at night, and bring back the nightmares, too, the ones of his father drunk and raging through the night. Having been murdered little by little by that man, he just couldn't stomach giving a killer the right of way. That's how the broken pieces of his psyche had set, what he had become. "The only client we ever really had was John Snow," he said. "I figure he's the only one who can call us off."

"If he does, let's hope it's long distance."

• 10:35 P.M.

Clevenger took the freight elevator to the fifth floor and started toward the steel door to his loft. He heard voices and occasional laughter coming from inside. He wondered whether Billy had invited a friend over, something he still had a habit of doing on school nights, despite Clevenger asking him to save it for weekends. He tried to pry his mind free from the investigation, to get ready to deliver a fatherly *Let's-call-it-a-night* speech—and something a little sterner once he and Billy were alone. But when he opened the door he saw J. T. Heller sitting with Billy at the kitchen island, drinking Cokes, like old buddies.

Heller stood up, walked over to Clevenger. He had a thick envelope in his hand. "Sorry to make myself at home," he said.

"Not at all," Clevenger said, taken aback.

"I was dropping off the records you asked for. Snow's inpatient psychiatry admission."

"Thank you."

"I wanted you to have them ASAP," Heller said. "You forgot to leave me your address today. I got this one from the Mass Medical Society. Billy said you'd be right back." He held out the envelope.

Clevenger took it. "I appreciate it."

"Looks like you keep the same kind of hours I do. I just finished a six-hour run in the O.R."

"You schedule people this late?"

"No. This guy came in to see his neurologist with the worst

headache of his life. They rushed him down to rays, like they should, grabbed an angio. Big-ass aneurysm sitting right on the superior cerebellar artery. No time to waste."

"How did he do?"

"When I opened, the thing was already leaking. If he'd waited one more hour to come in, he would have been history. I clipped it nice and tight and closed. Should be good for another hundred thousand miles." He winked, glanced up toward the ceiling. "God willing."

"Good for you."

"The day ended a lot better than it started, I'll tell you that," he said. Saying so seemed to bring him back to the morning. He suddenly looked as tired as a man should after losing one patient and barely saving another. "I should get going," he said.

"It's early," Billy blurted out, then looked down self-consciously, as if he'd dropped his veneer of cool somewhere near his feet.

Clevenger wasn't sure he'd ever heard him this excited to talk to an adult.

"I'm out of steam," Heller said to Billy. "Another time, though. Without fail." He winked at Clevenger. "Billy and I figured out we have a few things in common."

Billy looked up, again, beaming.

"That's great," Clevenger said. "Like what?"

"My road to the healing arts had a few twists and turns in it, including being put up for adoption."

"Not only that," Billy said.

Clevenger looked at Heller in a way that invited him to fill in the blanks.

"My biological parents left me at the hospital after my mother delivered. Walked out late that night and left the state. A couple from Brookline ended up taking me in. He was a doctor—at Mass General. She was a nurse. They couldn't have kids themselves." He glanced at Billy, then looked back at Clevenger. "I got to tell you, I put them through hell for years. Skipping school, stealing cars. I got nailed on an assault charge when I was eleven that bought me eight months in DYS lockup."

"Just like me," Billy said.

Billy had spent three months in Department of Youth Services custody about a year before, after he and a friend got into a beef with three other teenagers from nearby Saugus. The Saugus boys had all ended up in the E.R.

"What made the difference?" Clevenger asked.

"My religion," Heller said. "The nervous system." He let his words hang in the air a few seconds. "I started going to work with my dad—my adoptive father. He was a neurologist. He'd let me come by the hospital after school, hang out at his office, answer the phone now and then, occasionally sit with him while he examined patients—the really interesting ones."

"How cool is that?" Billy asked.

Clevenger figured Billy was thinking it was a whole lot cooler than he had been about sharing his forensic work. "And you ended up a neurosurgeon," he said to Heller. "You liked what you saw."

"I was fascinated by it. I was fascinated by him. In a real way, his giving me access to his professional life saved me. Until I saw what he could do for people, the power he had to help them, I didn't know we had that power inside us. The power for good."

"He said I can watch him in the O.R.," Billy glowed. "I can *scrub in*." He said the last words as though he had been admitted to a secret society with its own language. In a way, neurosurgery was that.

"I didn't exactly take that liberty," Heller said. "I told him I would check with you whether it might be alright."

Billy looked at Clevenger expectantly.

"Of course he can," Clevenger said. He felt a pang of jealousy, but knew it was irrational. After all, he was the one who had been wary of sharing his work. Billy would have been all over it.

"I'll call you with a couple of dates when I know we've got interesting cases," Heller said to Clevenger.

"Sounds good," Clevenger said.

"Next week, maybe, if we don't monkey with the schedule. I've got someone coming in who's been blind eleven years. She's thirty-three. Benign growth on the occipital nerve. If things go according to plan, and if I get a little lucky, she's gonna wake up, open her eyes and see."

"Jesus," Billy said.

"Jesus scrubs in on every case," Heller said to Billy. He turned back to Clevenger, nodded at the envelope in his hand. "Let me know if there's anything else I can do for you."

"Actually, if you've got a couple minutes," Clevenger said, "I wanted to bring you up to speed on a couple things on the Snow case. I can walk you out." He saw Billy's face fall. He hadn't meant to exclude him. And he certainly didn't want to look like he was competing for Heller's time. But he also didn't want to talk about Grace Baxter's murder in front of him. He tried to recover. "I'm sure you're as tired as I am, though," he said to Heller. "Why don't we talk first thing tomorrow?"

Billy got up from his seat. "You don't have to work around me," he said. "I got to lift, anyhow." He started toward his room.

"See you at the General," Heller said.

"That," Billy said.

Clevenger watched him disappear into his room.

"Is there a new development in the case?" Heller asked Clevenger.

"There is," Clevenger said. "Grace Baxter was found dead tonight."

"Grace Baxter . . ." Heller said, trying to place the name.

"Her husband George Reese is President of the Beacon Street Bank."

"Snow's Grace."

Clevenger nodded. "I just left Reese's house on Beacon Street."

"How did she die?"

"Her wrists were slashed, and her throat was cut."

"She killed herself." He squinted at Clevenger. His lip curled slightly. "You think she killed Snow? What is this, some sort of petty murder-suicide, love triangle bullshit. That's what I lost my patient to?"

"I don't know," Clevenger said, struck again by how Heller viewed everything through the prism of self-interest. Snow having lost his life didn't seem nearly as important to him as the fact that he had lost his star patient. "I didn't bring this up when you mentioned her earlier today in your office," Clevenger said, "but Baxter was a patient of mine. A new patient. I saw her once."

"You treated her?"

"She came for her first psychotherapy session this morning."

"That's strange."

"She probably booked the appointment because she was depressed Snow had left her."

"Did she talk about the affair?"

"No."

"She had threatened suicide over it," Heller said. "I think I mentioned that today."

"I wish I had known her psychiatric history," Clevenger said, his words barely sailing through the stiff resistance of his guilt. "I should have asked her more about it."

"You blame yourself for her death," Heller said. He looked directly into Clevenger's eyes.

What was it about Jet Heller that made for instant camaraderie, instant trust? Was it his own willingness to open up? Was it that he lacked rigid boundaries—dropping in for a late night visit, inviting Billy to the O.R.? Or maybe it was simply how comfortable he seemed with everything up to and including death. Would anything rattle a man who opened up other men's heads every day for a living? "There were questions I didn't ask," Clevenger said. He didn't mention the fact that he wasn't sure Baxter had killed herself in the first place.

"C'mon, Frank. Doc-to-doc. You think you killed her."

Clevenger cleared his throat. "She contracted for safety."

Heller nodded. "I've lost twenty-seven patients on the table," he said. "You want to know how many of them I screwed up on?"

"Listen, you don't have to . . ."

"Six. Possibly seven. They're dead because of my limitations as a healer."

Clevenger found himself fighting to listen to Heller more as his psychiatrist than his patient. "And what do you think about that?" he asked.

"I think I have one tough motherfucker of a job, which I happen to love, and I think I'm human, no matter what the newspapers say about me. If I can't stomach my failings, I have no business going inside anybody's head."

Clevenger swallowed hard.

"How about you, Frank? Are you human? Or are you starting to believe your own press—that you can heal anyone, solve anything?" He reached out and squeezed Clevenger's arm.

When you grow up with a father who shows you no love, a man reaching out to you can make you freeze or make you melt. Clevenger looked away as his eyes filled up.

"Right answer, brother," Heller said. "I've gone home the way you're feeling right now half a dozen times, and I'll go home that way a dozen more before I'm too old to hold a knife steady."

Clevenger took a deep breath, looked back at him. "Thanks," he said.

"Keep me up-to-date on this thing, if it doesn't violate any rules," Heller asked. "And if you end up thinking someone did this to Snow other than himself and need more dough to chase that fucker down, just ask. If somebody stole his life from him, they robbed me, too."

"I'll let you know anything important," Clevenger said. He had to remind himself he really didn't know Heller very well. "Anything that isn't classified. You understand."

"We all have our codes," Heller said. "I'll never ask you to violate yours." He nodded toward Billy's room. "Your boy's gonna be fine, by the way. He's got a really good heart." He shrugged. "You never know, he could be a neurosurgeon underneath all that hair and those piercings."

"You never know."

"Good night."

"Good night."

Heller turned and walked out.

Clevenger walked to Billy's room. His door was closed. No light seeped from under it. Either he was sleeping or pretending to. Clevenger stood there a few seconds, wanting to go in and wake him up, to try to do better at sharing Billy's excitement about Heller and the O.R. But he knew he'd get the usual, "Later, okay? I'm beat."

He walked to his desk facing the wall of windows that looked out onto the Tobin Bridge, sat down and opened the envelope Jet Heller had given him. He flipped to the Admission History and Physical, written by a Dr. Jan Urkevic, and read the section labeled "History of Present Illness."

Dr. Johnathan Snow, a 54-year-old, married, father of two, with epilepsy, is admitted for a competency evaluation prior to undergoing neurosurgery that carries very serious potential risks, including blindness and speech loss. He is a voluntary patient who states he is complying with the wishes of family members—especially his wife—in seeking this evaluation. "She needs to know I'm thinking rationally, that in deciding whether to move forward with the surgery, I've weighed its benefits and risks—even if she disagrees with my position."

Dr. Snow describes the planned procedure as "experimental." Discreet parts of his brain will be excised by Dr. J. T. Heller in an effort to remove the seizure foci responsible for Dr. Snow's epilepsy, a condition he describes as a "life sentence, with the prison inside me." He states, "My brain is broken. It short-circuits when my mind generates my best thoughts. My neural pathways can't handle the electrical current driven by my imagination."

In stating this, Dr. Snow understands he is using a metaphor to describe his condition. He is fully aware that removing the seizure foci in his brain—even if this procedure cures him of epilepsy—may or may not result in increased intellectual function. He is willing to accept the risks of surgery (which he lists accurately) whether or not he experiences any gain in that realm.

Dr. Snow holds a Ph.D in aeronautical engineering and works as an inventor at a company he co-founded (Snow-Coroway Engineering). There is no indication that he has become unable to perform tasks requiring memory, concentration or rational decision-making.

Clevenger scanned down to the section labeled "Past Psychiatric History," noted that Snow denied suffering any psychiatric illness in the past, or having seen a psychiatrist. Under "Mental Status

Examination," Urkevic had recorded his denying any suicidal or homicidal thoughts or any hallucinations. In his conclusions, he found Snow competent, pending psychological testing.

Clevenger fanned pages until he found a "Psychological Testing Report" by Dr. Kenneth Sklar. It was the part of Snow's medical record that would offer the best window on his intellect and inner emotional life, including any conscious or unconscious wish he might have had to die. The assessment included a battery of tests, including intelligence testing, personality profiling, and ink blots.

He started reading.

ASSESSMENT PROCEDURES:

> *Interview*
> *Rorschach Ink Blot Test*
> *Thematic Apperception Test (TAT)*
> *MMPI-2*
> *Wechsler Adult Intelligence Scale-III*
> *Bender-Gestalt Test (BGT) with recall*
> *Dementia Rating Scale-2*

OBSERVATIONS OF BEHAVIOR:

Dr. Snow was seen in my office on Ellison 7 at the Massachusetts General Hospital for all testing. He is a tall, attractive man who was affable throughout our meetings. His flow of thought was normal and he showed a marked absence of anxiety (See below). He was curious about the rationale for each of the tests being administered, but not intrusive. He did show a tendency to question whether this evaluator was skilled in psychological assessment, including asking my educational history and number of years of experience. That said, he was compliant and forthcoming in every regard.

RESULTS OF TESTING:

Results of Dr. Snow's WAIS-III intelligence testing reveals an extremely bright and intellectual man. Verbal and nonverbal reasoning is in the extremely gifted range, with an IQ score well into the range of genius, at 165.

The WAIS also disclosed an ability to think in both a data-oriented way, as well as a more abstract way. His technical know-how, in other words, does not limit his creativity. This duality is highly unusual and no doubt explains Dr. Snow mastering a complex scientific discipline and then being able to apply that discipline in new and "inventive" ways.

Results of projective and objective personality testing (including the MMPI), however, did reveal certain limitations. He displays a marked tendency toward self-criticism and criticism of others. He dwells far more on his own deficits than his strengths and is similarly focused on the failings of others. He defines many of the characters in stories presented to him as "flawed" or "not worthwhile." People are held to ideal, rather than realistic, standards of conduct. Intelligence is lauded, but only when it reflects genius. Any lower level of intelligence is denigrated. Ideals of physical beauty are prized. Physical shortcomings are exaggerated.

These themes continued to be evidenced on the Rorschach. Dr. Snow saw many of the cards as representing "chaos" or "a storm," indicating his lack of comfort with the symmetrical, but randomly generated patterns. On one of the most colorful cards, he commented, "Maybe a garden. Not well-conceived. A hodgepodge. One thing bleeding into another."

Interestingly, disorder did not cause Dr. Snow to experience anxiety, but rather a heightened level of activation closer to irritability. He likened the emotion to that he experiences while inventing. He stated that thinking up the right answer to a problem requires rejecting the wrong ones, including those that are strictly correct, but mediocre solutions. These imperfect ideas, he said, "do make me angry, angry enough to kill them off—especially when they're mine." It is a feeling he enjoys and which he links quite directly with the onset of his creative genius.

This emphasis on the need for perfection and order can lead Dr. Snow to ruminative, self-absorbed thinking. People are expected to "make everything they can of themselves" and to keep their emotions from ruling their intellect. When they do not, they are seen as "weak" or "damaged," particularly if their behavior causes him additional stress.

Dr. Snow's Thematic Apperception Test stories bear this out. For example, he generated the following narrative in response to a picture of a young child pondering a violin:

> He's thinking about Mendelssohn, what he did with a violin, and wondering if he could make music like that. There's always hope. Maybe he's gifted. And there's no way to find out other than to play. But it takes a lot of courage. I mean, who really wants to find out you fit in with the high school band?

When I challenged Dr. Snow on this type of elitist thinking, he justified his feelings as reflecting that of society as a whole, "even if no one cares to admit it." In his words:

> Why don't they broadcast pickup games of basketball at the local park? Because nobody cares. They're irrelevant. All that really matters is the NBA, and then only the world champions, and then only the superstar at the center of that team. That's what every pickup game and high school game and college game across America is feeding. All that energy gets

sucked to the very top, like a root system, so that we can witness a three-point shot in the last two seconds of the final game on CBS and stand on our feet, which is a way of worshiping—worshiping greatness, which is just a reflection of God.

Dr. Snow views his own work in precisely the same way. He shuns group process, is his own harshest critic, and judges his performance against the likes of Benjamin Franklin, Albert Einstein, and Bill Gates.

SUMMARY

In conclusion, it could certainly be said that a different man might tolerate Dr. Snow's epilepsy and reject the risks of surgery which he accepts. He has always considered his seizures "a profound weakness," going so far as to label them "grotesque." But this harsh vision of his pathology does not rise to the level of a delusion and should not impact his ability to consent to a procedure designed to remedy it.

Dr. Snow's intellect, memory and concentration are intact. There is no clear evidence suggesting a thought disorder or psychotic condition. I consider him competent.

Should Dr. Snow be denied his surgery by the Ethics Committee, I would be concerned how his mental status might be impacted. There is some chance he could come to reject the notion of living out his days with his disorder.

More than ever, Clevenger had trouble believing Snow would end up alone in an alleyway the morning of his surgery, having lost courage. Neither Urkevic nor Sklar had detected any depression, or history of it, that could explain him becoming suicidal. He wasn't an anxious man. He had a positive, perhaps even grandiose self-image, and his anger was directed at his imperfections, many of which he was about to rid himself of. He was not only killing off the parts of his brain responsible for his seizures, but the parts of his memory responsible for much of his suffering, the parts that tied him to flawed relationships. He had to feel euphoric.

The phone rang. He picked up. "Clevenger."

"How you doing?" Mike Coady asked.

Clevenger heard something genuine in Coady's tone. "Hanging in there," he said.

"Good. That's good." He paused. "I'm down here at the Medical Examiner's office with Jeremiah Wolfe. He's into the autopsy on Grace Baxter."

"And?"

"She had food in her stomach. She ate within an hour of her death."

Which didn't exactly square with a suicidal panic. But it didn't absolutely rule it out, either. He wondered why Coady was really calling. "So she decided to have a last meal," he said. "So what?"

"I'm sure that happens."

"Without a doubt."

"But it's strange, all the same."

He wasn't sure where Coady was headed, or why he wouldn't go straight there. "Okay, it's strange."

"So Jeremiah took a very close look at her stomach contents. He came up with a pill fragment, matched it up with one of those photos in the doctor's reference book."

"The Physicians' Desk Reference," Clevenger said.

"Turns out this pill fragment he found looks like a match with a vitamin pill—something called Materna."

Clevenger's heart sank. "That's a prenatal vitamin," he said softly.

Coady didn't answer right away. "The ultrasound shows she's, uh . . . She was about three months. Maybe a little more."

85

"Three months," Clevenger repeated.

"So, I don't know, maybe there's something to what you were saying. I'm no psychiatrist, but I don't see a woman taking one of those vitamins before she kills herself. And I can't quote the stats, but I wouldn't think pregnant women kill themselves all that often, to begin with."

"No. No, they don't."

"Because they've got the birth to look forward to and all that. Right? There's another life to think about."

Clevenger thought he heard Coady's voice break toward the end of that sentence. He wanted to give him the chance to say what he was feeling. "I don't think I'll ever get used to this work," he said.

Coady didn't take him up on the invitation. "There is the suicide note, though."

"I'd like a copy of that."

"I'll get it to you." He cleared his throat. "I have no hard evidence implicating George Reese in his wife's death," he said. "And I still think it's a huge stretch to figure him for a double homicide in a twelve-hour period. It would be an incredibly foolish plan, and he's no fool. I still see Snow alone in that alleyway."

Clevenger didn't want to argue the point. "George Reese isn't the only one who might have been enraged over the affair," he said. "I haven't interviewed anyone in Snow's family yet."

"When will that happen?"

"I'd like it to happen tomorrow."

"I'll set it up. I can bring Reese in for questioning anytime. But the more we know about his wife's relationship with John Snow from other sources, the better."

"Sounds like we're on the same page," Clevenger said.

Coady didn't grab that olive branch, either. "One other thing," he said. "Reese made a threat after you left."

"What kind of threat?"

"He said you should be on your way to the morgue, not his wife."

"Thanks for letting me know."

"I can offer police protection based on that," Coady said. "He's a man with resources."

"Thanks, but no," Clevenger said.

"I didn't think you'd take me up on it." His voice trailed off. "Three, three-and-a-half months, you can't save a child, right? Even four."

Clevenger closed his eyes. He realized Coady was worried whether he could have done anything to save Grace's baby. It was an irrational thought—he hadn't even known she was pregnant at the time—but the irrational thoughts were the ones with the power to burn holes in your gut. "No," Clevenger said. "The child couldn't have survived." He knew Coady would need something even more definitive than that for when the doubts came back in the night—maybe not that night, maybe in six weeks, or six years. "No chance," he said. "Zero."

" 'Course not," Coady said, recovering. He cleared his throat. "Talk to you tomorrow."

EIGHT

Clevenger got a call just after 7:00 A.M. from Mike Coady telling him he was cleared to meet with the Snow family at their home on Brattle Street, in Cambridge, at 10:00 A.M. Before starting over, he stopped at police headquarters and picked up the envelope Coady had left for him. Inside was a copy of Snow's journal, along with five floppy discs of the files found on Snow's laptop.

He got to Harvard Square at 9:35 and parked on Massachusetts Avenue, half a mile from the Snows' house. He opened the envelope, took out the hundred or so sheets of paper.

The first thing that struck him was the heading on the first page: Renaissance, French for rebirth. The second was Snow's handwriting: The printed characters were so small they were barely legible. There had to be a thousand words to a page. Some were circled, some boxed, some underlined. Sentences blew past the margin, climbed to the top of the page, flipped upside-down and streaked across the top, continuing down the other side, as though Snow's thoughts met no resistance.

Clevenger fanned the pages, saw the text interrupted in places by schematic drawings and mathematic calculations.

Then Clevenger noticed something else: There were no mistakes—not a single word crossed out or written over. Each and every tiny letter was perfectly inked. Amidst what looked like chaos there was absolute order, like a puzzle of a hundred-thousand pieces fitting together to form a perfect maze.

He started reading, sometimes turning the page sideways or upside-down to follow the text.

RENAISSANCE

We exist inside our bodies, but separate from them.

By law, a person of sound mind is allowed to let his body die, to refuse medical care that would sustain it, in accordance with his or her religious beliefs. Because that person's religion asserts that the survival of the soul is paramount.

We exist inside our bodies, but separate from them.

A fetus lives inside a woman. But by the law of the land, that woman can decide to remove that part of her biology as inconsistent with her life story.

One step further. What if the spirit residing inside the body of a man or a woman wishes to be rid of the particular biology binding him to all relationships from the past? For biology and nothing more does so, nests of neurons in the cingulate gyrus, temporal lobe and hippocampus. What if the memories encoded there are no longer consistent with his sense of self? What if he knows this spiritually with the same fervor that a woman can know she is not compatible with the life stirring inside her womb?

The man knows his spirit could still soar if not shackled to the past. He suffers greatly for his bondage, unable to move in the direction of his dreams. Why is that man worthy of less concern than the others? Why should his soul not be set free? Why should his spirit age and die in lock step with the body, when in truth it can be reborn by simply removing the appropriate obstacles in the nervous system?

I am this man, strangled by tethers that bind me to a loveless marriage, to children I am no father to, to friends and a business partner who are those things in name only. I wish to be free of them all.

My story has gone wrong, and I long to write another.

Let them have their lives and let me have mine. But let me truly begin anew, unencumbered by even a distant memory of them. Because then they will have no claim on me.

The man they knew will be dead.

And I will be reborn.

The medical science to achieve this personal renaissance is at hand. Do I have the right to use it? Is it moral to cleave myself from the past, to move cleanly on from my current life story to begin another?

Snow had stopped writing there, filling the next few pages with drawings and calculations. The drawings were three-dimensional and highly detailed, depicting a cylinder in various positions—lying flat, at a thirty-degree angle, a forty-five degree angle, upright. In one rendering Snow had drawn arrows to indicate the cylinder spinning counterclockwise, in another clockwise. In still others, it tumbled end-over-end.

The calculations looked like lengthy solutions to physics equations. Beneath them, Snow had written, "Every Action Causes an UNEQUAL and Opposite Reaction."

Clevenger flipped the page and stopped short. Midway down the right-hand side, surrounded by calculations, was a two-inch by two-inch drawing of a woman's head and shoulders—Grace Baxter's. Snow had obviously lingered over it, spending time shading in her hair, eyes, lips, capturing subtleties of her beauty.

The portrait was imbued with emotion missing not only from Snow's schematics and calculations, but from his writing. There was real passion in it.

Clevenger turned page after page—more cylinders and numbers, more philosophical reflections.

He checked his watch. 10:47. He started the car and drove to Brattle Street, pulled up in front of 119, a majestic brick colonial on half an acre, behind fifty yards of stone wall and a semicircular driveway shaded by massive oaks. The place had to be worth at least $5 million. A Mercedes limousine, a Land Cruiser and three police cruisers were parked outside.

He got out of the car and walked toward the front door. A cop named Bob Fabrizio got out of his cruiser, headed over to him. Clevenger knew him from working another Cambridge case—a Harvard professor who'd murdered his wife. "What's with the show of force?" Clevenger asked him.

"Paid detail," Fabrizio said. "The widow feels uneasy."

"Enough to order up three cruisers."

"Four. We had three available."

"I guess you can't blame her," Clevenger said. "Her husband was shot about thirty hours ago."

"Hey, I don't mind the work," Fabrizio said. "But it gives this whole thing a little O.J–JonBenet feeling, if you ask me."

"Meaning?"

"Four cruisers? Who does she think is coming for her, the frickin' Mossad? You said it yourself: a show of force. Maybe this is all show. Maybe she wants to *look* good and scared, keep all eyes off her—or the son."

"You know anything about him?"

"Like every other cop in Cambridge. Two arrests, cocaine possession. One arrest, A and B. One malicious threatening. He called in a bomb threat to his prep school in Connecticut. He had a crude device on him, wouldn't have ignited a Duraflame log. All charges were dismissed or continued without a finding. Fancy lawyers. Kid's basically a hothead, but you never know. I mean, either this guy Snow killed himself, or he got killed by someone with access to his gun. Either way, the compass in my gut points right here."

"Thanks for the consult."

"No charge. Hey, how's Billy doing?"

"Fine," Clevenger said, a little taken aback by Fabrizio's interest. He sometimes forgot Billy had gotten famous from the Nantucket murder case that cost him his baby sister. Once his name was cleared, just about every national magazine ran a story about him. And when Clevenger adopted him, the feeding frenzy only intensified.

"Good to hear it," Fabrizio said. "We're all rootin' for him." He headed back toward his cruiser.

Clevenger walked up to the front door, rang the bell. Half a minute later a very pretty young woman with straight, long, light brown hair, and deep brown eyes opened the door. She was dressed in a tight-fitting, black, V-neck sweater and tighter Levi's. She looked about twenty-two, twenty-three. "You're from the police?" she asked.

"That's right," he said, offering his hand. "Frank Clevenger."

She shook his hand in a halfhearted way, let it go. "Mom's waiting for you in the living room."

Could she be just eighteen? he wondered. "You're John Snow's daughter?"

"Lindsey."

"I'm sorry about your dad."

Her eyes filled up. "Thank you," she said, just above a whisper. She stepped aside. "Straight ahead."

Clevenger walked along an oriental runner that took him past a turned staircase and down a hallway with white wainscoting and widely striped wallpaper of deep green and olive hues. Antique architectural drawings of Cambridge landmarks hung on the walls—probably Snow's wife's choice, as the architect in the family. The hallway ended in the living room, framed on either side by six-foot-high fireplaces with limestone mantels carved with angels blowing trumpets. Above them hung two magnificent oil paintings. And above them, the ceiling was bordered by intricate crown molding a foot deep, carved with oak leaves and acorns.

The room was so imposing it took Clevenger a few seconds to notice a slim woman about five-foot-two, standing at an arched window, looking out at ice-covered gardens that glistened in the late morning sun. She wore gray flannel pants and a simple light blue sweater that almost made her fade into the gray-and-blue-striped wallpaper. "Excuse me," he said.

She turned around. "I'm sorry. I didn't hear you. Please, come in." She motioned toward a pair of love seats in the center of the room.

He met her at the love seats. "Frank Clevenger," he said, extending his hand.

"Theresa Snow." She shook his hand stiffly, then let hers go limp and fall away. She was elegant looking, though not beautiful. Her eyes were the light blue of her sweater, her hair prematurely gray, worn just off her shoulders. There was an angular quality to her face—her cheekbones and jaw—that made her look as though she was concentrating very hard. She smiled for an instant, but it did nothing to soften her. She sat down.

He sat opposite her.

"Detective Coady told me you'll be helping with the investigation," she said.

"That's right," Clevenger said.

"Thank you. We appreciate it more than you could know." She laced her hands together beneath her chin, as if praying.

"I need to learn as much about your husband as possible," Clevenger said. "I need to understand him, in order to understand what might have happened to him."

"You mean, whether he committed suicide," she said. She let out her breath.

"That's part of it."

"Detective Coady said as much." She leaned forward, placed her hands on one knee. "You have to believe me: My husband would never commit suicide."

Clevenger noticed she wore no jewelry other than a modest diamond solitaire and slim wedding band. "Why do you say that?" he asked.

"Because he was a narcissist."

That was no compliment, but Snow's wife didn't sound bitter. She sounded like she was stating a fact—her husband was in love with himself. "He didn't care about other people?" Clevenger asked.

"Only so much as they confirmed what he wanted to believe about himself and the world around him. He used people like mirrors, to reflect his own self-image."

"Which was what?" Clevenger asked, glancing at the painting hanging over the mantel behind Snow. It was the silhouette of a naked woman, standing behind a lace curtain, looking out on a lanterned Boston street at dusk. It looked familiar, like he might have seen it in a book or something.

"That he was infallible, all powerful," Snow said. She settled back in her seat. "I'll miss him terribly. I don't quite know how to go on without him. But I don't want to candy-coat our lives together. He was a complicated man."

"What will you miss?"

"His confidence. His creativity. He was brilliant. Truly. Once you've been in the company of that kind of mind, it's very hard to imagine being in any other company. At least it is for me."

Not only did Clevenger detect no bitterness in Theresa Snow, he detected very little grief. She sounded like a newscaster bidding farewell to a famous politician she'd covered for a couple decades. "Self-consumed people aren't immune from suicide," Clevenger said. "Sometimes they can't bear the difference between how they see themselves and how the world sees them."

"That makes sense for someone who cares about the world around him," she said. "But John didn't give anyone that kind of power. He never wondered whether his thoughts and feelings about himself, or anyone else, were justified. Maybe that's why I never saw him depressed. He always believed the problems in his life were outside him, never inside."

"Did he tend to get angry?"

"He had a temper."

"How did he express it?" he asked. He glanced at the painting, again.

"By making people feel dead," she said.

"Excuse me?" Clevenger asked, focusing on her again.

"If you didn't match John's vision of reality, he simply didn't treat you as though *you* were real. There were times shortly after we married when we would argue—over nothing terribly important—and he wouldn't speak to me for weeks. He had the ability to pretend a person had disappeared off the face of the earth."

Which was essentially what John Snow was planning to do with everyone in his life, courtesy of Jet Heller's scalpel. Clevenger didn't need to ask Theresa Snow why she had stayed married for twenty-odd years to someone so self-consumed. The answer had to be that she wasn't psychologically prepared for a deeper relationship. Living with Snow had given her the trappings of family, including a gracious home and children, but it all came with a guarantee she would be left alone emotionally. That kind of trade-off can work to sustain a marriage between two limited people, but it can also set the stage for trouble: If Theresa Snow came to believe her husband had become truly intimate with someone else, violating their code of mutual isolation, she might feel branded as the only damaged one, abandoned to her solitude. And that could make her very rageful.

Clevenger wondered just how much, if anything, Snow's wife knew about Grace Baxter. And that question made him realize what seemed so familiar about the painting over the mantel. It reminded him of Baxter. But not in death. That wasn't the reference point. It was the drawing he had seen in John Snow's journal. Snow had drawn Grace's head and shoulders from exactly the same perspective. He had been brazen enough to bring her portrait into his home.

"Like it?" Theresa Snow asked.

"Excuse me?"

"The painting," she said. "You seem taken by it."

"It's very fine work."

"John found her." She glanced back at the portrait. "She is magnificent, isn't she?"

Was she being coy, Clevenger wondered, speaking in code about Baxter?

"The artist is local," Snow went on. "Ron Kullaway." She nodded over Clevenger's shoulder. "That one is his, too."

Clevenger looked behind him at the painting over the other mantel, a winter scene of the Public Garden skating rink, crowded with skaters. "Remarkable." He turned back around.

"John hadn't been terribly interested in art, until recently. He became very knowledgeable very quickly. He collected several significant pieces."

"That must have been nice for the two of you," Clevenger said, hearing how hollow his own words sounded.

"I think John enjoyed it a great deal," Snow said, matter-of-factly. "I never fully grasped his passion for it."

Clevenger wanted to open the door to Theresa Snow telling him she knew about Grace Baxter—if she did. "You considered him a good husband, in spite of his narcissism?" he asked her.

She stared at Clevenger several seconds, her face blank. "He was *my* husband," she said, finally. "He wasn't the perfect man he imagined himself to be. But I forgave him his shortcomings. I didn't expect him to be normal. He was extraordinary."

That didn't answer Clevenger's question. "I wondered whether the two of you were getting along," he pressed. "His driver took him to the hospital the morning of his surgery."

"And?"

"I wondered why."

For the first time, Theresa Snow looked a little angry. "You wonder because of your own frame of reference," she said. "You believe when people are facing a danger like surgery, their families should be with them—physically. Most people share your view. I happen to, as well. But John's vision of reality was of himself as invulnerable. He would never have tolerated me or the children seeing him at a moment of weakness, or fear, pre-op or post-op. The support we could give him was to leave him alone. He told me Pavel would be driving him, and I knew not to press the point."

"Or else he would pretend you didn't exist?"

"I was happy to be able to kiss him good-bye and wish him well."

"You understood the man you married."

"I'm not sure anyone understood him. I forgave him his limitations. That may have been selfish, on my part."

"Why do you say that?" Clevenger asked.

"I married a genius. I never regretted it. What John lacked in interpersonal skills, he more than made up for with his intellectual abilities. He could literally startle you with his brain power. It was magnificent to be close to. I can't really describe it. I suppose it was a little like being close to any other force of nature. A sunrise. A storm. Maybe like living on a beach, mesmerized by waves that could sweep the foundation from under your home. But my daughter didn't approve of that trade-off, and she had to live in our home, too. I think that made life very difficult for her."

"In what way?"

"The constant pressure to be perfect," Snow said. "She's very fortunate. She's beautiful and she has a mind nearly the equal of her father's—when she decides to use it. He utterly adored her. But I think the constant effort to please him was a burden. She hadn't been trying quite as hard lately, and things weren't going quite as well."

"What changed?"

"I think she's been distracted, in a very good way. She's become very committed to her studies." She smiled, almost bashfully. "And she may have finally discovered boys." The smile was gone. "She used to literally be John's shadow. She'd do her homework in his office here, while he did his own work. She would call him at Snow-Coroway several times a day to check in. That was all falling by the wayside."

"How about your son? How did living with your husband affect him?"

"That's a different story." A mixture of sadness and frustration showed in her face. She let out her breath. "Kyle could never win his father's love, no matter what he did."

"Why is that?"

"He has . . . learning differences."

She didn't seem to like saying the words. "Dyslexia?"

"That, and problems with concentration."

"How did that interfere with his relationship with your husband?" Clevenger asked. He knew the answer from the psychological testing in Snow's medical records. Snow's focus on ideals of beauty, strength and intelligence wouldn't mesh with a child battling "learning differences."

"John saw Kyle as fundamentally flawed. Broken. He doted on him as an infant and a toddler. He was an absolutely stunning child. But when it became apparent he was different . . . At first John went to the ends of the earth to find a solution—to fix him. Mass General. Johns Hopkins. He even took him to London for a program that focuses on computer-assisted learning. When he found out he couldn't make him normal, he began to avoid him."

"How did he manage to do that?"

"He arranged to send Kyle to special schools, starting at a very young age. The first of them was in Portsmouth, New Hampshire. He was seven. They were long days, with the commute and all. He'd leave at 7:00 A.M. and return at 7:00 P.M., sometimes later. From grade six, he lived away at school in Connecticut. He's only been here with us full-time since graduating high school in June."

Clevenger nodded. "You didn't object to the schooling?"

"I didn't love the idea," Snow said. "But I thought—still think—it was better for him than the alternative. He would have been completely destroyed if he had been here more of the time, with John ignoring him."

"Your husband wouldn't have become more accepting of him over time?"

"Not John. No."

It didn't sound like Theresa Snow had ever confronted her husband, even when he banished their learning-challenged son to a decade of private schooling out of state. But Clevenger knew she had stood up to him at least once, forcing him to have his mental competency evaluated prior to surgery. Was that because she knew it was her last chance to keep him in her life? Did she know he was leaving her? "Didn't you take a big risk forcing your husband to undergo a psychiatric evaluation?" he asked. "That had to be a serious challenge to his self-image. He could have cut you off."

"You've been to see Dr. Heller," she said. "Do you have John's medical records?"

"Yes," Clevenger said.

She nodded to herself. "Forcing the evaluation carried that risk," she said. "I knew he might never speak to me again. But I had to know if he was being rational. He was putting his speech and his vision on the line. And he had been acting oddly before he decided in favor of the surgery—nearly euphoric. It had been building for months." She shrugged. "John didn't put up much resistance to the evaluation. I'm sure he knew all along the testing would prove he was thinking clearly. If it hadn't, I might not have heard from him ever again. He was magnanimous in victory, much less so in defeat."

"Tough person to be in love with."

"No," she said immediately. "He was easy to love. I understood him. He spent all his tolerance for imperfection in one place: his seizures. He could barely cope with that. Any other lack of order was unacceptable to him. That's another reason he would never have committed suicide. He had the chance to be seizure-free. He was ecstatic about it."

"He didn't share any of your second thoughts about the surgery?"

"He had complete confidence in Dr. Heller. He knew the potential side effects, but he didn't believe he would suffer them."

Clevenger nodded to himself. There was one side effect John Snow fully expected to "suffer"—loss of memory. "If your husband didn't take his own life," Clevenger asked, "who do you think did?"

She hesitated, but only a few seconds. "I've urged Detective Coady to focus on Collin," she said.

That was a more definitive answer than Clevenger had expected. "Why Collin?" he asked.

"John and he had come to an impasse over the company. Collin was enraged over it."

"Whether Snow-Coroway would go public," Clevenger said.

"That was a major part of it. John would never have allowed that to happen."

"What was the rest?"

"An invention of John's."

"What sort of invention?"

"John was a good deal of the way toward inventing a system to make a flying object invisible to radar. He called it Vortek."

"A flying object, meaning a plane?"

"The system was designed specifically for missiles. The way John explained it, missiles actually do three things in addition to moving forward: They spin, tumble end-over-end and tilt side-to-side. Radar works by identifying any of the three motions. He had developed an array of gyroscopes that would prevent all of them. The company expected a windfall from military contractors."

"But . . ."

"John had second thoughts. He was an inventor, and he loved the fact that his brain had generated an idea as elegant as Vortek, but he saw that he was creating a monster. He knew it would ultimately cause the deaths of many, many people. He wouldn't sign off on selling the intellectual property."

"He had veto power?"

"Every major decision at Snow-Coroway required two signatures—his and Collin's."

"And in the event of your husband's death . . ."

"His ideas become the property of the company. All control shifts to Collin."

"In other words," Clevenger said, "Collin Coroway is free to move forward with the project now."

"Yes. And John was certain Vortek would generate more than a billion dollars in revenue. It would make an initial public offering of the company's stock a sensation. Now nothing prevents Collin from going ahead with it."

Clevenger felt Theresa Snow pushing hard to shift the thrust of the investigation toward Collin Coroway. Could that be because she didn't want any suspicion swirling around her? Her son? "Did you agree with your husband?" he asked. "You felt his invention should stay under wraps?"

"Of course."

"That's a very moral position—and a very expensive one."

She didn't miss the subtext of Clevenger's comment. "You're asking whether I would trade my husband's life for a larger inheritance?"

"I didn't mean . . ."

"It's a good question," she said flatly. "I'll give you a very direct answer. Between my husband's equity in Snow-Coroway, our other assets and his life insurance policy, I expect to inherit approximately a-hundred-and-fifty-million dollars. Not less than a-hundred-and-twenty million. I can live on that."

Clevenger had the impulse to ask whether Snow's children were also represented in his will—particularly the son he had never been able to love. But he held back. "Would you mind if I spent time over the next few days talking with Kyle and Lindsey?" he asked.

"To what end?"

"I'm sure they have their own perspectives on your husband. A complete family history is standard in an evaluation like this one. *Not* speaking to them would be very peculiar."

"By all means, then," she said. "We'll do anything we can to make the investigation go smoothly." Her jaw tightened, giving her face an even harder edge. "Whoever took John's life," she said, "robbed me of my husband. But he robbed all of us of the fruits of John's intellect. If Collin is that person, I don't want him rewarded. I want him to pay."

"Have you suggested Detective Coady consider any other suspect?" Clevenger asked.

"I haven't. If Collin can prove he wasn't near Mass General yesterday morning, I don't have any idea who could have done this. I'll have to rely on the police—and you—to find out."

"Do you think Collin might try to hurt you?" Clevenger asked. "I saw the cruisers out front."

"It's foolish, I know," she said. "I don't see why anyone would have any reason to hurt me or the children. But the truth is I don't know what to expect, anymore. John made the world seem very predictable and manageable, almost as though he could invent his future—and ours—singlehandedly. He was obviously wrong about that."

NINE

Clevenger was almost back to his car when a woman called out his name. He turned around, saw Lindsey Snow jogging toward him.

She walked up to him. She hadn't put on a jacket and was hugging herself to stay warm. "Do you have one minute?"

"Of course."

"You saw my father?" she asked quietly. I mean . . . after."

Clevenger hadn't expected Snow's daughter to suddenly hand him the weight of her grief. He felt his breathing and heart rate slow and wondered again why sharing the pain of others steadied him. "Yes," Clevenger said. "I saw your father."

"I know you're just starting to figure out what happened." She hugged herself tighter. Her eyes filled up.

"It's cold. Let's talk back at the house."

She shook her head. "My mom doesn't want me talking to you at all."

"Why is that?"

"Let's just drive somewhere."

Clevenger wasn't about to drive away with a teenager he had just met. "We can talk in my truck," he said.

"Okay."

He walked her over to the truck, opened the passenger door for her. She climbed inside. He got in the driver's side, started the engine and got the heat going.

She looked straight through the windshield, the way Billy sometimes did when he was upset. "I guess what I'm asking, even though you probably can't say yet, or wouldn't tell me . . ." She swallowed hard, closed her eyes. "I want to know whether my dad killed himself." She looked over at him, then quickly away. "I need to know." She drew her legs up close to her body, rested her head on her knees.

For the first time, she looked more like a troubled kid than a woman. "That's the most painful question for you?" Clevenger asked her.

Tears streamed down her face.

"Is that because you think you know the answer?"

She nodded, and the tears really started to flow. "I feel so alone," she managed.

Clevenger felt the impulse to hold her and comfort her, like a father would. But that would dissolve professional boundaries he needed to keep in place. If he started out by thinking of Lindsey as someone to protect, he might never be able to see the Snow family dynamics for what they really were.

He wondered why Lindsey seemed so comfortable sitting in his truck, opening up to a complete stranger. Why had she suggested driving off together? Was she trying to draw him in? "You don't have to tell me what you're thinking," he said, to see whether pulling back would bring her closer.

It worked instantly. "I have to tell someone," she said. With her arms still wrapped around her knees, she turned her face toward Clevenger.

That simple movement, spilling her shiny hair over her cheek and neck, showcasing her deep brown, wet eyes and full lips, changed her again—from girl back to woman. "I killed him," she said.

Clevenger looked into her eyes, saw some of the same emptiness he had seen in the eyes of killers. And he suddenly felt danger of another kind sitting there alone with Lindsey Snow. He pressed his leg against the door, made sure he hadn't forgotten to strap his pistol to his shin before leaving Chelsea. Just as he did, he saw Lindsey's eyes fill with despair and vulnerability, and she morphed again from woman to girl, killer to victim. "You're telling me you shot your father?" he asked her.

She looked out the windshield again. "I made him shoot himself," she said.

"You made him?"

"I . . ." She looked as though the words were excruciatingly painful for her to speak. "I made him feel like he should be dead."

"How did you do that?"

"I told him I wished he were."

"And you think telling him that would be enough to make him end his life?"

Her eyes went cold and empty again. "Yes."

Lindsey Snow obviously believed she wielded extreme power over her father—the power to sap his will to live. That probably meant Snow had made her feel entirely responsible for his happiness. "Why did you want your father dead?" Clevenger asked her.

She curled into a tighter ball than before, let her hair fall back over her face. "He lied to me," she whispered.

"About . . . ?"

"Everything," she said, a hint of rage creeping into her voice.

Did Lindsey know of Snow's love affair with Grace Baxter? Or did she know her father was preparing to leave everyone—including her? And who might she have told? Her mother? Her brother? "Which lie made you the most angry?" Clevenger asked.

She shook her head.

"You can tell me."

She reached for her door handle.

"Lindsey, wait."

She pulled open the door, jumped out and started jogging back toward the house.

Clevenger watched her slow to a walk as she came within view of the cruisers in front of the house. As she passed them, her mother walked out the front door. And getting a glimpse of the two of them together made Clevenger realize they were opposites in many ways—one reserved, one highly emotional; one beautiful, one much less so; one very forgiving of John Snow's foibles, one enraged by them.

Lindsey hung her head, walked straight past her mother and disappeared inside the house. Her mother followed her. The door closed.

Clevenger started the car and began the twenty-minute drive back to his office in Chelsea. He thought again of Mike Coady's caution that the list of viable suspects in a case like Snow's could be long, even if Snow had actually committed suicide. He wondered whether North Anderson had gotten anywhere ruling out Collin Coroway. He dialed him up.

"Hey, Frank," Anderson answered.

"Anything on Coroway?"

"Plenty. He took a US Air shuttle to D.C. at 6:30 A.M., yesterday," Anderson said. "No reservation, got to the ticket counter at 5:50 A.M. And he hasn't made the return trip."

"Snow was getting shipped to the morgue, and he was on a flight out of state," Clevenger said.

"And didn't rush back to comfort Snow's wife or rally the troops at Snow-Coroway. He's still checked into the Hyatt."

"He's got motive. I found out Coroway inherits control of all the intellectual property of the company. He used to need Snow's signature to make a move. They had a very hot invention in the pipeline that Snow wanted to bury, and Coroway wanted to sell to the military. It was key to Coroway pulling the trigger on taking Snow-Coroway public."

"Now Snow's getting buried," Anderson said. "But if we're thinking double homicide, he isn't our man. He was already in D.C. when Grace Baxter died."

"Unless we're dealing with two killers," Clevenger said, automatically. He didn't much like hearing his own words.

"Less likely," Anderson said. "Snow and Baxter were lovers. All in all, I still like George Reese for both murders. A jealous husband is an ugly thing."

"Just the same," Clevenger said, "maybe I make the trip down to D.C., catch Coroway a little bit off balance."

"Good luck. I hear he's a very cool customer."

"Did he take a limo to the airport?"

"Don't know," Anderson said. "You're thinking his driver could tell us if he looked rough?"

"Or let us check for blood on the back seat."

"If he took a limo, I'll make that happen. If he left his own car in the airport garage, I'll wander by. I'm sure Coady can pull a search warrant if there's anything worth taking a close look at."

"I just came from talking to Theresa and Lindsey Snow," Clevenger said.

"Anything I should know about?"

"Snow had both of them wrapped up, in different ways. They worshiped him. The thought of losing him could have made either of them feel like she was losing everything."

"The thought of losing him to another woman or to the neurosurgery?" Anderson asked.

"Either way." Clevenger remembered the portrait over the mantel. "Snow had a painting of Grace Baxter on the wall of his living room."

"What?"

"An artist by the name of Kullaway. I couldn't tell whether his wife knew it was of Baxter or not. She didn't let on whether she'd gotten wind of the affair."

"A portrait of your lover in plain view of your wife and kids? Kind of sick. What's that all about?"

"I'm not sure. If I had to guess, I'd say it's about how little John Snow was able to relate to his family as real people."

"What do you mean?"

"He expected them to be perfect. The flip side of that is that he didn't see them as human, with both strengths and weaknesses—and *feelings*. He wanted to be close to Baxter, so he brought her home. Period. I picked up his journal from Coady. It's mostly sketches and calculations, some of his thoughts about the surgery. But he'd sketched Baxter in there, too. Real detail, real emotion to the way he drew her. It's almost like she had a way of breaking through defenses he used to keep everyone else at a distance. I think he might have loved her in a very different way than he loved his work or his wife or even his daughter. A deeper way."

"You didn't mention the son."

"I didn't see him," Clevenger said. "His mother talked about him a bit. He has a learning disorder. Snow couldn't relate to him at all. Sounds like he pretty much ignored him all his life."

"Snow was no prince. I mean, nobody deserves what he got, but he wasn't the nicest guy in the world."

"No," Clevenger agreed. He thought again of Billy, how devastating it had been for him to have a father who dismissed him as damaged goods. "It looks like Snow was much more comfortable with things that were predictable and hardwired than he was with relationships. When you have seizures as a kid, when you know you can lose consciousness at any moment and land on the floor in con-

112

vulsions, you can get obsessed with keeping things under control, working just right. He could do that with a missile or a radar system. It's a lot tougher with a son or a daughter—or a lover."

"But he had the emotional bandwidth to deal with more than one woman."

"*Deal with*, sure. But *love*, I don't know. I really wonder whether the only one who tapped his passion was Baxter."

"The guy was fifty years old. You're telling me nobody else ever really got to him?"

"It's possible," Clevenger said.

"But why Baxter? Snow was famous. He was rich. Good looking. He had to have attracted plenty of women."

"Maybe she was his *lovemap*."

"His what?"

"*Lovemap*. I had this professor in med school named Money. John Money. He interviewed kids in first and second grade, showed them photographs of little boys and girls, asked them who they thought was cute—and why. If one of the little girls said she liked a particular photo of a boy, Money would ask her *what* she liked about it. Maybe she'd say it was the way the kid was smiling, the left side of his mouth a little higher than the right. So Money would put all her responses, all the little quirks she liked, on a database. Hers, and a thousand other kids. Then he followed up with the same kids thirty years later. Turns out what they liked at seven and eight—their ideals of beauty—hadn't changed much. The little girl who liked the little boy with the crooked smile married a man with that smile—a little higher on the left than the right. Some of the kids never found what they were looking for and were just never very happy in their relationships."

"So there really is a perfect love out there for each of us."

"According to Money, there is. He thinks you're born with a

lovemap—a set of physical characteristics encoded in your brain that represents your ideal mate. If you ever get the physical part right, and someone connects with you psychologically, you have a lock-and-key fit. True love, forever. Maybe only one person in a million can really do that for any other person. Maybe Baxter did it for Snow."

"Think you'll ever find yours?" Anderson asked.

"My *lovemap*?" Clevenger asked. He laughed.

"Do you?"

The image of Whitney McCormick, the FBI forensic psychiatrist who had helped Clevenger solve the Highway Killer case, came to his mind. The relationship had gotten personal, then gotten complicated, then faded way into the background as Clevenger tried to be a decent father to Billy, before anything else. It had been a year since he'd seen her. "I don't know," he told Anderson. "Getting the physical part right would be a hell of a lot easier than the psychological part. I've got some strange curves to my psyche that would be pretty hard to match up."

Anderson laughed. "Same here, my friend. I love my wife, don't get me wrong. But I guess it's possible I could get hit by a Mack truck with my *lovemap* on it one day."

"What do you figure you'd do?"

"Not shoot myself, I can tell you that."

Clevenger smiled. "Call me if you get anything on Coroway's car, huh? I'll let you know what I come up with in D.C."

Clevenger caught the 12:30 P.M. US Air Shuttle to D.C. He'd called Billy on his cell and arranged for him to wait at the Somerville Boxing Club until he made it home, probably around 6:30. That got a "no problem" from Billy. If it were up to him, he'd hang at the gym 24/7.

Once the plane had taken off, Clevenger opened John Snow's journal and began reading the next entry:

Does a man have the right to begin life anew? Is he the full owner of his existence, or is he merely a limited partner?

A man is born to parents. He is <u>their son,</u> and their life stories unfold alongside his own, mingling with it, so that the plot of each is partly dependent on the others. They change his diapers, hold his hand as he goes to school the very first day. They worry endlessly with him and about him for decades, celebrate his victories, suffer his defeats. But what if their vision of him has little to do with his true nature? What if they do not know <u>the real him?</u> Would it be fair for him, their son, to pull the thread of his identity loose from the pattern of <u>family life,</u> to find himself by losing them? Is a man at liberty to forget from whence he has come, so that he can proceed unfettered to the place his soul tells him he must go?

Another example. A woman married twenty years with teenage children and a husband. A home. Pets. Photo albums and scrapbooks brimming with memories. What happens when such a woman no longer feels any passion for a shared future with her husband and children? What if she feels nonexistent?

Is she depressed? Does she need Zoloft? A higher dose? Two medicines? Or is it possible her life has carried her so far from her internal truth that she is, for all intents and purposes, a zombie—one of the living dead?

Is that woman within her rights—morally and ethically—to leave her home and family and friends, leave them so com-

115

pletely that she has no memory of them? Having brought her children into the world, does she owe them the rest of her days or is she free to celebrate the past and move on to create a new future without them?

The answer must be a resounding "yes."

A person can be spiritually deceased, the carcass of his or her soul adrift inside a cage of skin and bone that has outlived him. What sort of mother or father, sister or brother, husband or wife would put his or her attachment to a shared past above that person's future — his or her rebirth?

True love would never exact such suffering.

Clevenger put the journal down. He realized the difference between John Snow's view of the world and his own. Clevenger believed people could change and grow, no matter what circumstances conspired to limit them. Given the right motivation and the right guidance, and, yes, even sometimes the right medicine, they could reinvent themselves and overcome the past. That was what living a successful life was all about. It could be painful, sometimes excruciating, but it was their pain to deal with. Passing that suffering along to others by surgically removing themselves from one drama to start another did seem immoral. It might restore the blood volume of one person's soul, but it would leave a dozen others hemorrhaging from the procedure.

He thought of Theresa Snow's assessment of her husband as a narcissist, unable to balance the needs of others against his own. And maybe that was the heart of the matter. But the question still had to be asked: What had brought John Snow to the point of believing he was a dead person inside a living body, that his story was at an end?

Something had killed John Snow before he took a bullet in that alleyway.

Clevenger flipped through more of the journal. The next ten or so pages were full of calculations and drawings obviously related to Vortek, Snow's last invention, now in the hands of Collin Coroway. Clevenger looked at the missile, drawn larger in some places, smaller in others, sometimes with wings, sometimes without. In a few of the drawings it was splayed open, and Snow had sketched coils inside it.

Clevenger turned another page and found himself staring at a page filled with a chaos of letters, numbers and mathematical symbols. The characters were even tinier than Snow's usual hand, clustering together into dashed lines here, curves there, even amorphous clouds of letters and numbers. He held the page farther away, kept staring at it. And then what seemed like chaos slowly began to take form. Hair. Eyes. A nose. Lips. He looked longer and harder. And then he realized with amazement that he was looking at Grace Baxter's face.

THE FOUR SEASONS

• A SPRING DAY, NINE MONTHS BEFORE.

Everything seemed brand new. The days were long, and the sun was bright, and the flowers in the Public Garden bloomed pink and blue and white at the edges of the pond where the Swan Boats floated beneath whispering trees.

The windows of the suite were open, the drapes pulled back, the gauze curtains billowing as a warm wind streamed in. Lying naked atop the bed, the breeze as their blanket, lost in white noise from distant traffic, Grace Baxter and John Snow could almost imagine they were outside together, lying in soft grass at the Park.

It was his turn at the game Grace had taught him, a game of intuition in which one of them imagined what the other wanted, divining where to kiss or touch by listening for the slightest change in breathing, watching for hairs to stand on end, for muscles to relax or tighten. A sigh. A shiver.

He had been no good at it the first or the second or the tenth time they had played it, and they had laughed together over that. He could not sense her needs. She had to put his hand where she wanted him to touch, pull him closer when she wanted him to hold her, whisper the secrets to her excitement in his ear. But he was better at it now. He was developing the kind of emotional, sexual radar Grace herself had.

He propped himself on one elbow beside her, transported by the sight of her auburn hair fanned across the white sheet, by the way her eyes turned emerald when sunlight found them, by her long, graceful neck, her perfect breasts, the rise and fall of her abdomen.

Three months of meetings—sometimes once, sometimes twice a week—had done nothing to lessen his desire for her. More than a hundred hours on the phone had only left him thirsting to hear her voice again. Being drawn to Grace had drawn him out of the isolation he had known most of his life, and the crumbling of the walls he had built around him was exhilarating.

He rested his hand on Baxter's knee, felt her thigh press against his own. He ran his hand a few inches up her leg. Her knee slipped between his legs, her thigh pressing against his groin. He leaned over and kissed her gently, leaving her mouth a little hungry, the way she liked it. Seeing her tilt her head back slightly, he kissed the line of her jaw, then her neck. Her breathing quickened, and she let out a sigh halfway between pain and pleasure. He saw her shoulder blades fan wider and moved his hand over her breast. She ran a foot halfway up his shin. He knew what that meant, too. He kissed his way down her abdomen. She let her knees fall open. And he kissed his way still lower.

Later, he lay with his head on her stomach, rising and falling with her breathing, a hypnotic rhythm. And he remembered the question she had asked him the very first time they met at the hotel: Why was he so focused on what could be seen and what could not be seen? Why had perfecting radar, and designing ways to evade it, become his life's work? He hadn't had the answer, until that very moment. "It was easier," he said quietly.

"Hmm?" she purred.

"When we had dinner at Aujourd'hui, that first time we met here, you asked me why I was so interested in detecting what's out there—in the sky, in space."

"I remember."

"I think I wanted to avoid looking inside myself."

"Why?"

"Because," he said, "I was never sure there was anything to see."

She ran her fingers into his hair. "Of course there was. You just lost sight of yourself somehow."

"Somehow."

A few seconds passed. "How?" she asked.

He thought about that. "As a child I fascinated people," he said. "I fascinated myself. What I could do with my brain."

"What was it you could do?"

"Calculations. Problem solving. Complicated scientific equations."

"A little genius," she said.

"That's what people said."

"Your parents were proud?"

"Very," he said.

"So what you could do passed for who you were."

How was she able to see straight to the heart of things? Snow wondered. And how was she able to summon the precise tone of voice that reassured him he was safe telling her his truth. "Yes," he said.

"They loved your brain."

"When it worked," he said, with a short laugh, his smile quickly fading away.

She didn't laugh at all. "What if it hadn't?" she asked. "What if it had stopped working? Would they have still loved you?"

Snow thought back to his first seizure at age ten. He remembered how much he liked being in the hospital, how his father and mother had spent more time with him in that white-walled room than ever before. And he realized why. They were there because his brain was sick, not because *he* was. The thing they were proud of had short-circuited. "I don't know," he told Grace. "I don't know if they ever loved me."

"I'm sorry," she said, running her fingers through his hair. "If you don't know that for certain, it's hard to be certain of anything, ever."

"It's all right," he said.

"It is? Why do you have to be so brave, John? You could fall apart a little and still be okay."

Part of Snow wanted to tell Grace the rest of the story—how his brain had short-circuited again and again, how it took four medicines to keep it working reliably even now, decades later. But he still wanted things to be perfect between them. He wasn't willing to be seen by her as weak. Maybe that was because he didn't believe she loved him, either. Maybe she was right about everything she had said, even about the way he could finally answer the question of whether he was worthy of her love, or anyone's, including his own—by falling apart a little, letting her know his imperfections, letting himself be human with her. But he just couldn't bring himself to take the risk. He closed his eyes, let the motion of Grace's abdomen rock the pain away. "How about you?" he asked. "Have you been loved?"

Another deep breath. "No," she said. "I don't think I ever have."

"As a child?"

"You were a genius. I was pretty."

"And that's all anyone could see?"

"I was *very* pretty." She laughed.

This time, it was Snow who refrained from laughing. "Your parents had to know how intelligent you are. You can see things— understand things—other people can't."

"Maybe that was the problem."

"What do you mean?"

"I could see them."

"And what did you see?" he asked her.

"You're getting good at this."

He was good enough at it to feel Grace's reticence about saying more.

She ran a fingertip over his forehead, along the rim of his ear, down his cheek. "Tell me about your wife," she said.

He propped himself on one elbow, again, looked up at her. "Where did that come from?"

"I'm just wondering about her. What is she like? What is it like living with her?"

He didn't answer immediately.

"You can tell me," she said.

He pulled himself up toward the headboard, laid beside her. He had to think hard to come up with anything meaningful to say. "She's a better person than I am," he said.

"In what way?"

"She's been there for my son and daughter in ways I haven't."

"How could you? You haven't been there for yourself. Your brain has been too busy."

"That's no excuse."

"Yes, it is," she said. She leaned and kissed his cheek. "Do you still make love with her?"

"I don't think I ever did," he said.

This time she kissed him on the lips.

"How about your husband?" he asked. "Do you still make love with him?"

"I'm not even in the room. I go somewhere else, in my mind. A deserted beach. A road through the mountains. Somewhere I can be alone."

Snow kissed her gently on the forehead. "Why don't you come here."

She closed her eyes, rested her head on his shoulder. "I could try," she said. "If you will, too. I mean, when you're with her. That way, they only bring us closer."

"I will."

"Good," she said. "Now, lie down." As he did, she propped herself on an elbow. "My turn," she said. She touched his knee with one fingertip, then slowly began moving her hand up his thigh.

TEN

Clevenger landed at Reagan National just before 2:00 P.M. He checked his cell phone, saw he had two messages. He listened to them on his way to the taxicab line. The first was from Detective Coady, saying he had some interesting news from Grace Baxter's autopsy. The second was from J. T. Heller saying he had fast-tracked to that evening the surgery of the blind woman whose vision he hoped to restore. She was experiencing new migraine headaches that made him worry her tumor was growing rapidly. He wondered whether Billy might like to scrub in.

Clevenger dialed Heller's office first, got his receptionist Sascha. "It's Frank Clevenger, returning Dr. Heller's call," he said.

"He told me to put you right through," she said. "But I wanted to thank you first."

"For . . . ?"

"What you told me—about John Snow. How sometimes you can't save someone. How letting them know you care about them might be the most you can do."

"And very few people do that."

"Are you coming in again?"

Clevenger heard real warmth in her voice. And part of him would have liked to ask the next question—whether Sascha wanted to see him. But he knew her answer wouldn't tell him much. He had offered her absolution from her guilt, and that was probably what she was hungry for. The message, not the messenger. "I'm sure I'll be by at some point," he said.

"Well, then, I hope to see you," she said, more formally. "Hold on."

"Frank," Heller boomed, seconds later.

He sounded like he'd downed about thirty cups of coffee. "I got your message," Clevenger said. "I think that would be great for Billy."

"Bring him by the General, say, four o'clock?"

"Unfortunately, I'm out of town," Clevenger said. "I'll try to arrange for a friend to grab him from boxing practice and get him there—assuming he's up for it. He could probably even take the 'T.' "

"I can pick him up," Heller said. "I've got nothing on my agenda until that case. I could use the drive to unwind, anyhow. I get pretty worked up when I'm about to go in. I keep going over my moves, you know?"

"Your moves . . ."

"My strategy. Every surgery is a war, brother. And that tumor wrapping itself around my patient's ophthalmic nerve wants to win every bit as much as I do. It wants it all the way back to the progenitor cell that first broke free of the program God wrote for it and struck out on its own, planting itself where it had no right to be. It's trying with every bit of its protoplasm to take Nature's design and reconfigure it according to its own warped, murderous plan. But you know what?"

Clevenger wondered whether Heller might have crossed over from grandiosity into mania. "What?"

"Today is Judgment Day."

"For the tumor."

"For the tumor. For disorder. For entropy. Today, with God's grace, I restore what He in his ultimate wisdom intended." He laughed at himself. "What do you think, Frank, a little lithium for your new friend?"

At least Heller knew he sounded like he needed medication. And maybe it wasn't fair to question his stability at all. Maybe opening a woman's head and dissecting parts of her brain required the energy of a warrior, the conviction you were fighting against evil. "Why would you think you only need a little?" Clevenger joked.

"Good point," Heller said. "So, what do you say? Shall I pick him up? I just bought a Hummer. Black on black. He'll get a kick out of it."

Clevenger felt the same discomfort he had felt when he found Billy and Heller chatting in his loft. Was that because Heller was triggering a protective instinct in him? Or was it because he was triggering his jealousy? He had to admit it was probably more the latter. After all, people routinely put their lives in Jet Heller's hands. And Billy could take care of himself, in any case. "I'll ask him if that would work for him," Clevenger said.

"If he's game, I'll shoot over to Somerville in about forty-five minutes."

Clevenger was taken aback that Heller knew to find Billy in Somerville.

Heller must have sensed his discomfort. "He told me all about the Club," he said. "Golden Gloves. Pretty hot stuff. You do worry about head trauma, though. I have patients who boxed four or five years and can't remember what they had for breakfast."

"I do worry about that," Clevenger said. He had the feeling again that Heller was trying to out-father him. "He wears head gear." He knew he didn't need to explain himself, but couldn't stop. Having had a father who was no father at all had left him wondering whether he could ever be any good at it himself. "Billy's gotten his share of concussions, but none in the ring."

"I've had seven, myself. Lost consciousness three of the times.

127

All before my sixteenth birthday. I know exactly what you're dealing with. I was right where Billy is. On the edge. Getting him into a boxing ring was a great idea."

How much could two people have in common? And why did hearing about it bother him so much? "I just hope everything turns out as well for him as it did for you."

"If you call opening heads for a living a good result," he said. "When are you back in town, by the way?"

"With any luck, end of the day."

"I don't think we'll be out of surgery until about nine o'clock. Maybe you and I could grab a beer when I drop Billy off."

Now driving Billy home was part of the plan, too. "Sure." He didn't want to leave Heller assuming Billy would abandon boxing practice to bask in his shadow. "I'll let you know in the next hour whether he's gonna take you up on your offer."

"You got it."

"Thanks."

"And, Frank?" Heller said.

"Yeah?"

"I hope you don't think I'm being strange or pushy, offering to show Billy what I do. I just see myself in him. Probably like you do. And I think he's a good kid, underneath it all. But if you'd rather I back off . . ."

In that instant, Clevenger realized Heller had a remarkable way of dissolving another person's resistance by voicing it himself. Hearing him speak your objection made you object less. Was that manipulative? Or was it his way of being up-front? "No need to back off," he said. "I think watching surgery will be wonderful for him."

"Just wanted to clear the air."

"Done. I'll get back to you."

Clevenger hung up. He grabbed a cab for downtown and called

Billy's cell phone en route, figuring he'd leave him a message. School wasn't out yet.

Billy picked up. "Whazzup? In D.C. yet?"

"Just now. Where are you?"

"Headed to Somerville. My last class got canceled. Teacher went home sick. They let us go."

"I got a call from J.T. Heller. He's doing surgery today on that woman—the one he thinks could end up getting back her sight. He wants to know if you'd like to scrub in."

"I'll take the 'T.' I can skip the gym."

"No need," Clevenger said. "Dr. Heller said he'd swing by and pick you up at the Club. You can get in an hour of practice, then head over to the General with him."

"Unreal."

Clevenger hadn't heard that kind of enthusiasm from Billy in a long, long time. "I'll see you at home when you're done."

"Definitely," Billy said. "Cool." He sounded as pumped as Heller. "Thanks."

The thank you was new, too. "No problem," Clevenger said.

He dialed Heller back, gave him the thumbs up to take Billy over to the hospital and drop him back home. Then he dialed Boston Police headquarters, got Coady on the line. "What's the news?" he asked him.

"Jeremiah Wolfe called. He's into the microscopic anatomy on Baxter."

"And?"

"He's not buying the carpet knife as the blade that caused her wrist lacerations," Coady said.

"Why not?"

"He says the tissue was splayed open by something with a finer edge. There isn't quite enough damage at the borders, or whatever. He figures a razor blade is more like it."

"Which we don't have."

"There are razor blades in that bathroom, but none of them have any blood on them."

"And Wolfe thinks the carpet knife is consistent with the wounds on her neck?"

"He does," Coady said. "I don't figure many people commit suicide using two different blades. But I don't think many killers switch weapons, either."

"Unless the razor blade just wouldn't do the trick," Clevenger said. "Let's say she was passed out, drunk. Somebody looking to make this look like a suicide might have started using a razor blade on her wrists, hoping she wouldn't wake up, die in her sleep. That way, he'd get away easy. But maybe she wasn't as deep as he thought. She started to struggle. He needed to stop her. Maybe he had the carpet knife handy, just in case."

"Maybe," Coady said. "And flushed the razor blade?"

"Or cleaned it off."

"I'll get the lab to test every sharp piece of metal in that bathroom. Let's see if they come up with any trace blood on those new blades. I'll also have them take apart the plumbing. See if we find anything caught in the pipes."

"Sounds like the right idea."

"Let me ask you a question," Coady said.

"Shoot."

"How about this scenario? She starts cutting her wrists . . ."

How had they slipped back into the suicide theory? "You know I don't think . . ." Clevenger broke in.

"Hear me out."

Clevenger felt his pulse begin to race. His jaw tightened. "Alright."

"She starts cutting her wrists in the bathroom. She's drunk. The blood's trickling out. She stumbles around. She's thinking how

Snow is dead, her love affair is over. Or maybe she's even freaking over how she killed him."

Coady segueing into the murder-suicide idea only made Clevenger grit his teeth harder.

"Maybe she hates herself for what she's done," Coady went on. "And she looks at the blood still trickling out. She starts crying, screaming how her life is over. Either she dies now or she dies in prison. Either way, she's lost Snow. She sees the carpet knife, probably left there by one of the workmen using the john. She grabs it..."

"And cuts her throat, killing herself and her baby," Clevenger said. "I thought we were past that. Remember the prenatal vitamin? Materna, right?"

"Right. Ya. We were past that. But then I kept thinking. And I thought, what if it was *his* baby? Snow's."

Clevenger hadn't thought through whose baby Grace had been carrying. And that blind spot made him wonder whether there really was an angle to the case he didn't want to see. Was it possible he felt so guilty about not hospitalizing her when she visited his office that he was shutting down? At the back of his mind did he think he had caused two deaths—Grace's and her unborn child? "Let's say the baby was Snow's," he said, the anger gone from his voice.

"Then I start to think maybe she could have done what maybe she did. I mean, I can picture her taking that vitamin an hour before offing herself. It's part of her routine. She's trying to get things back to normal, get over what she lost in that alleyway, or what she *did* in the alleyway. Then, even with the booze on board, it all really starts to sink in. She's carrying Snow's child. She murdered the father of her baby. She's living a nightmare. And it's never gonna end. She looks down, can't believe what she's done to her wrists. How can she be a mother? All her rage, grief, guilt funnel together..."

"And she just wants it to stop."

"No more trickle. She wants it over."

"The carpet knife," Clevenger said. The cab stopped outside the Hyatt.

The doorman opened his door. "Good to see you, sir. Any bags?"

Clevenger waved him off. He paid the driver, got out, closed the door. He didn't feel the cold air on his face.

"All I'm saying is that theory might be worth considering," Coady said. "I don't know if the psychology fits."

That was a question. "It might," Clevenger said. "I think it could."

"Not that we're ruling anything in or out," Coady said, obviously emboldened. "We'll still bring George Reese in—and any other suspect."

"Right."

"Did you get everything you needed from the Snows today?"

"I didn't get to talk with the son, Kyle," Clevenger managed. "He wasn't around. At least that's what Theresa Snow told me. I think she may be trying to keep him away from me."

"Why?"

"I don't know."

"I can grab him off the street right now," Coady said.

"For what?"

"His urine drug screen came up dirty at probation today. Opiates. That's a violation. You want to come in later and take your shot with him?"

"I just got to D.C.," Clevenger said.

"D.C.? What's down there?"

"Collin Coroway flew here yesterday."

"Who tracked that down?"

"What difference does it make?"

"Were you planning to let me know?"

"Like I said, I just got here. It was a last minute thought." He knew that didn't answer Coady's question. "I should have called it in to you," he said.

"It is my case."

"It's your case."

Coady was silent a few seconds. "Not that you'd quit," he said. Another couple of seconds. "I need you on this more than ever. I may have a theory about what happened, but I'm not even close to being able prove it. And I could be very wrong. I get that."

"I don't quit cases," Clevenger said, conscious of the effort to sound convincing.

"I'll set Kyle Snow up for first thing tomorrow. How's 9:00 A.M.?"

"I'll be there."

"See you then."

Clevenger hung up and walked inside the Hyatt lobby. He tried to focus on finding Collin Coroway, but his mind kept replaying what he had just heard. Because the picture Coady had painted was anything but outlandish. If Grace Baxter had been carrying John Snow's baby, her hatred of him for abandoning her and their child was a credible motive for murder. And her desperation after his death could have led to a complete psychological implosion.

He remembered telling Coady why Baxter's slashed throat didn't fit with a female suicide. Men chose the more violent methods, *except in cases where a person—male or female—was delusional*. He had given an example: a woman who believed the devil's blood flowed through her veins. But what if the thing Grace hated and had to be rid of was no demon, but the new life growing inside her. What if Snow's death made her think of the baby as an invader, of its blood as his blood, mingling with her own, poisoning her? She would be desperate to bleed out.

He was still reeling from that thought as he walked up to the reception desk.

"Can I help you?" a kind-looking Indian man in his thirties asked him.

"Would you mind phoning Collin Coroway's room and letting him know I'm here?"

The man checked his computer. "Who shall I say is calling?"

"Dr. Clevenger. Frank Clevenger."

"One moment." He picked up the phone, rang the room, listened. Ten, fifteen seconds went by. He shook his head. "He doesn't seem to be in."

Clevenger figured he was better off coaxing one employee to do as much legwork as possible. It would raise less concern than poking around the place himself. "Would you mind asking the concierge whether Mr. Coroway might have called a car service? Maybe I can still catch up with him."

"Let me check." He dialed the concierge and asked whether he knew if Coroway had left the property. He got his answer, hung up. "You're in luck. He took a car to 1300 Pennsylvania Avenue. The Reagan Building. Would you like me to call one for you?"

Wonderful service at the Hyatt. "Please," Clevenger said. "The same company, if that's all right."

For the first time, the man looked at him slightly askance.

"Expense accounts," Clevenger said, with a wink.

"Of course. Not a problem, sir."

Fifteen minutes later Clevenger was headed to 1300 Pennsylvania Avenue in a black Lincoln Town Car from Capitol Limousine. "Where you from?" the driver, a burly man about sixty asked in a baritone.

"Boston," Clevenger said. "You?"

"Los Angeles." He chuckled. "Couldn't stand the weather."

Clevenger knew the joke was an invitation to ask the real reason behind his move. He would have liked to ignore it, to stay completely focused on Snow and Baxter. But he had never built up any resistance to the life stories of others. "Too hot out there for you," he said.

"Manner of speaking."

Another open door. "Not the weather, you mean."

The driver shook his head. "A woman."

"Things went badly?"

"Worse than that."

The story was gaining momentum. "Oh?" Clevenger asked, settling back to listen.

"Two kids, when I met her. But I had a thing for her right off. You know? So I go with her a little over a year. Everything's good. She loves me. I love her. The kids are already calling me Dad, which I maybe should of seen as a problem, seeing as the real father is in prison." He raised a finger to highlight his next point. "For armed robbery, I thought."

"Armed robbery," Clevenger said.

The finger, again. "I marry her. Now, the little girl is eleven. Out of the blue, the mother accuses me of fawning her."

"You mean, fondling."

He ignored the edit. "I did nothing. On my parents' souls. Nothing. I brought her a towel after her shower. I opened the bathroom door two inches, turned my head out of respect for her privacy. Her mother is down the hall. She sees this, starts screaming. I mean, at the top of her lungs. Long and short of it, I'm arrested."

"For what?"

"Indecent assault and battery. My wife says I forced the door. And the girl, who I just happened to ground for getting three C's, two D's, says I touched her." He ran a hand over his chest. "*Never happened.*" He looked in the rearview mirror, presumably checking whether Clevenger believed him. He seemed satisfied. "I had to get a lawyer, give him thirty grand to get found innocent, which I was. But a case like that, there doesn't need to be any evidence, only the word of the victim. She took it all back on the stand." He nodded to himself. "Three guesses what the old man was really in jail for."

"Indecent assault and battery on the girl."

He looked in the mirror. "You're good. See, I was taking the heat for him. He did something out of the way, so she and the mother jumped the gun, figured I was the same way."

"If he was that way," Clevenger said.

"What do you mean?"

"Maybe the first husband touched the girl, maybe he didn't. Maybe your wife's own father touched her when she was ten or eleven. Maybe it happened in the bathroom of the house where she grew up. Then you open that bathroom door a few inches, and she sees it happening all over again—this time, to her daughter."

"Never thought of that."

"You moved away," Clevenger said.

"It was in all the papers out there. Big headlines when I was arrested. No headline when I was cleared. Plus, I got beat up in the divorce. And, get this . . ."

"Child support."

"Right, again." He turned to glance at Clevenger.

Clevenger saw for the first time that his eyes were pale green and remarkably gentle. He looked at his hand on the steering wheel, saw he was wearing a wedding ring.

"So, I left broke," the driver went on, "my name dirt."

"You're remarried?" Clevenger asked him.

"Never."

"You wear a wedding band."

He shrugged. "Craziness, I know. I've never taken it off. Not when I went to trial. Not when I was found innocent. Not when I got the divorce papers."

"Why not?" Clevenger asked.

"I still love her." He shook his head. "I still love the kids. Some things, you never, ever get over."

Some things you don't, Clevenger thought. He fought off another memory of Whitney McCormick. But you go on. If the driver was telling the truth—and he seemed to be—he had lost the woman he loved and two step-children he cared deeply about, lost his reputation, spent all his money on a lawyer to overcome charges of sexual assault, then moved across the country to start over. Why couldn't John Snow do the same? Even if his marriage was at an end, even if his relationships with his children were strained to the point of fracturing, why couldn't he start fresh? Were his feelings for Grace Baxter ultimately too unwieldy, too threatening? Was his neurosurgery as much to remove her from his mind as anyone else? "Ever think of getting in touch with them again?" Clevenger asked.

"I send a letter every month, tell them what I'm up to," he said. "I tell them I forgive them. Twenty-one letters so far. Almost two years."

"Have they ever written back?"

"Not yet. But the letters don't get returned. They're getting through."

"I guess that's something."

"It is to me." He pulled over in front of the Reagan Building, a massive granite complex of three million square feet on eleven acres. "Thirteen-hundred Penn." He turned around. "Call it twenty bucks. Thanks for listening to my bullshit."

Clevenger handed him a hundred. "Maybe you can help me with something," he said.

"You know I'm gonna try."

"A man named Collin Coroway took a Capitol limo from the Hyatt over here. Any way to find out whether he's still in the building?"

"You some kind of detective?" the driver asked, checking Clevenger out more closely. "You listened real good—like you knew where I was going before I got there."

"I'm a psychiatrist," Clevenger said.

"Good one." His broad smile said he wasn't buying that for a second. "None of my business. Forget I asked." He picked up his cell phone, dialed. A woman answered. "Katie, Al here," he said. "Collin Coroway, the Hyatt to Thirteen-hundred Penn. Any return?" He listened. "Take your time. I'll hold."

Half a minute passed before Katie was back on the line. She rattled off a phone number.

The driver grabbed a pen, jotted it down. "I owe you," he told her. He clicked off, then dialed the number. When someone answered, he hung up. He turned back to Clevenger. "He's still here. And our contact number for any problems with his return trip goes through to a secretary for something called InterState Commerce."

"That all went pretty smoothly."

"My gift to you," he said, with a wink. "One gumshoe to another."

"You're a private detective?"

"Licensed in Cali. Gotta make a living though, right?"

"Right."

"Take care, my friend." He handed Clevenger his business card. Clevenger read the name—Al French. "You take care, too, Al."

He got out of the car, walked into the Reagan Building and found InterState Commerce on the directory in the lobby. Tenth floor. The penthouse. He took the elevator up.

InterState was one of just two suites on the floor. Each of them had to run fifteen, twenty thousand square feet. Clevenger walked to the InterState entrance, a set of massive, frosted glass doors with a five-foot letter *I* etched on one door and a matching *S* etched on the other. He rang the buzzer.

"May I help you?" a woman asked.

"I'm here for Collin Coroway."

The door clicked. Clevenger pulled it open, walked inside.

The reception area was ultramodern, with stainless steel walls and giant flat-screen monitors hanging on massive concrete columns. CNN Headline News was playing on one. The other showed a map of the world, with a hundred or so cobalt blue spheres, each imprinted with *IS*, glowing like a storm of Ping-Pong balls over all six continents. Between the monitors, a beautiful black woman wearing a headset sat behind a cobalt blue glass desk, faking a smile.

Clevenger walked up to her. "I'm Frank Clevenger," he said.

"I don't believe Mr. Coroway called for a car yet."

Mistaken for a brain surgery patient by one receptionist, for a driver by another. "I'm not from the car service. Could you let him know I'm here to see him?"

"Will he know you?"

"I'm working with the police on the death of his partner, John Snow."

No reaction. "He's expecting you, then?"

"He'll want to see me."

An even more synthetic smile. "Wait here, please." She disappeared behind a corrugated, translucent blue plastic wall that set the lobby off from the rest of the suite.

Clevenger spotted a stack of brochures for InterState on her desk. He picked one up. The cover was a collage of photos—a fighter jet, an oil tanker, a nuclear power plant, a camouflaged soldier talking into a walkie talkie. He opened to the first page, read the company's mission statement:

InterState is dedicated to forging responsible partnerships between corporations and government agencies, across a

broad range of industries, including construction, transporta-
tion, pharmaceuticals, and public utilities.

And military hardware, Clevenger thought to himself. He flipped through page after page of testimonials from CEOs of major corporations superimposed on inspirational photos of waves, sunsets, lightning. Beside each photo was a case study of Inter-State's role in marrying a particular need of the government to a particular product. Getty oil fueling the U.S. Navy. Merck's antibiotics healing the good and vanquished people of Iraq. Viacom satellites transmitting the Voice of America.

"He'll see you now," the receptionist said, stepping out from behind the plastic wall.

Clevenger followed her down a long, wide corridor with glass-front offices along one side and dozens of framed photographs of world leaders lining the other. In each photo, a politician or military officer was shaking hands with a tall man with a shaven head, always wearing the same black suit. He looked about seventy, but remarkably fit. And he looked familiar. "Your CEO?" Clevenger asked, pointing at the man as they passed one of the photos.

"Yes, that's Mr. Fitzpatrick," she said.

That helped Clevenger place him. Byron Fitzpatrick had been secretary of state during the last year of Gerald Ford's presidency. He'd obviously brokered his connections in a big way.

Clevenger's cell phone rang. He looked at the display. North Anderson. He answered it. "I'm about to go into a meeting with Collin Coroway," he said quietly.

"Drove himself to the airport," Anderson said. "No blood stains on the car, so far as I can tell, but the grill is smashed in."

"The conference room is right around the corner," the receptionist said, clearly put off by Clevenger taking a call.

"I've got ten seconds," Clevenger told Anderson.

"Coady checked for accident reports. Coroway blew through a red light and hit a *Boston Globe* delivery truck yesterday. Guess when and where."

"Three seconds."

"Storrow Drive, fifty yards from Mass General. 4:47 A.M."

"Puts him at the scene."

"Here we are," the receptionist said, stopping in front of another set of frosted glass doors.

"Watch your back," Anderson said.

"Will do," Clevenger said. He hung up.

She pushed open one of the doors, held it for Clevenger. "Mr. Coroway, Frank Clevenger."

Coroway stood up from his seat at the far end of a long, black conference table. He was an elegant-looking man, about fifty-five, around six feet tall, with neatly styled silver hair, broad shoulders and a slim waist. He wore a charcoal gray, pinstriped suit, white shirt with French cuffs, club tie. "Please, come in," he said.

Clevenger walked in.

"Thank you, Angela," Coroway said, his voice as smooth as the silk of his tie.

The receptionist left.

Coroway walked up to Clevenger, extended his hand. "Collin Coroway."

Clevenger shook his hand, noticing the confidence in his grip and the fact that he wore a large, gold academic ring with a sapphire center, the sides engraved *Annapolis, 70.* The Naval Academy. "Frank Clevenger."

"Your reputation precedes you. I'm glad you're here. The team looks a hell of a lot stronger with you on it."

Coroway was acting as though he'd summoned Clevenger to D.C. He didn't seem even a little shaken. "What team is that?" Clevenger asked him.

141

Coroway pursed his lips, nodded to himself. "I know John's death is being investigated by Detective Coady. Senator Blaine's office was kind enough to look into that for me. No doubt he's a very competent man. But he does have quite a few open cases."

"This one's a priority," Clevenger said.

"Let's hope that's true." He motioned toward the conference table, surrounded by black leather swivel chairs. "Please." He walked back to his seat.

Clevenger took a seat halfway between Coroway and the door. "Thank you for seeing me on no notice," he said.

"Not at all. I let John Zack in the Senator's office know where to find me. I was surprised I hadn't heard from someone sooner. That's one of the reasons I have my doubts about Detective Coady. I should be pretty high on any list of suspects." He leaned forward, exposing gold cuff links shaped like fighter jets. "I don't mean to be glib, or overly critical. But John was more than a business partner to me. He was like a brother."

"Tell me about him."

"The most creative, intelligent, decent man I have ever known or expect to know. He was my best friend."

So why wasn't Coroway visibly shaken by his death? Why hadn't he returned to Boston? "Was he a very complicated person?" Clevenger asked

"Quite the opposite. He was simple. He loved to invent. He loved being able to imagine something and see it come to fruition."

"But not everything he imagined," Clevenger said.

Coroway settled back in his seat. "You visited with John's wife."

"I did."

"She told you about Vortek."

"She told me you and John disagreed on whether to market it or bury it."

"And now I have carte blanche—with John's death. I can just

put Vortek into production, call Merrill Lynch and announce a public offering of Snow-Coroway stock."

"That's her understanding."

Coroway was silent several seconds. "Would you like to know why I'm here in D.C.?" he finally asked.

Part of Clevenger wanted to say it seemed like as good a place as any to wait for powder burns to disappear from his hands, but he held back. "Sure," he said, and left it at that.

"InterState funded a significant portion of the research and development costs on Vortek. I just returned about half of the twenty-five million they invested in us."

"Why?" Clevenger asked.

"Because we can't deliver. I don't believe what John imagined can ever be achieved. Vortek was an overblown fantasy."

"He never finalized a design?"

"We tested two prototypes. Both failed miserably."

"His wife told me his work was complete. He just wouldn't let go of the underlying intellectual property."

Coroway smiled, nodded to himself. "Saint John, defender of the downtrodden, enemy of all weapons of mass destruction." He sat back in his seat. "Does Theresa really have three cruisers in front of the house?"

"I'm sure you already know."

"She really believes there was nothing he couldn't conquer with that big brain of his. I half-believed it, too. Until the last six months."

"Because he couldn't deliver Vortek."

"Because he couldn't come close. Not with twenty-five million in funding. Believe me, there isn't any public offering in the wings."

"Why would Theresa lie?"

"I think she sincerely believes what John was telling her. He had conquered radar, created a ghost of a missile, capable of flying right through the enemy's defenses. He was just too kind-hearted to let his invention see the light of day." He paused. "The truth is John would have been the first in line to sell the United States government the patents on Vortek—if he had ever managed to come up with them. That pacifist bullshit he fed his wife was his way of saving face."

"He had given up on it?" Clevenger asked him.

"No. That would have meant he wasn't all-powerful. It would have meant his mind couldn't change the laws of physics." He paused. "Instead, he blamed his brain."

"Meaning?"

"Every time he felt he was close to a breakthrough on Vortek, he'd have another seizure. I think that's why he started this odyssey to the O.R. with Jet Heller. He believed the surgery would unlock brain power he couldn't access because of his epilepsy."

"What do you think?"

"Honestly? I think it would have been easier to get rid of Grace Baxter. He was distracted by her."

"John told you about her."

"We didn't keep secrets from one another."

It sounded like Snow hadn't kept Grace Baxter a secret at all. Heller knew. Coroway knew. Her portrait was hanging in his house. "I'm investigating her death, as well," Clevenger said.

"I know that."

No surprise. Coroway seemed to know everything about the investigation. "Any thoughts?"

"I think she couldn't live without him."

"You think she took her own life."

"Unless there's hard and fast evidence to the contrary. She had threatened to."

"When was that?"

"The first time John told her it was over, about a month ago. She said she'd cut her throat."

Clevenger's heart sank.

"And that was only the latest and greatest way she threw him off balance," Coroway said.

She said she'd cut her throat. The words echoed in Clevenger's mind. He stared at Coroway, but saw Grace Baxter in her bathroom, carpet knife in hand.

"You all right, Doctor?"

Clevenger forced himself to focus. "How else did she throw him off balance?' "

"She was in his head. That's the only way I can put it. He was obsessed with her, like a goddamn fifteen-year-old." He settled himself down. "It was a completely new thing for John. You have to understand, Theresa and he lived together. They had children together. But they were never *together, together*. John loved his brain. So did she. It was a ménage à trois. Once he fell in love with another person, everything came unglued. He suddenly felt like a man, instead of a machine."

Which also could have threatened the bottom line at Snow-Coroway. The company relied on Snow's brain for its profits. "Were you happy for him?" Clevenger asked.

"For a while, sure. It was tremendous to watch. Everything changed. His mood improved. His energy was at an all time high. He bought himself decent clothes, for God's sake. He was fascinated by things he had shown absolutely no interest in before. Art. Music. Even his son. He came alive."

Theresa Snow hadn't mentioned her husband's renewed interest in Kyle. "But his work . . ."

"His work went to hell."

Coroway's analysis of Snow made sense, given what Clevenger

knew of him. But his contention that Vortek had veered off course wasn't easy to confirm. For all Clevenger knew, Coroway could have patented the invention an hour before. And he hadn't forgotten Coroway had driven into a truck while speeding away from Mass General, as John Snow lay bleeding to death. "Had you seen John in the last twenty-four hours?" he asked.

Coroway leaned forward again. "Don't be delicate with me. If you hadn't found the accident report by now, I'd be as worried about you and North Anderson as I am about Detective Coady."

Coroway might or might not be guilty of murder, but no one would convict him of being indirect or poorly informed. "Okay. Did you see him at the General yesterday morning?"

"I couldn't find him. I called his cell phone. He didn't answer."

"Why were you looking for him?"

"I wanted to try one last time to get him to reconsider going under the knife," Coroway said. "It was a last-minute impulse. That's why I was taking my car to the airport, in the first place. I had a limo all set to pick me up at 5:45 A.M. back home in Concord. Then I got this feeling . . ." He shook his head.

"What?" Clevenger asked.

"I'm gonna sound like a refugee from the Psychic Hotline."

"We'll keep it between us."

"I got this feeling I needed to protect him." He paused. "All I could make of that—that feeling—was that I needed to protect him from himself, that if I went down there, told him once and for all that he was being a fool, then . . ." He stopped himself. "He needed me to protect him from someone else."

"You don't think he killed himself?"

"I heard Coady was running that idea up the flagpole," Coroway said. "I hope he's let it go. Otherwise, it's time for him to go."

That made it clear how much influence Coroway believed he had with the Boston Police Department. "Isn't it remotely possible he committed suicide?" Clevenger asked him. "It was his gun. Very few people had access to it."

"John was no quitter," he said flatly.

"People get sick," Clevenger said.

"He was getting rid of what ailed him. At least what he thought ailed him. He was getting his brain cut apart to take out the bad circuit boards. He was going to prove to me and everyone else that Vortek wasn't any figment of his imagination, that he could make it real."

What Snow was really about to prove was that he could leave everyone behind, including Coroway. "The two of you had put legal work in place to cover the potential that John might not be able to continue at the company."

"He was going in for brain surgery. Anything could have happened."

It was time to get a little more specific. "Where exactly did you try to find him at Mass General?" Clevenger asked.

"Good. Let's get the minutiae out of the way," Coroway said, with characteristic detachment. "The lobby, first. Then the cafeteria. The cashier saw me—Asian woman, forty or so, slight build, wearing glasses."

Coroway's Navy Seal training seemed to be kicking in.

"I called Heller's office," he went on. "There was no answer. I figured John might have gone into surgery early. So I headed back to the parking garage, where I paid six dollars at the exit booth. Young guy. Twenty, twenty-two, thick glasses. Curly, black hair."

"Quick trip."

"I had a plane to catch."

"At six-thirty," Clevenger said. The accident report had Coroway leaving Mass General just before 5:00 A.M. Logan was about fifteen minutes away.

"I left something I needed at the office."

Or did he need to clean himself up? "So you drove to Snow-Coroway."

"After I drove into a truck. Security at the company will confirm I arrived there about 5:20. I didn't get to Logan until just before six o'clock."

"Did you hear a gunshot when you were at the hospital?"

"No. But I heard sirens. At the time, I didn't know what all the commotion was about." He stopped, closed his eyes, rubbed his thumb and forefinger into them.

Clevenger let a several seconds pass. "Why didn't you want him to go through with the surgery?" he asked.

"I didn't want a partner who was a blind mute."

"You thought the risks were too high."

Coroway looked at him. "For no real gain? You better believe it. Vortek was D.O.A. I had written it off the books as a total loss. That's why I was headed here in the first place, to return Inter-State's money. I didn't believe for one second the operation would achieve what John thought it would."

"Had you told him so directly?"

"A hundred times." His eyes locked on Clevenger's. "But I hadn't told him everything. I hadn't told him what I really believed about his seizures. I promised myself I would—at the hospital yesterday morning."

"What were you going to tell him?"

"That I didn't believe they were real."

"The seizures?"

"The whatever."

"You think he was faking?"

"Not consciously," Coroway said. "I think when he became stressed, when a problem was greater than his ability to solve it, he had a way out. I think he'd gotten in that habit as a kid. Because nobody ever told him it was okay to fail. Then it just became automatic. A reflex."

Coroway was describing pseudoseizures, fits that looked like epilepsy but were really a kind of hysterical reaction to stress. People's eyes might roll back in their heads, their limbs might jerk back and forth, but nothing much was actually wrong with their brains.

"I'm not saying John wasn't overcome by these *fits*," Coroway went on. "I think it was more like when someone passes out over bad news. It isn't from low blood pressure, as I understand it. It's an *emotional* collapse."

"His medical records from MGH say he bit through his tongue more than once during his convulsions. That takes a whole lot of emotion."

"John needed to convince all the people around him he was sick, beginning with his family when he was a child. But more than that, he needed to convince himself. I think he would have bitten his tongue clear off if it meant avoiding the truth."

"The truth . . ."

"That he had limits."

"You don't think Jet Heller confirmed whether the epilepsy was real? You think he'd perform neurosurgery on someone whose brain was essentially normal?"

"My guess? The evidence was slim. John interpreted any abnormality on a CAT scan or EEG as proof that his nervous system was betraying him. I think Heller saw things the same way. And I think that's the real problem the Ethics Committee at the General had with the surgery. They had a cowboy neurosurgeon on their hands so hungry for headlines he would have cut up John's brain to stop him from sneezing."

"And John was that afraid of failing with Vortek?"

"Vortek was only a symbol," Coroway said. "What he was afraid of was being human."

That was a whole new perspective on Snow's quest to go under the knife. But it didn't change the facts. Coroway had sped away from the same city block where his business partner had been shot. He had flown out of state. And he hadn't returned. He could take off from D.C. to Paris to parts unknown, if the spirit moved him. "Are you planning to come back to Boston soon?" Clevenger asked.

"Probably tomorrow," Coroway said. "Maybe the next day. I wish I could be with our employees, but John's death leaves me with more work than ever. And a lot of it's here, with our vendors and clients, including folks on the Hill. They need to be reassured we're still in business."

"Are you?" Clevenger asked.

Coroway's lip curled ever so slightly. "No one is indispensable," he said. "I built Snow-Coroway at least as much as John did. He was a genius, but we do have very talented people who were working right under him." He didn't look like he was buying his own lines. "And I do have to remind myself," he said, "that as creative as John was, he made us spin our wheels for months on Vortek. We should have walked away from it much sooner."

Clevenger's eyes traveled back to Coroway's cuff links—the little, gold jets. His question had been naive. Business was business. The show would go on without Snow. "Who do you think killed him?" he asked.

"I have no idea," he said immediately.

That was about the only thing Coroway didn't seem to know. "No suspicions?"

"That's your job."

"That's why I'm asking."

Coroway got up, walked to the window. "Maybe we're all a little guilty."

That mea culpa seemed vaguely reminiscent of Lindsey Snow's peculiar confession. "How so?"

"We all needed John in our lives—for different reasons," Coroway said, his voice softer, less self-assured. "Grace, Theresa, John's kids. Me. Maybe nobody's hands are clean."

Clevenger wanted to push Coroway a little harder. "Tell me about yours," he said.

He turned back to Clevenger. His face was pale. "I told Lindsey about Grace Baxter."

Clevenger pictured the girl's cold, empty eyes. "You told her her father was having an affair?"

"I'm not proud of it."

"Then, why . . ."

"She's a very convincing girl," Coroway said. "She was in tears, questioning what had changed between her and her father. She'd been the only person in his life who could compete with his work for attention. He worshiped her. All of a sudden, she was sharing him."

"With Grace."

"With Grace. With Kyle—her brother. With Heller. With the whole fricking United States, if you really think about it. Her father was a celebrity, all of a sudden. It was difficult to watch her suffering." He shook his head. He looked genuinely disgusted with himself. "Grace had called the house to arrange delivery of an oil painting from the gallery. Lindsey got weird vibes off her. She asked if there was anything going on. I told her."

"You could have lied."

"I should have."

"Why didn't you?"

"Because Baxter was no good for him," he said immediately. The answer didn't seem to satisfy him, any more than it did Clevenger. "I wanted him back. It sounds pathetic, I know. I was worried about the business. And I missed my friend."

"Are you telling me you think Lindsey killed her father?"

"John was playing a dangerous game. Three women were hung up on him."

"Theresa, Grace and Lindsey."

"As for Theresa, she wanted his brain. I don't think she much cared what he did with the rest of his anatomy. Grace seemed to be more self-destructive than anything else, threatening to cut her throat and all that."

To cut her throat. The words didn't hurt any less the second time Clevenger heard them. "Which leaves Lindsey," he managed.

A faraway look came into Coroway's eyes. "She was so enraged," he said. "I knew the minute I told her. . . . I knew she'd never get over it."

"She broke down."

"No, she didn't. That's what bothered me. She just got very quiet. Very still." He focused on Clevenger again. "Then she said something I really didn't understand."

"What was that?"

"She told me I had no idea how much Kyle hated his father." He shook his head. "I didn't get why she was making that leap, from her to her brother. But now, I think maybe I do."

ELEVEN

Coroway offered to call a car for Clevenger after their meeting, but Clevenger told him he had an early dinner just blocks away with an old friend. He wasn't about to get into an unmarked sedan ordered up by a man with fighter jets for cufflinks and a business partner shot dead in an alleyway. He walked three blocks, flagged down a taxi, got in and told the driver to take him back to Reagan National.

The first call he made en route was to his assistant, Kim Moffett. The media had gotten wise to the fact that Clevenger had been hired by the Boston Police Department to find Snow's killer. Over a dozen reporters had phoned the office. Camera crews were milling about in the parking lot. Moffett was so caught up in that chaos that she waited until the end of their call to tell Clevenger that Lindsey Snow had stopped by about twenty minutes before.

"Did she say what she wanted?" Clevenger asked.

"No. But she said it was *no emergency*. She wasn't crying or upset or anything."

Moffett was being extra cautious in the wake of Grace Baxter's telephone calls, which only made Clevenger feel worse about having missed them. "She leave a number?"

"Her cell. 617-555-8131."

"I'll give her a call."

"Can I tell you something weird about her?" Moffett asked.

Clevenger had learned not to be distracted by Moffett's youth, blond curls or sweet voice; she was as savvy as they come. "Shoot."

"She talked to me like she knew me. And she talked about you like it was totally expected she'd just drop by. Like she does it every day. She could be my instant best friend. Add water and stir. I mean, is she living in some sort of fantasy world?"

"I don't know," Clevenger said. "Whatever world she's in, steer clear."

"I get that."

"Anything else?"

"North isn't here, but he said to remind you to call him when you're out of your meeting, which you must be, since you're calling me."

"Will do."

Clevenger checked in with Anderson and quickly updated him on the meeting with Coroway. They decided Anderson would stop by MGH during the 11:00 P.M. to 7:00 A.M. shift with a photograph of Coroway off the Web. It was worth checking whether any employees there remembered seeing Coroway in the lobby or cafeteria or parking garage—or near the alleyway where Snow was found.

His next call was to Lindsey Snow.

"Hello?" she answered.

"It's Dr. Clevenger," he said.

"Hey, are you in your office?"

Her tone was inappropriatcly familiar. "I'm not," Clevenger said. "I heard you stopped by."

"When will you be there? Can I come see you?"

Clevenger checked his watch. 5:10. If he caught the six o'clock flight back to Boston, he could be in the office by eight o'clock. Billy wouldn't be home from the O.R. until later than that, anyhow. He knew he was going behind Theresa Snow's back to talk to her eighteen-year-old daughter, but there wasn't anything forbidden about that in a murder investigation. And he could probably arrange for Moffett to stay late, to have a third person around. "Sure," he said. "Why don't you come by at eight?"

"I'm not doing well," she said, her voice suddenly close to despair. "I feel so empty."

"You've lost your dad."

"I've lost everything."

She sounded like she was at the end of her rope. "Lindsey, if you need to talk to someone right away," he told her, "there's no shame in heading over to an emergency room. I'll meet you at Cambridge Hospital."

"I can't talk to most people."

"Can you promise me you'll be all right for the next couple of hours?"

"I'll be fine," she said, very quietly.

Clevenger felt like he was locked in a replay of his meeting with Grace Baxter, asking for another *contract for safety*, as if that guaranteed anything. But he also knew Lindsey hadn't said anything that would warrant getting the police to take her to a hospital against her will. "You're sure?" he asked her.

"You're worried about me," she said, speaking through tears now. "That's so nice." She cleared her throat. "You don't need to be. I kill *other* people, remember?"

"Lindsey . . . Where are you?"

"I'll see you at eight." She hung up.

Clevenger dialed back once, got her phone message. He tried again. Same result. He thought about calling Cambridge Hospital, getting them to send a crisis worker to the Snows' house on Brattle Street. But he didn't have the right to do that and he knew most of his anxiety wasn't even about what might happen to Lindsey. It was about what had already happened to Grace Baxter.

He closed his eyes and let his head fall back against the seat, but that just brought Collin Coroway's words back. *She said she'd cut her throat.* He opened his eyes, stared out the window of the cab at the bare trees rushing by. The sun was falling, and the sky looked darker to him than it had just minutes before.

He wanted to sleep on the plane, but couldn't. He took out John Snow's journal, glanced through it. Most of the entries sandwiched between Snow's drawings and calculations were rehashings of his central question—whether he had the right to exit his own life story. But midway through the journal was a passage scrawled in especially tiny letters, written diagonally down the lower half of a page. And it began with the word *Love.*

> *Love is the greatest obstacle to being reborn. In love, one stakes claim to another human being, incorporating that person into his or her own self-image. Lovers not only find it hard to imagine either existing without the other, they become a third entity—the couple. This is why love feels so liberating when it blooms.*
>
> *But is there not in every coupling also a slow death of each individual, a disappearance of the man and the woman into one another? Is this what people mean when they speak of loving someone to death?*
>
> *I just love you to death.*
>
> *Is the couple truly more worthy of survival than the two individuals?*

156

Technology offers us a solution. When love fades, a properly guided scalpel can wholly reconstitute the individual, cleanly freeing him or her from the tentacles of another rooted so deeply in his or her soul.

The singular human spirit can be set free from the crushing weight of shared emotion and experience under which it is buried.

The individual can be reborn with no guilt or sadness, for there is no memory of others left behind, only the brightest horizon ahead, the infinite potential of an entirely new story.

Clevenger put the journal down. Snow's fear of engulfment was everywhere in his writing, his worry that the "tentacles" of his lover would reach deep inside him and never let go, that romantic love was a kind of intoxicating cancer that consumed the souls it linked. Was that what falling in love with Grace Baxter felt like to him? Had he ultimately decided to end their relationship and proceed with surgery out of terror that he would cease to exist if he fell in love with her completely? And how would he have responded had he learned that a part of him was already growing inside her womb?

He took a deep breath and shook his head. A profound sense of sadness settled inside him. He wondered why. At first he thought he was beginning to actually feel for Snow, to empathize with him, a man convinced that being embraced was always the prelude to being suffocated. A man who had married in order to be left alone. But then the image of Whitney McCormick came to him again. She was only with him a split second, but that was long enough to help him see that he wasn't sad only for Snow. He was sad for himself. Because living through his own kind of hell as a child hadn't left him much better off. Ultimately, he was alone, too. He could care about his patients. He could love his son. But he wasn't at all sure he would ever let himself be loved.

With a delay into Boston, Clevenger got to Boston Forensics ten minutes before Lindsey Snow, driving right past three die-hard reporters who must have been lurking outside the chain-link gates for hours.

Cary Shuman was one of them, a gritty street scribe who would have happily burrowed right under the asphalt of Chelsea's crooked streets if he thought there was any chance a story might be hidden there. "Any leads, Doctor?" he yelled out, as Clevenger walked toward the entrance.

Clevenger didn't stop.

"Is it true Grace Baxter was your patient?"

That broke Clevenger's stride, but he forced himself to keep walking.

"You made it," Kim Moffett said, coming out from behind her desk as he walked through the door. She had agreed to stay late. She had on a black leather jacket, torn Levi's and a pair of Prada leather sneakers—a pretty typical getup for her.

"Thanks for hanging out," Clevenger said.

"No problem."

"Everything all right?"

"Just great. I've got plenty of company if I get lonely," she said, nodding toward Shuman and friends on the street outside.

He smiled, started toward his office.

"You know, you don't look good," she said. "Have you been sleeping?"

"I'm okay," he said. He stopped, turned toward her. "Thanks for asking." Nobody did, anymore.

"Want me to order you dinner?"

"I'll just grab something on the way home."

"Liar."

He smiled at her, turned and walked into his office. He had barely taken off his coat when the intercom chimed. "Lindsey Snow here to see you," Moffett said.

"Send her in." He opened his door for her.

Lindsey glanced shyly at him as she walked past him, into the office. She was dressed in the same tight jeans and black sweater she had been wearing at the house, but she had pulled herself together, putting on makeup and perfume and tying her hair back.

"I'm glad you came by," Clevenger said. He motioned toward the chair Grace Baxter had sat in. "Please."

She sat down.

He sat in his desk chair, swiveled around to face her and saw she was crying.

"Why can't I keep it together?" she asked.

"Maybe because you're not supposed to," Clevenger said.

She wiped her tears away, but they didn't stop.

He let her cry. Watching her, he saw again how she teetered between adolescence and adulthood, with a raw sensuality that had to deposit her in a kind of no-man's land—too much a woman for boys her own age, too young for fully adult men.

She seemed cried out after a minute or so. "I didn't tell you everything today," she said.

Clevenger waited, remembering that pushing her had made her pull back.

"I did something terrible."

More bait. He didn't take it. "Are you sure you're comfortable talking to me about it?" he asked.

She just shrugged.

Several seconds passed. He wondered whether he was being too aloof. "You won't scare me away."

She closed her eyes, swallowed hard, then opened them and looked straight into his eyes. "I didn't just tell him to die. I made him *want* to die. I mean, I took something away from him that made him want to live."

"What was that?"

"A *woman*." Her cheeks flushed. She looked down at the floor. "He was seeing someone else."

From the bitterness in her voice, it sounded like she felt her father had been cheating on her, not her mother. "Who?" Clevenger asked.

"Her name was Grace Baxter. She ran an art gallery." She pressed her knees together. "She killed herself, too. Right after my dad." She hung her head. "I'm a pretty bad person."

"How did you find out about her and your father?"

"She called the house once," Lindsey said, looking back up at him. "She was, like, all strange on the phone. Like she knew me or something. And the way she said his name . . . It was sickening. I asked Collin, my dad's business partner, about her."

That squared with what Coroway had told Clevenger. "And what did he tell you?"

"That she was . . . you know . . . with my dad."

"How did you feel?"

"Like I told you, that my dad was a liar."

Clevenger stared into her eyes.

She held his gaze. "And that she was a fucking whore."

The bulk of Lindsey's rage was clearly directed at Baxter. That made psychological sense. John Snow had a passionless marriage, but a daughter he considered perfect. That imbalance could have easily led Lindsey to consider herself the most substantial female in his life. There was no healthy Oedipal competition in the house. She owned her father—until Grace Baxter showed up.

"I went to the gallery once," she said.

"Did you find her?"

She looked nauseated. "How could I miss her? I had been looking at her for months. Did you see the painting over the mantel in
the living room? The naked woman behind the window?"

Clevenger nodded.

"It's of her. That's how twisted she was. She made him bring her
home to his family."

"How did it feel, seeing her in the gallery?" Clevenger asked.

"I wanted to vomit."

"Did you tell your father you knew about her?"

"Not exactly. I told him he was a liar. I told him I wished he
would die."

The lie, of course, was that Snow would be Lindsey's were it
not for his rather lifeless marriage. As the only female he adored,
her developing psyche was deprived of coming to the healthy conclusion that her father was completely unattainable as a mate
because he was *in love* with her mother. Grace Baxter's arrival on
the scene showed Snow was willing to go outside his marriage, to
be passionate—but not with Lindsey. He would never be hers.
"And what did he say when you told him you wished he would
die?" Clevenger asked.

"He said . . ." Her eyes filled up. "He said maybe I'd get my wish."

"When was that?"

"A few months ago."

"And had the two of you talked since then?"

"Not about anything important. Not much at all. There wasn't
anything to say." She fought against her tears. "Then I found
something."

"What was that?"

"A note."

"From your dad?"

She shook her head. "From that . . ." She stopped herself. "From her. A suicide note."

Clevenger's pulse started to race. "Where did you find it?"

"In his briefcase."

"You were looking through his briefcase?"

"That's where he kept the receipts from the Four Seasons Hotel," she said bitterly. "They used to meet there. I followed them once. I wanted to see if they'd been there again."

"Do you remember what the note said?"

"This crap about how she didn't feel alive without him. How she hoped he would forgive her for killing herself. And some really disgusting stuff."

He didn't want to make Lindsey shut down, but he needed to know. "Such as?" he asked.

She looked truly nauseated now. "She said that when he '*entered* her,' she '*entered* him.'"

Lindsey was describing the suicide note found on Grace's night-stand. "What did you do with the note?" he asked her.

She looked away.

He waited.

"I should have just put it back in his briefcase."

"But . . ."

She looked at him with something new in her eyes—a self-righteousness he hadn't seen before. "I gave it to her husband, George Reese. I had my brother bring it to his office at the Beacon Street Bank."

"You told Kyle about Grace Baxter?"

"He'd been getting all cozy with Dad the last three or four months. Like they were best friends, all of a sudden, even though Dad basically blew him off his whole life. I didn't want him getting sucked in, then finding out we were all getting ditched for her."

Kyle's evolving connection with Snow clearly would have

threatened Lindsey's special place in Snow's life. By telling Kyle about Grace Baxter, she not only torpedoed her father's affair, she destroyed any chance for a meaningful father-son relationship. "When did he bring George Reese the note?"

"A week ago."

That information was all Coady would need to bring Reese in for questioning. He had motive for one or both murders; he knew his wife was having an affair, and with whom. And he knew it was no fling. She was in love. She didn't want to live without Snow.

"It ended everything between her and my dad," Lindsey went on.

"How can you know that for sure?"

"His cell phone. Kyle went on-line and figured out how to look at the outgoing calls. He didn't call her once after that day."

"I guess you got done what you were looking to get done."

Lindsey shrugged. "I guess she finally went through with it," she said, without much emotion.

Passing the "suicide note" to Reese really might have set wheels in motion that ultimately resulted in John Snow's death—and Grace Baxter's. But Lindsey didn't seem particularly remorseful. "I'm glad you told me," Clevenger said. "It takes a lot of courage to admit something like that."

She brought her knees up to her chest, like she had in his truck, rested her head on them. "I feel so comfortable with you," she said. "I could tell you anything. Do you make everyone feel that way?"

"Not everyone," Clevenger said.

"I guess it's sort of like a chemistry thing. I mean therapy is a pretty intimate relationship."

"This isn't therapy."

"What is it?"

Clevenger didn't answer. He wasn't Lindsey's psychiatrist, but he had invited her to the office. Maybe that had been a mistake.

"Who do you tell stuff to?" she asked.

Clevenger felt her trying to further blur the boundaries between them. Now she wanted to be *his* therapist, or something more. When you have a father who seems to hold out the possibility of complete union, you can end up chasing that illusion everywhere you go, with every surrogate father you can find. "I wouldn't burden you with my 'stuff,'" Clevenger said.

"I don't mind."

"You don't need to worry about me," Clevenger said. "I'll be okay."

She looked at him even more warmly. "I bet you don't have anyone to lean on. You're a loner. You listen to other people's secrets, but you don't let anyone in on yours." She caught her lower lip between her teeth. "Am I right?"

In that moment Clevenger realized how psychiatrists sometimes lose their way. Because what Lindsey Snow was saying about him was partly true. It felt good to hear it, to be understood, even by an eighteen-year-old. And even with her being eighteen, it would be easy to forget the psychological dynamic making her say it—the transference to her father. It would be easy to believe the two of them really did have a special bond. "Any therapist would be wrong to talk about himself with . . ."

"But I'm not your patient."

"No. Not exactly."

"Okay, then. So . . . What am I?"

"You're the daughter of a man who died yesterday. I'm investigating that event. If I can be helpful to you, I'm glad to be, but . . ."

"Listen to you. Round and round and round. It's all circular logic. I can't be your friend, but I'm not your psychiatrist, but if I can help you. Blah, blah, blah. You sound like Dad, the way he used to spin his wheels talking through physics problems. No way you're gonna let yourself *feel* your way through anything. It's all by the numbers." She let go of her knees, slowly straightened up in her chair. Then she stood up, joining her hands over her head and arching her back like a cat. Her sweater rode up past her pierced navel, over the slopes of her perfect abdomen. She finished the stretch, shrugged. "I'll be okay, too. Thank you."

"Did you drive here? Can I call you a taxi?"

"Careful. You don't want to start worrying about me, either." She turned around and headed out of the office.

Clevenger watched her leave the office, then the building. She walked over to a lapis blue Range Rover, climbed inside and drove off. And he was struck again by how quickly she seemed to have tucked in the loose edges of her sadness and guilt. Was that because, underneath it all, she really did want her father to pay with his life for his transgression—for essentially cheating on her? Was her rage that much in ascendance over her conscience?

Then Clevenger had another, even more troubling, thought. What if her story about George Reese wasn't true? What if she had found Grace Baxter's suicide note and kept it until she or Kyle Snow had the chance to leave it by Baxter's bed, after one or both of them made her pay for stealing their father?

"If looks could kill," Kim Moffett said from Clevenger's door.

He turned to her.

"I don't know what you told that girl, but she definitely does not want to be my friend, anymore. She looked at me like I stole her honey." She smiled, cocked her head to one side. "Honey."

"She's dangerous. Keep that in mind."

She touched her forehead, winked. "Good night."

TWELVE

Clevenger called Mass General, got put through to the O.R. and learned Heller was still in surgery. He dialed Mike Coady's cell phone.

"Yup," Coady answered.

"It's Frank."

"You back?"

"A couple hours ago."

"How was it?"

He told Coady how unflustered Coroway had seemed, even while being questioned about Vortek. And he told him that Coroway had confirmed for Lindsey Snow her suspicion that her father was having an affair with Grace Baxter.

"Then you have to think the mother knew, too," Coady said.

"Probably. But here's the most important part. I just met with Lindsey. She told me she found Baxter's supposed suicide note— the one you found at the scene. She quoted it word for word. That note wasn't written to George Reese. It was written to John Snow. Lindsey found it in his briefcase about a week ago."

"Grace Baxter wrote that note a week ago?"

"And either gave it to Snow, or he found it. Whatever he ended up saying or doing, it must have been the right thing. She didn't go through with it—not while he was alive."

"So if Lindsey Snow found the note, how did it end up back with the corpse?"

"Lindsey had her brother deliver it to George Reese. She obviously wanted to end the affair, once and for all."

"That would do it," Coady said.

"If she's telling the truth, it looks like Reese put that note at the bedside—after he killed his wife."

"Looks that way." Coady was silent a few seconds. "Unless he was scared someone would think he had. I mean, Baxter did write that note. She was in pretty bad shape when she came to see you. He could have found her dead, then panicked and dressed up the scene a bit."

She was in pretty bad shape. . . . Coady kept wanting to paint Grace Baxter's death as a suicide. And Clevenger had to wonder whether he, himself, was equally intent on seeing it as a murder. Was something clouding Coady's vision, or was guilt clouding his own? "I guess that's possible," he said.

"I'm just trying to think the way his five-million-dollar defense team would think," Coady said. "But I'll arrange to have him come in for questioning."

"I'll look forward to talking with him, again."

"We just got to be real careful with this Beacon Street Bank thing."

"Careful?"

"It's a major bank. A major employer. The stock is gonna tank when the *Globe* runs with Baxter being a focus of the investigation, which should take about four seconds, given the number of reporters on this thing. I'm gonna hear from Mayor Treadwell, if not the Governor. They'll want to make damn sure I don't have my head up my ass."

"Nobody can say you pulled the trigger too fast. There are real questions he's got to answer. What did he do with that note? What did he think about his wife sleeping with John Snow? Where was he at, say, 4:30 A.M. yesterday?"

"Like I said, I'll set it up."

"Fair enough," Clevenger said.

"Kyle Snow is all ready for you, too. He's waiting at the Suffolk County Jail, anytime you want him."

"He's in jail?"

"He didn't like the idea of dropping by the station to be questioned, so I got his bail yanked on account of his dirty urine."

Lindsey hadn't mentioned her brother being arrested. "When did you pick him up?"

"About an hour ago. Maybe you can open him up now that he's locked down."

"I'll give it a shot. I'll stop by tomorrow morning."

"Let me know how it goes."

"Will do."

Clevenger drove home to wait for Billy and Jet Heller.

It was 9:20 P.M. He turned on his computer and slipped in one of the five floppy discs that held files copied from the hard drive of John Snow's laptop. He called up a directory, saw the usual Microsoft operating system files, along with several other standard program files like Word and Norton AntiVirus. But mixed in with those were twenty files starting with *VTK*, numbered sequentially—*VTK1.LNX* through *VTK20.LNX*. Those certainly looked like files related to Vortek. He opened the first. It was pages and pages of what looked like computer code. Either the files were corrupted, or they were programming lingo Clevenger couldn't make heads nor tails of. He slipped the next disc in, and the next, with the same results. There were a total of 157 *VTK* files, every one of them indecipherable.

Clevenger picked up the phone, dialed his friend Vania O'Connor at Portside Technologies, up north in Newburyport, close to the New Hampshire border. O'Connor was a thirty-five-year-old computer genius with a laundry list of Fortune 500 clients who probably never visited his windowless basement office, stacked wall-to-wall with hundreds of resource texts on computer programming and troubleshooting.

O'Connor answered on the first ring. "Mmm. Hmm," he hummed, in his trademark baritone.

"It's Frank. Sorry for the late call."

"What time is it?"

Clevenger looked at his watch. "Ten-fifteen." He wondered why Billy wasn't back.

"A.M. or P.M.?"

Clevenger smiled. He didn't doubt O'Connor lost track of night and day sometimes, working underneath the house where he, his wife, and three kids maintained a surprisingly normal existence. And that thought—of O'Connor serving his genius and his family at the same time—made Clevenger question again why John Snow had been unable to. "A.M.," he joked.

"Impossible," O'Connor said. "It's our day to bring snack to kindergarten. Nicole would have been screaming at me hours ago."

Nicole was O'Connor's magical six-year-old daughter. "You serve many masters."

"I know this," O'Connor said. "Let me guess. You're calling to figure out why opening an Explorer browser while using an Excel spreadsheet would preclude accessing the monthly forecast function—which is weird, because that's exactly what I'm working on this very minute."

"Sounds interesting."

"Like hell."

"How long you been at it?"

"I don't know."

"I hate to interrupt."

"Something tells me you'll get over it. What's up?"

"I have these floppies here with all kinds of files on them. They came off a laptop's hard drive. Some of them look pretty standard, but there are a hundred-and-fifty-seven others that start with the letters *VTK* and end with *LNX*."

"A hundred and fifty-seven."

"I opened every one of them. I can't figure out whether they're messed up by a virus or written in code. Either way, they make no sense to me." He heard the door to the loft being unlocked and headed toward it.

"Do not e-mail them to me," O'Connor said. "God knows what you're infected with."

He said it like Clevenger had about a day to live. "How about if I bring them by? I promise not to breathe on you."

"Any time."

"Tomorrow morning?" Clevenger asked.

"Before eight-thirty or after nine-fifteen. Like I said, it's our turn . . ."

"To bring snack." The door opened. He heard Billy and Heller talking.

"Blueberries," O'Connor said. "It's Montessori. They're into health food. Me, I'm into brain food. I'm on my third box of Hot Tamales tonight."

Billy walked in wearing scrubs and a jeans jacket, followed by Heller wearing scrubs and a black wool, three-quarter-length coat. He had on his black alligator cowboy boots.

"See you around eight," Clevenger told O'Connor.

"Large, cream, four sugars."

"Done." He clicked off. "So how was it?" he asked Billy.

Billy smiled, glanced at Heller. Heller smiled back at him. "Awesome," Billy said. "Completely, totally awesome."

"Stay a while," Clevenger said to Heller.

"Still up for that drink?" Heller asked. "I think Billy here is pretty tired."

"Beat," Billy said. He held up a book. "Bedtime reading."

Clevenger read the title. *Brain and Spinal Cord Structure* by Abraham Kader, M.D. He couldn't quite believe Billy was holding it in the same hand usually reserved for Marlboros and Eminem CDs. "That's a classic," he said.

"Kader is a friend of mine," Heller said.

But, of course, Clevenger thought.

"It's signed," Billy said. *"One healer, to another."*

"That's why I gave it to Billy," Heller said. "Could be true again."

"You should of been there," Billy said. "We close, and, like, thirty minutes later she wakes up in recovery and . . ." He glanced at Heller again, who nodded his okay to deliver the punch line. "She could see," Billy said, reverently.

"That's incredible," Clevenger said.

"Like I told Billy," Heller said, "we had nothing to do with it. God gave that woman her sight." He held up his hands. "He gave me these." He let them fall to his sides. "And if Billy turns out to be a neurosurgeon, that'll be because he had it inside him all along, just waiting for him to worship that fact."

Clevenger couldn't argue with the substance of Heller's soliloquy, but his delivery made it obvious he was still riding the manic wave that had swept him into the O.R. "Whatever your gift is, you have to respect it," Clevenger told Billy, hearing his words drowned out by the lingering echo of Heller's.

"Exactly," Heller said.

"I helped close," Billy told Clevenger.

"Fantastic," Clevenger said.

"Nobody with a passion for surgery can just watch," Heller said. "Billy held retractors for four hours straight. Not a peep out of him. He earned the right to throw in the last couple staples."

"Somehow I don't think this is the last time he's going to want to visit the O.R.," Clevenger said.

"No problem," Heller said. "He was a champ in there. Capable. Respectful. Everyone liked him."

"I'm gonna start diving into this," Billy said, holding the book up. He looked at Heller. "Thanks."

"Thank you."

Clevenger watched them shake hands.

"Night," Billy said to Clevenger, then headed off to his room.

"Night, buddy," he said. "Love you." He'd gotten used to the fact that Billy rarely hugged him or said he loved him; the kid had come from a family where all you got for being vulnerable was more pain. But he felt particularly distant from Billy with Heller standing there. "How about that drink?" he asked Heller. He really wanted one.

"Where to?"

"The Alpine? It's bare bones, but it's right down the street."

"I'm not exactly dressed fancy," Heller said.

They walked to the Alpine, a hole-in-the-wall where the bar took up almost half the square footage. When drinking had been most of what Clevenger was looking to do, the prominence of that bar had seemed fitting, even soothing. No one went to the Alpine for the coffee, or the decor—dark wood paneling, indoor-outdoor carpeting, a suspended ceiling. They went because it was a stone's throw from the triple deckers they called home, and because you could buy a beer for a dollar, a gin and tonic for two.

Heller ordered a scotch, straight up.

"How about you, Doc?" the bartender, early forties, six-foot-two and all muscle, asked Clevenger.

Clevenger hesitated. It would be easy to tell him to make it two—as easy as the first step off a tall building. He ordered a Diet Coke.

"We miss seeing you," the bartender said.

"Miss you, too, Jack," Clevenger said.

"Sounds of it you're doin' good, though. Got that big case. The professor who shot himself, or whatever."

"Right," Clevenger said.

"So gimme the inside scoop: Was it suicide or what?"

"We're still working."

Jack winked. "Keepin' it under your hat. I don't blame you." He looked at Heller. "What's with the pajamas?"

"He's a surgeon," Clevenger said. "Just out of the O.R."

"Two doctors in this joint," Jack said. He poured the drinks. "On me," he said.

"Thanks," Heller said.

"Keep it on account, case I get a hernia or an appendix."

"He's a neurosurgeon," Clevenger said.

"Neuro . . ." Jack said. "Brain." He squinted at Heller. "Wait . . . wait . . . wait a second. You were *his* surgeon. The dead professor."

Heller stiffened. "Right."

"Jet Heller."

"Yes."

"Must of been tough, all that pre-game hype over the guy's lobotomy, then he gets his brains blown out."

"It's been very difficult," Heller said.

"Would have been a nice notch in your belt. Sorry it didn't work out for you," Jack said.

"I wasn't worried about a notch in my belt," Heller said.

Jack reached under the bar for a bottle of Johnnie Walker Red. "Yeah, sure. I bet you hate headlines."

Heller's jaw muscles started working.

He started pouring Heller's drink. "You're talking to Jack Scardillo here. Behind this bar eleven years." He pushed his drink toward him. "Enough said?"

"More than enough," Heller said, staring at him.

Jack had been behind the bar long enough to know one thing for sure—when a customer was ready to come over that bar. He smiled a smile that showed a couple missing teeth. "Giving you a little shit." He held out his hand.

Heller shook it, but his stare stayed icy. "No problem," he said.

"Let's sit down," Clevenger said to Heller. "Everyone's had a long day."

Clevenger and Heller took a table by the front window, under a neon Budweiser sign.

"Sorry about that," Clevenger said.

"I don't have enough distance on losing John to joke about it," Heller said. He nodded at Clevenger's Diet Coke. "You don't drink?"

Clevenger could smell Heller's scotch, almost taste it. "Not today."

"Good for you. Mind if I do?"

"Not at all."

Heller took a long swallow of the scotch.

Clevenger drank down half his Diet Coke. "You won your battle in the O.R."

"Feels damn good," Heller said. "Because I remember each and every time I lost. I'm glad Billy's first outing wasn't one of those." He took another sip of his scotch. "How about you? Getting past the ugliness with Grace Baxter?"

"I'm still trying to understand it," Clevenger said.

Heller stared into his glass. "There's very little in medicine that's exact," he said.

Clevenger liked the direction Heller was heading. It felt like it could lead back to Snow's case. "In psychiatry, you mean," he said.

Heller looked up. "Every specialty. Take pathology. Now there's somewhere the general public would say the answers are crystal clear. You take tissue samples, mount them on slides and look at them under the microscope. You'd figure you could say *absolutely yes* that's a cancer, *absolutely no* that is not. But it isn't like that. You can get different readings from very competent pathologists on the same specimen. I've had to send tissue samples to four different labs before I felt confident I was dealing with cancer, not some peculiar-looking, benign growth. And even then, I end up taking one person's word over another. Mass General versus Hopkins. Hopkins versus the NIH. Because diseases are actually spectrums."

"Some are," Clevenger baited Heller.

"All of them. Look at diabetes. There are clear cases, but there are borderline ones, and subclinical ones. Maybe the patient has it, maybe he doesn't. You draw a blood sugar, and that gives you an equivocal reading, so you need a fasting blood sugar, then a glycated hemoglobin level. Maybe it's worth treating, maybe it isn't. Same with hypertension. There are plenty of obvious cases, but they have nothing to do with the real art of medicine. That comes into play when somebody's pressure is usually normal, but a little high with a cup of coffee, or with too much stress—where you have to judge whether the disease is there or it isn't." He downed the rest of his scotch.

"Epilepsy would be the same," Clevenger said, feeling his own throat warm wonderfully for a split second. He caught Jack's eye, pointed at Heller's empty glass.

Heller nodded, but said nothing.

"I mean, there must be people with abnormal brain wave activity that doesn't rise to the level of actual epilepsy," Clevenger said.

"Sure," Heller said. "Two, three percent of the people in this room would show some spike activity if we hooked them up to EEGs."

Clevenger smiled. "This room? Five, ten percent."

"That's why I'm hoping you're past your guilt over Grace Baxter. Forget about diabetes, hypertension and epilepsy. There's just no way anyone can predict with accuracy whether someone has a fatal depression. There's not even a microscope for that. No EEG. Nothing."

Jack came by the table with another scotch, left it in front of Heller. He gave him a little slap on the shoulder as he left the table.

Heller didn't acknowledge him.

"Let me ask you a question," Clevenger said: "How about Snow? What about his EEG?"

"What about it? He had it all. EEGs, MRIs, PET scans."

"Were the results crystal clear or did they require interpretation?"

"They were very clear," Heller said. He picked up his scotch, took a swallow.

"So he had a classic case of epilepsy," Clevenger led.

"If there's any classic case," Heller said. "He had tonic-clonic, fall down, bite-your-tongue seizures accompanied by abnormal electrical activity in multiple parts of his brain, including the temporal lobe and hippocampus."

Clevenger took a drink of his Diet Coke, cleared his throat. "And the pathology—the abnormal electrical activity—satisfied the Ethics Committee. They were only worried about the side effects of surgery."

"Listen, when you're dealing with a hospital committee, you know as well as I that everybody is raising every question in the book, real or imagined. Bottom line: It was Snow's life. He hated those seizures. He wanted to be rid of them."

That left open the question of whether one or more members of the committee doubted whether Snow's epilepsy was real. Clevenger decided to press the point. "What did the EEG actually show? You called it *abnormal electrical activity*. But, like you said, every illness is a spectrum. So where did Snow fall on that sort of spectrum? If he hadn't had such dramatic tonic-clonic muscle jerks and tongue-biting and all that, would you have diagnosed epilepsy based on the EEG alone?"

"But he did have them," Heller said. He paused. "What are you really asking me?"

"If I knew Snow really had pseudoseizures, I'd have to wonder about his psychological stability across the board," Clevenger said.

"You would," Heller said. He smiled, but tightly. "But that's not what you're driving at. What you really want to know is whether I would have performed experimental brain surgery on John Snow purely to free him from his relationships—from his past—epilepsy or no epilepsy. To give him a new life. Isn't that right?"

Clevenger hadn't had that specific question in mind, but it was clearly on Heller's mind. "Would you have?"

"Maybe."

"Even if the seizures—or pseudoseizures—were a result of stress?"

"Don't be so concrete, Frank. You're a psychiatrist. I don't know if it matters whether the precise pathology was in his brain or in his psyche. He was having big chunks of both removed. Damaged circuitry and highly stressful relationships. Presumably, he would have ended up symptom-free either way."

"Then what about a patient without any seizures at all?" Clevenger asked. "What if somebody just felt like he was at the end of his life and needed a way out, needed to hit the reset button."

"I don't know. Part of me thinks, who am I to deny that person?"

That answer took Clevenger by surprise. He had Heller pegged as a purist, someone who would be offended at the idea of using a scalpel to do anything other than cut away diseased tissues. "Wouldn't that be playing God?" Clevenger asked.

"Better than playing the devil," Heller said. He smiled, finished off his second scotch. "Tonight was grand. Truly. That woman can see again. But John could have *lived* again. She was blind. He was dead." He leaned forward. "Somebody stole that chance from him—and me. What that person did is as terrible as what John Wilkes Booth or Sirhan Sirhan did. Maybe worse. That person robbed us all of the chance to be reborn, resurrected. In a way, that person killed Christ himself."

Maybe Heller really was manic, Clevenger thought. "I guess you'll be looking for another John Snow, then."

Heller shook his head. "He was one in a million. An explorer. Columbus. John Glenn. I don't believe there's another man out there with his psychological stability and level of intelligence who would be willing to put his vision and speech on the line to start over again. And he did have sufficient brain pathology to satisfy the Ethics Committee. Barely enough, but enough. This was once-in-a-lifetime for me. This was my chance to make history."

Clevenger was taken aback again by how Heller took Snow's death as a personal assault on his legacy, not to mention his God. "I'm sorry," was all he could think to say.

This time Heller himself motioned Jack for a refill. He focused on Clevenger again. "I've answered your questions, how about you answer a few of mine?"

"I'll try."

"Billy said you were in D.C."

"That's right."

"Mind if I ask whether the trip was related to the Snow case?"

"I was following up on a lead," Clevenger said.

Heller nodded. "I spoke with Theresa Snow. She told me about her suspicions."

"What did she say?"

"She thinks Collin Coroway killed her husband—over Vortek, and taking the company public."

Snow's widow was pushing her version of his death pretty hard. "Okay . . ." Clevenger said.

Jack brought Heller his third scotch and Clevenger his second Diet Coke, then headed back to the bar, without a word.

"I put two and two together," Heller said. "Vortek and your trip to D.C. Did you happen to visit the patent office to check for recent filings under Coroway's name?"

"No. But why do you want to know, if you don't mind my asking?" Clevenger asked.

"When you told me Snow probably didn't kill himself, I started thinking of this as a crime of passion. Grace Baxter, distraught lover, kills my patient, then kills herself. Nobody's left standing. But you're better at this than I am. And you seem to be looking beyond that scenario."

"I'm not ruling it out."

"Does your gut tell you Collin Coroway killed Snow?"

"My gut and my experience both tell me to look at every possibility."

Heller downed half his scotch. "What are the other possibilities?"

"That's confidential," Clevenger said.

"Professional courtesy, one doc to another."

"Help me understand why being inside the investigation is so important to you."

Heller ran his finger around the lip of his glass. "You already understand." He looked Clevenger in the eyes. "You saw Grace Baxter for about an hour, right? And you've got a head of steam to find out who killed her. I know that isn't just because you want to soothe your conscience. It's because you feel you owe it to her, even after that single hour. Because she was your *patient*. That's a mystical, immeasurable connection. Try to explain it to someone who isn't a physician—and a goddamn good one—and you'll get nowhere. Am I right?"

"Yes."

"Well, I worked with Snow over a year. I put my career on the line for him. I was more than his surgeon. I was his confessor. And I was the one who ran his code in the ER. I was the one who put my hand inside his chest and pumped his heart."

Clevenger stared into Heller's eyes, searching for deceit. But he looked sincere, like he had lost a brother, or a son. "Whatever I ultimately find out, you won't have to read it in a newspaper," he told him. "I'll let you in on it as soon as I possibly can. You have my word."

"I'll trust you on that," Heller said. "And please remember my offer: If you need more money to dig deeper, just let me know. I'd be willing to put up a reward, too, if you think that would help."

"I'll keep that in mind."

He threw back the rest of his scotch. "Third one's a charm," he said. "What do you say? Ready to head out?"

"You all right to drive?" Clevenger asked.

Heller got up, stood on one foot, then the other. He ran the ball of his right foot up his left calf, without wobbling a bit. "I'll be fine. I hate to admit how many three scotch nights I've had in the last six months. I lived and breathed John's case."

Heller was talking a lot like an alcoholic. "The case is over," Clevenger said, standing up.

"No," Heller said. "You get whoever got Snow. Then it's over."

Clevenger got back to the loft a few minutes after midnight. No light seeped from under Billy's door. Apparently, *Brain and Spinal Cord Structure* had put him to sleep.

He walked over to his computer, saw that the display was still glowing, with the code or gibberish from the last VTK file he had looked at still splashed across the screen. That was odd; the computer was set to default to screen saver after five minutes. He reached down and touched the seat of his desk chair. Warm.

He felt angry and disappointed. Billy had gone through his files. He looked at the door to his room, again. Maybe a bedtime chat about respecting each other's privacy was in order. Maybe grounding him would drive the lesson home. But another feeling unexpectedly eclipsed the rest. He felt victorious—over Jet Heller, over Abraham Kader, over neurosurgery itself. Because while Heller and he were at The Alpine, Billy probably hadn't been reading about the nervous system. He'd been at the computer, trying to get closer to Clevenger and his work. And while Clevenger did fear losing him to the darkness of murder cases, he couldn't deny that his son's curiosity felt good.

He didn't knock on Billy's door or yell for him to come out. He sat down in the desk chair and closed his eyes, knowing Billy had been there just moments before.

THE FOUR SEASONS

● A SUMMER DAY, FIVE MONTHS BEFORE.

6:00 P.M.

Grace Baxter knocked on the door to their suite, uncertain whether he would be there. They had scheduled their meeting a week before, but she had not heard from him since, despite phoning him a dozen times. She knocked on the door again, waited ten, fifteen seconds, then turned to leave.

He opened the door.

She turned back to him and was shocked at what she saw. He was unshaven, his eyes bloodshot, dark circles beneath them. His white shirt was wrinkled and stained with sweat. She stepped inside, closed the door behind her. "John, what's wrong?" she asked.

He shook his head, gazed at the floor. "I'm sorry." He looked back at her. She was luminous in a fitted, black shift and high-heeled, black sandals. "I haven't been . . ." He rubbed his eyes.

She took his hand and led him to a velvet love seat.

"I didn't want you to see me this way," he said.

"We agreed never to hide from one another."

He looked through her. "Things haven't been good."

"What things?"

He shook his head. "Just . . ."

"What things? Please, John, tell me."

"My mind," he said, barely focusing on her. "My work. I'm at a dead end."

183

She leaned toward him. "You said it helps when we see each other more. I'll see you every day, if you want me to."

He closed his eyes.

She moved his hand up the inside of her thigh, until the tips of his fingers touched the lace of her thong. "Something's in your way, again. That's all. You're blocked. We can get through it."

He could feel her warmth, her wetness. And part of him wanted to move inside her, to tap the energy that had helped him clear so many creative hurdles in the last six months, bringing Vortek closer and closer to reality. But the last time they had been together had left him no stronger, no less barren. He was convinced that even she could not fuel his imagination any longer. He was empty of ideas. And for John Snow, that was no better than being dead.

She leaned closer, kissed him on the mouth.

He barely felt her lips. He was beyond her reach and slipping farther away. He felt suddenly lightheaded.

She kissed his neck.

He felt a crown of shivers ring his scalp. His arms and legs felt stiff. He looked at her, saw her sitting ten feet away on the love seat. Yet he still felt the warmth of her lips. How could that be? he wondered.

"I love you," she whispered in his ear.

He heard her words as a distant echo. And then he knew what was about to happen. The unspeakable, unthinkable treachery of his brain short-circuiting. A loss of all control, all light, all love. He felt himself pulling away from her. Or was he falling away?

"John," she said. "What's happening? My God."

He watched it happen like a third person in the room, his eyes rolling back in his head, his neck craning, his limbs shaking, the awful twisting in his back, like he was a rag being rung dry. He saw his grotesqueness reflected in the horror on Grace's face. And yet, even as his jaws clamped shut, even as he tasted blood streaming from his tongue, he saw her reaching for him, felt her holding him tight.

He awakened on the floor, in her arms. She was crying, rocking him like a baby. He looked up at her.

"John?" she said, running her hand over his cheek. "It's okay. It's going to be alright."

He tried to speak, but his mouth felt like it was full of razor blades. His pants felt strange against his skin. He had wet himself.

"Don't," she said. "You've bitten your tongue. Don't try to talk."

He lay quietly, still dazed, looking up at her.

She kept rocking him. "You can't do this to yourself," she said. "Do you understand? You have to let this project go. Forget about it. You can come back to it in a year, or five, or never. It doesn't matter."

He felt her tears on his face.

"It's just an idea," she said. "You can't let it destroy you. I won't let you. I love you."

It seemed strange to him that he would feel the real power of her devotion at his worst, rather than his best, odd that she would love him despite his collapse. Yet another part of him knew he could never have received her gift in any other way. Because he was utterly certain now that she loved *him*, not his brain. John Snow. The man, not the machine. And in the way that pure and unconditional love truly can heal, truly can inspire, he knew in his heart that he wasn't even close to giving up the fight to create what so many others insisted was just a fantasy. Because in her arms at that moment—unshaven, bloodied, barely in control of his limbs—absolutely anything and everything seemed within reach.

THIRTEEN

• JANUARY 14, 2004

Clevenger made it up to Vania O'Connor's house, a big colonial on a quiet Newburyport side street, just before 8:00 A.M. He parked, got out of his truck. It was two degrees above zero. With the wind chill it felt like twenty below. The air sparkled with a dusting of shimmering snowflakes.

O'Connor's wife, a pretty blonde with a head for numbers, was backing out of the driveway. She worked as the controller for a Boston-based hedge fund. She lowered her window. "Vania's waiting for you," she called to Clevenger. "He said you were bringing coffee."

Clevenger held up the cup. "Large, cream, four sugars."

"He needs it. He's been up most of the night. Could you please remind him . . . ?"

"To bring snack to the Montessori. I heard all about it."

She smiled, rolled up the window and drove off.

Clevenger walked the bluestone path that led to the bulkhead door at the side of the house. He knocked, pulled it open. "Vania?"

"I think so," O'Connor said.

Clevenger climbed down the narrow concrete steps to O'Connor's lair, saw him hunched over a keyboard typing, the glare from the monitor in front of him the brightest light in the room. Clevenger hadn't been there in about a year, and the place had only gotten more crowded with computers, books and software, piled high on every surface.

Clevenger walked up behind O'Connor, looked at the computer screen, full of numbers, letters, asterisks, arrows, ampersands. He put the coffee cup down beside the keyboard. "All that actually means something?" he asked.

"That's the problem. It doesn't want to add up to much of anything." He picked up the cup, flipped open the lid, took a sip.

"It's going around."

O'Connor smiled up at him. "You sound tired, man." He held out his hand.

Clevenger shook it. "You *look* tired." That wasn't true. O'Connor looked full of energy, younger than he had a year ago.

"How's Billy?"

"Fine."

"Remember, I can spot a faulty line of programming across a frigging room," he said, looking at him askance. "What's wrong?"

"Nothing's wrong. It's a challenge. That's all."

"Was there any chance of you taking on a kid who wasn't a challenge?"

Clevenger thought about that. "No."

"Exactly. You'd be wasted on a kid who was coasting."

O'Connor was right. But Clevenger wondered why it had to be that way. Why had surviving his own childhood traumas bound him so inextricably to other broken people? "Coasting once in awhile might be nice."

"Trust me, you'd hate it. You're a full-time healer. Like it or not." He nodded at the discs in Clevenger's hand. "What kind of trouble are we in, partner?"

"These are the files I told you about. They're from John Snow's laptop. The inventor."

"The guy who was killed, or shot himself, or whatever."

"Yes."

"He's half of what they talk about on the news." He nodded at the discs. "You're not thinking he was killed because of what's on those, are you?"

"I don't know. But I haven't told a soul I'm giving them to you." He saw O'Connor's face lose some of its exuberance. "You don't have to do this."

O'Connor stared at the discs a few seconds. "I already drank your coffee," he said. "Tell me everything."

Clevenger told him about Vortek.

"So we're talking engineering, physics, force, momentum. All that."

"All that."

"Let's pop one in."

O'Connor slipped the floppy into his desktop and called up the directory. He opened *VTK1.LNX*, stared at the field of numbers and letters silently for a minute or so. "Right," he said finally.

"You understand that?"

"No. But I can tell you why. It's highly encrypted, C++, Visual Basic language."

"I'd hate to see what gets an *A*."

O'Connor laughed.

"Can you decode it?" Clevenger asked him.

"If I get lucky. Even if I do, a hundred-and-fifty-seven files is gonna take some time."

"And money."

"That, too. Enough to spread around a little. I know a guy retired from NASA who lives on a farm in Rowley. I may need his help with some of the calculations."

"Whatever it takes," Clevenger said. "I wouldn't show this guy all your cards, though. Like I said, I don't know if what's in those files got Snow killed. And I don't know your friend—or who he knows." He reached into his pocket, handed O'Connor twenty hundred-dollar bills.

"That'll get us started," O'Connor said. "I need more, though."

"I'm good for it. That's what I had on me."

"Not money," O'Connor said. "Information. Snow's date of birth, social security number, dates his kids were born, his anniversary. Some of these guys use that kind of info as keys to unlock encrypted data."

"I'll get you everything I can."

"I'd watch yourself here, Frank," O'Connor said, scrolling down the screen. "Snow went to a lot of trouble to keep people from seeing whatever's behind this code. Maybe nobody knows I've got these discs, but you gotta believe they know that you do."

Clevenger started the drive back to Boston to meet with Kyle Snow at the Suffolk County Jail. He saw that North Anderson had called his cell phone and dialed him back.

Anderson picked up. "Hey, Frank."

"Anything new?" Clevenger asked.

"Coroway's story checks out, on one level. The parking attendant and the cashier in the cafeteria both remember him."

"How doesn't it check out?"

"I talked to the driver of the *Boston Globe* delivery truck he hit. Guy named Jim Murphy. Thirty-something. He says Coroway was beside himself, real shaken after what only amounted to a fender bender. Coroway tried to pay him cash not to file a claim. Five hundred."

"People do that," Clevenger said. "And Coroway says he was in a rush. He had that shuttle to catch."

"Sure. But Murphy really felt leaned on. He told him he couldn't make the deal, it being a *Globe* truck and all, but Coroway wouldn't take no for an answer. He upped his offer to a grand, kept at him until Murphy finally called the police to take a report. Coroway left the scene before the cruiser came."

"Interesting."

"So what's next?" Anderson asked.

"We need to track whether Coroway filed any patents with the Copyright Office in D.C.," Clevenger said. "I want to know whether Vortek was really a bust or not." He looked in his rearview mirror, saw a dark blue Crown Victoria about fifteen yards behind him. He thought he'd seen the same car as he was traveling up Route 95 to Newburyport. He had a bad feeling someone had tailed him all the way from Chelsea. He moved into the fast lane, accelerated to seventy-five mph.

"Would inventions for the military be recorded?" Anderson asked.

"Let's find out," Clevenger said. He remembered Jet Heller's question about whether he had been down in D.C. to visit with military contractors. "It'd also be nice to try to get a handle on whether Coroway licensed Vortek to Boeing or Lockheed or whatever." The Crown Vic hadn't changed lanes, but was keeping up with him. He cut across three lanes, figuring he'd take the next exit and quiet his paranoia.

"I'll get the names of the board members for the biggest companies in the industry," Anderson said. "We can check them against our contacts, see if there's a way in. Maybe one of my friends from Nantucket can help."

Anderson had been Nantucket's Chief of Police before coming to work with Clevenger. "Great. I'll call you after I talk to Kyle Snow. I'm headed to the jail now." He took the exit. The Crown Vic took it with him.

"Cool."

"Hold on. I think I got somebody following me," Clevenger said.

"Where are you?"

"Up near Newburyport."

"You dropped the discs with O'Connor?"

"Yeah. Can you get somebody on the force up in Newburyport to go by his house? Fifty-five Jackson Way. They may have followed me up there."

"You got it. Stay on the highway. Don't get off for anything."

"Too late. I just got off in Georgetown. Route 133."

"Get back on 95. I'll call you in one minute." He clicked off.

Clevenger heard a siren behind him. He looked in the rearview mirror, saw a flashing blue light on the dash of the Crown Vic. He could make out the figures of a male driver and male passenger. He pulled over, pulled his pistol out of its holster and wedged it under his thigh.

The driver stayed behind the wheel. The passenger, a tall man about fifty-five, with thinning hair and glasses, walked up to his window.

He rolled it down.

"Dr. Clevenger?"

"Who's asking?"

"Paul Delaney, FBI."

"Pleasure to meet you. You could have called my office for an appointment."

Delaney smiled. "I'm very sorry. I'm going to need to search the truck, Doctor."

"Not without a warrant, you're not."

"Got one." Delaney reached into his suit jacket. Before Clevenger had a chance to make a move, the nose of a pistol was pressed against the back of his neck. "Eyes in the back of your head?" Delaney asked. "Read my warrant." He nodded toward the Crown Vic.

Five seconds later the passenger door of Clevenger's truck

opened, and Delaney's partner, a rotund man at least six feet tall, leaned into the cabin and started searching under the seats, in the glove compartment. He lumbered into the passenger seat. "Got to pat you down, Doc'," he said.

Clevenger's phone started to ring. He glanced at the caller ID. North Anderson.

"We'll be done in no time," Delaney said. "You can call back."

The fat man ran his hands over Clevenger's chest, arms, legs. He found the gun, held it up for his partner.

"Just leave it in the glove compartment," his partner said.

"If you tell me what you're looking for, I might just give it to you," Clevenger said. "We can skip the Dragnet routine."

"The computer discs. You were given them in error."

Clevenger's phone started ringing again.

"Whose error?"

"Detective Coady's," Delaney said. "Amateur move. They should have been turned over to the FBI." He nodded at Clevenger's cell phone. "Answer it, if you want. Maybe Billy needs you."

Clevenger knew how famous his son was, but hearing Delaney use his name didn't sit well with him. "If you're threatening my son, you'd better be authorized to pull that trigger."

Delaney didn't bat an eye. "I apologize. This has nothing to do with your son. I'm sorry I mentioned him. But to answer your question, I am authorized to pull the trigger if you refuse the search and resist being taken into custody."

The phone stopped ringing, then started right up again.

"I guess those files are pretty important," Clevenger said. "I don't have them." He nodded at the phone. "You mind? That's Billy now."

"Go ahead."

Clevenger clicked the phone on.

"Frank?" Anderson said.

"Five blue discs. Next to my computer in the loft. Go . . ." He felt a flash of pain as Delaney smashed the butt of his gun into the back of his head. Then he blacked out.

He woke up shivering, slumped in the passenger seat of his truck, in an empty corner of the parking lot of a Shaw's Supermarket at the Georgetown Plaza strip mall. His head felt like someone had used it in a game of volleyball. He ran his hand over his scalp, felt something sticky and looked at his fingers. He was bleeding. Delaney, or whatever his real name was, had pistol-whipped him. He looked at his watch. 9:40. He'd been out about twenty minutes. He looked for his cell phone, couldn't find it.

He threw the door of the truck open and stumbled to the pay phone outside Shaw's. He fed in three quarters and dialed Anderson.

"Where are you?" Anderson asked.

"Georgetown Plaza. They knocked me out, drove me here in my truck and left me. You alright?"

"I'm fine. It looks like they had three teams. One got to the loft before I did and took the discs. Your computer, too."

"Billy alright?"

"Yeah. I called his cell. He had left the loft right after you."

"How about Vania?"

"They had to be tailing you the whole way up to his house. They took all his software and hardware, including the discs. But he's all right—physically. He was taking his little girl to kindergarten when they ransacked the place."

"Where is he now?"

"He bundled up and went sailing."

"C'mon."

"Really. Guy must be some sort of Zen master. He said there's not much he can do until the FBI returns his property. His boat's still in the water."

"Where are you?"

"The office. They came here after the loft."

"They take the computers?"

"The computers. All our discs. They went through the files, but didn't seem to find anything interesting. They wanted Kim's BlackBerry, but she basically told them to fuck themselves. They took a look at it, then backed off."

"I don't blame them," Clevenger said. He smiled, in spite of everything, which triggered a bolt of pain to shoot from the base of his skull into his forehead. He closed his eyes.

"You there?"

"I'm here."

"Are you all right to drive or should I come up and get you?"

"I can drive. I'm gonna find Coady. He had to know this was coming down. Then I've got Kyle Snow at Suffolk County."

"I'll work the Board of Directors issue, and all that."

"Let's meet at the office. One o'clock all right?"

"See you there."

The desk sergeant at Boston P.D. walked Clevenger to Coady's office, then disappeared as Coady stood up from behind a gray metal desk piled high with case files.

Clevenger walked up to the desk. His head was pounding. His eyes hurt whenever they moved. "Did you know this was coming down?" He gripped the edge of the desk to keep himself steady.

"Did *I* know?"

"You brought me close to keep me away? Were you worried Theresa Snow would hire me to really work the case?"

Coady didn't respond.

"Someone pay you?" Clevenger pushed. "Coroway?"

Coady stood up. "You've been hanging around crazy people too long."

"When did you first bring the FBI in?"

Coady's neck reddened. "I've been straight with you from the beginning. Where do you get off . . . ?"

"You want to try to sell me the double suicide theory again? Or maybe you're ready to settle for murder-suicide."

"I'm not trying to sell anything. What kind of show are you putting on here, anyhow? If anything, you sold me out."

"Right. I'm subverting your fine investigation."

"I'm not the one with contacts in D.C.," Coady seethed.

"What the hell are you talking about?"

"You know exactly what I'm . . ." He stopped, looked toward the door.

Clevenger turned around and was left speechless. Standing in the doorway was beautiful Whitney McCormick, MD, the FBI forensic psychiatrist, the woman who had risked everything with him to reel in the Highway Killer, a.k.a. Jonah Wrens. The woman who still visited him in dreams.

Coady walked past her and out the door. He shut it behind him.

"I asked North where to find you," McCormick said, in a gentle, almost vulnerable, voice. "I made him promise not to tell you."

"He didn't." He couldn't take his eyes off her. She was thirty-six, slim, with long, straight blond hair and deep brown eyes. Anyone would describe her as pretty. But for Clevenger, she was more than beautiful. She was a key to something locked up inside him.

He saw she was wearing the same pale rose lipstick that she had been wearing the first time he met her, a year before. He remembered how amazed he had been that day at the way she surrendered not one iota of her femininity while briefing him on the carnage Wrens had inflicted as he crisscrossed the country.

"I'm working at the Agency, again," she said. "The past month."

McCormick had resigned as Chief of Forensic Psychiatry after her direct supervisor, a man named Kane Warner, Director of the Bureau's Behavioral Sciences Unit, discovered she and Clevenger had been lovers while tracking down Wrens.

"Same position?" Clevenger asked.

She shook her head. "I have Kane's old job."

"I'm impressed." He wondered whether McCormick's father, an ex-Senator, had had anything to do with her replacing the man who had pressured her to quit. "Does your new job include giving me a little therapy after I get pistol-whipped for doing mine?"

"I'm not here on assignment," she said.

He nodded. It would be so simple to go to her, take her in his arms and kiss her. His attraction to her was magnetic. She steadied him. His pulse slowed in her presence. His anxiety about the world and his place in it all but disappeared. He thought about his old professor John Money, about his *lovemap* theory. Maybe McCormick was his.

But even a *lovemap* doesn't take you neatly past every obstacle. There was the fact that Whitney was so close to her father that there might not be room to be truly intimate with another man. There was the fact she was back working for a law enforcement agency Clevenger had gone to war with more than once. And above all else, there was the fact that Clevenger was committed to fathering Billy Bishop, which left him little time for romance.

"So why did you come here?" he asked her.

"To make things easier for you."

"How?"

"By getting you to forget the discs, for one thing."

"I thought you weren't here on assignment."

"I want to be here," she said. "No one sent me. But you should know those discs were confiscated because they have implications for national security. It's nothing personal."

"It's hard not to take a pistol-whipping personally."

She smiled. "What I'm trying to say is that no one wants to stop you from finding John Snow's killer. That's not what this operation was about. It was about plugging a leak."

"Did they take the discs out of evidence here at the station?"

"Those discs don't exist. You'll never see them or hear of them again," she said. "Not them, not the journal."

Clevenger had left his photocopy of the journal beside his computer. No doubt the FBI had grabbed that, too. "Why are you involved in this?" Clevenger asked. "A murder investigation in Boston wouldn't usually travel to the Behavioral Sciences Unit in Quantico."

"I'm not involved. My dad is."

"Ah . . ." Senator McCormick had been an integral part of the Intelligence Community before running for office. Apparently, he still was. "Why am I not surprised?" Clevenger asked.

"Don't get started. I don't need you playing psychoanalyst with me."

"What if I need those discs to solve my murder case?"

"We're talking about missile technology, Frank. A bunch of highly encrypted data. Mathematical equations. What difference would seeing them make?"

"I don't know. That's what bothers me."

"So be bothered," McCormick said. "But move on."

"Or?"

"You don't want to be part of the problem when it comes to national security. Not these days."

That was a pretty clear warning. "And no one told you to tell me this?"

"No. You already took one blow to the head. I want to save you the trouble of running into brick walls."

"I get the message," he said.

She looked genuinely worried he would ignore her advice.

"I hear you," he said. "Okay?"

She nodded.

"So what do you say? You around tonight? We could get a late dinner."

"I am, if you want me to be."

"Nine o'clock? I want to make sure Billy's home and settled."

"He's home by nine these days?"

"Almost never. But I always have hope."

"Good for you—and him."

"Where do I pick you up?"

"I'll check into the Four Seasons."

Clevenger had to smile at that coincidence.

"What?"

"Nothing. I'll make a reservation at Aujourd'hui."

They stood there in silence several seconds. Then McCormick walked toward him, stopping a foot away. "See you later," she said.

She didn't have to say anything more. The smell of her was part of their lock-and-key fit. He pulled her toward him.

Clevenger found Coady pouring himself a cup of coffee from a dilapidated Mr. Coffee outside the interrogation room. "Sorry about what I said in your office," he told him. "Looks like we're both caught in something we can't quite control here."

"We'll see about that," Coady said, stirring in three packages of Equal.

"Meaning?"

Coady leaned back against the cracked Formica countertop.

"Fucking FBI," he said. "They've been steamrolling this department for too long. I can't believe it's still going on."

"What do you plan to do about it?"

"I'm not backing off, that's for sure." He looked around, checking that no one was in earshot. "There are a couple things you need to know."

"Shoot."

"Kyle Snow was spotted downtown Boston at 3:10 A.M. the morning his dad was shot. He was buying ten Oxycontin tablets from his dealer."

"How do you know that?"

"Kyle rolled on him when I threatened to leave him in jail to serve out the rest of his probation. I went to visit this guy—a college kid from B.U. He was just as much of a stand-up guy. Told me what he'd sold Kyle, and when."

"How can you know he's on the level?"

"He sold it to him in the Store 24 on the corner of Chestnut and Charles. Kyle's on the surveillance tape buying a sandwich and a carton of milk after the deal went down."

"People actually eat those sandwiches?"

"They buy 'em. I don't know if they have the courage to eat 'em."

"So we have him approximately four blocks from the shooting, about an hour and a half before it happened," Clevenger said.

Coady nodded. "Second thing: I'm gonna bring George Reese in for questioning at the end of the business day. No warning. That should put these people on notice. I'll cuff him and drag him in here. You free?"

This was a whole new Mike Coady. Sometimes when you push someone, you find out who that person really is. "You know I am," Clevenger said.

"The suits come down from D.C., take evidence out of my case file? No notice? No respect? I let 'em do it to me this once, pretty soon I won't respect myself."

"You're worrying me."

"How come?"

"We're starting to think alike."

FOURTEEN

Kyle Snow was a wiry sixteen-year-old with fine, almost feminine features and longish black hair he kept flipping out of his blue-gray eyes. He could barely sit still. He was wearing the standard issue orange jumpsuit of the Massachusetts Department of Corrections. He tapped his heel on the floor as he sat across the table from Clevenger. His pupils were dilated. Tiny beads of perspiration covered his forehead. He needed a fix.

"Yeah, I gave him the note," he said, in response to Clevenger's question about delivering Grace Baxter's suicide note to her husband, George Reese. "So what?"

"Did he read it?"

"Sure."

"What was his reaction?"

"He said 'thank you,' real cool like that. He wasn't upset or whatever. You ask me, he knew she was doing her own thing. He's probably been doing his own thing, too."

"Did he ask you anything?"

"Just how I got it."

"Did you tell him?"

"Nope."

"Why did you bring it to him?"

"I don't know."

"Were you angry about your father and Grace Baxter?"

Kyle started tapping his feet. He looked toward the door of the interview room. "They ever getting me that methadone?"

"Couple more minutes," Clevenger said. He waited a few seconds. "Were you angry at your father?"

"Not particularly."

Clevenger decided to take another tack. "You and your dad didn't have much of a relationship, until recently."

"He hated me," Kyle deadpanned. "That's a kind of relationship."

Clevenger knew that firsthand, from his own father. "Did you hate him back?"

Kyle smiled. "I used to fantasize about killing him. Does that answer your question?"

"Killing him, how?"

"Shooting him." He smiled, shook his head. "Weird how things work out."

Clevenger stayed silent.

Kyle wiped his brow. "I'm not holding together."

Clevenger stood up and walked to the door. He opened it, motioned for the guard seated in the corridor outside.

The guard stood up, walked over.

"How about that methadone?" Clevenger asked him.

"Should have been here, Doc," the guard said. "I'll call the infirmary again."

Clevenger walked back into the room, sat down across from Kyle. "You were spotted close to Mass General around the time your dad was killed."

"Too bad I didn't know. I could have watched."

Clevenger looked into his eyes and believed him. Maybe Kyle Snow had seen his father shot, maybe he hadn't. But he certainly would have enjoyed it. "Do you know anything about the project your father was working on when he died?" he asked him.

"I don't know what it was. I know it had him tied in knots until the last month or so."

"How do you know that?"

"He got real uptight when things weren't flowing. He'd stay up the whole night, pacing around, walking the neighborhood. He was doing all that shit. Then it all seemed to turn around. Like maybe he had some sort of breakthrough, or something. You could see it in the way he walked. A little lighter on his feet. And his brow. It could stay furrowed for months, like he was trying to read fine print that was just too small. But when he finished a project, that would go away, too. And it did."

"You could read him pretty well," Clevenger said.

"All those years he wouldn't talk to me, would hardly look at me, I was watching him, trying to figure out what he was thinking, what was wrong. Stupid."

"Why?"

" 'Cause it didn't matter. I was trying to find a way in. There wasn't one. Not for me, anyhow"

"How about Lindsey?" Clevenger asked.

"What about her?"

"Did she feel the same way about your dad?"

" 'C'mon. She worshiped him. He worshiped her. Until all this."

"The affair."

"That wasn't the whole story. He was different. More human. Hooking up with Grace Baxter was just part of it. The fact that he was getting along with me, all of a sudden—that was another part. And being more of a person, he happened to have some issues with my sister. Like her staying out all night with boys. He tried to lay down the law. Before, he wouldn't even notice when she walked in at four, five A.M. Let me tell you, she didn't like any of it."

"Why didn't she want you to get closer with your father?"

"Listen, I'm not stupid. I just standardize-test that way. She hated my dad paying attention to me. All those years when he wouldn't give me the time of day, she had him to herself." He shifted nervously in his seat. "She kind of set me up here, if you want to know the truth."

That felt like a fracture line Clevenger might be able to split open. "By having you deliver the note to George Reese's office?"

He nodded. "My dad was bound to find out I did it. Which probably explains why he didn't talk to me the last couple weeks."

"Did that bother you?" Clevenger asked.

"I'm used to it," he said. But his voice made it obvious that deep down, beneath the last traces of Oxycontin, he was in all kinds of pain.

There was a knock on the door. A male nurse opened it, stepped inside. He was carrying a little paper cup filled with clear liquid— Snow's methadone. He walked over, handed it to him.

Kyle drank it down, handed back the cup. "Thanks."

Clevenger waited for the nurse to walk out. "I would think it would hurt—being ignored by your father again, after finally connecting with him."

"I never really bought the new him," he said, unconvincingly.

"No?"

"I mean, somebody wishes you were never born, then all of a sudden wants to be your best buddy? I don't think so. He was riding a wave, that's all. He was high on Grace. So he spread the joy around a little. But it was never about me. It was about him—and her."

"Did you know about the portrait in the living room?"

"Lindsey told me when she found out. She was all messed up over it."

"How about you?"

"I thought it was cool, actually."

"Cool?"

"You still don't get it. My dad's been nothing but a machine. A computer. Data in, data out. My parents' marriage was a sham. I don't know how she did it, but Grace Baxter brought him back to life. He should have worn her portrait as a goddamn sandwich sign, if she'd asked him to."

Clevenger stared at Kyle for several seconds. "Bottom line," he said finally, "Are you glad he's dead?"

Kyle didn't respond.

Clevenger waited.

"I miss him, I guess," he said. "But I've missed him my whole life. Having him dead makes it better, actually."

"How does it make it better?"

"He's not blowing me off anymore."

Kyle Snow was presenting a psychological motive for murder. Killing his father would have removed from his life the man whose presence was a constant reminder that he was broken and unloved. Maybe the pain of his father coming close, then pulling away again was just too much to bear. Maybe it was enough to make him strike out. But Kyle also seemed acutely aware of his feelings—and painfully honest about them—in a way that argued against him resorting to murder. And his access to Oxycontin meant he had a steady supply of a drug to suppress his rage. "Do you think your dad killed himself?" Clevenger asked him.

"He may have fired the gun. But that's irrelevant."

"What do you mean?"

"Even if he pulled the trigger, we killed him. Lindsey, me, his partner Collin." He smiled. "Have you met Collin?"

"I have," Clevenger said.

"He's a piece of work. You know he told Lindsey that Grace and my dad were lovers?"

"Yes," Clevenger said.

"That's good. You're doing your homework. So here's how I figure it. He came alive there for a while with Grace, started breathing for the first time. Kind of like being reborn. And we cut off his air supply, strangled him."

"You drove him to suicide."

"You got it. Which is why I said what I said about the whole thing being so weird. There I was wanting to shoot him, and I didn't have to."

Clevenger nodded. That was a consistent theme. Collin Coroway, Lindsey and Kyle all believed they had conspired to make life unlivable for John Snow. Perhaps that was what finally drove him to choose surgery. Perhaps, for a time, he truly had thought he could be reborn in the love of Grace Baxter. And when his life closed around him like a noose, he decided a scalpel was the only way to cut himself free.

But one major question remained: If Grace Baxter loved John Snow enough to write a suicide note when she lost him—if she was his *lovemap* and he was hers—why hadn't that love been great enough to overcome everything else? Why would exposing their affair end it?

A piece of the puzzle was missing.

Clevenger looked into Kyle Snow's eyes, saw his own reflection. And while he knew he was there to investigate two deaths, while he knew Kyle was a suspect, not a patient, he couldn't help seeing the world of pain he was in. He could actually feel it in his gut. Such was his gift, and his cross to bear. He was permeable to the suffering of others. It was the thing that had once driven him to drink and drug and gamble himself into oblivion. And it was the thing that was keeping him in his seat right now. Because he had everything he was going to get from Kyle Snow. Now he felt the need to give something back. "You think your father being gone is going to make you feel better? Is that right?" Clevenger asked.

"Pretty much."

"Well, you're wrong."

"The only one who ever cared about me was my mother. Now we're a single-parent family. I feel better already."

"Maybe you will, for a week. Maybe two. But the truth is that taking your father off the planet doesn't change the fact that he's still inside you."

"I never went in for all that New Age shit."

"That's why you use the Oxys, by the way. You're feeding them to the part of you that's your dad, the part that thinks you're worthless, that you should never have been born."

"Plenty of Oxy out there."

Clevenger smiled to himself. He'd once thought the same way, that he didn't have a problem so long as he had enough booze and coke to feed it. "There isn't enough Oxycontin in the whole world to put down that feeling. Not in the long run. The only way to do that is to start thinking—and feeling—for yourself."

Kyle rolled his eyes, looked away.

"My father used a belt to convince me I shouldn't be alive. I think that was actually easier to deal with than being ignored would have been. Being ignored, you start to wonder if you even exist. I knew. Just the bruises alone . . ." He closed his eyes, remembering. When he opened them, Kyle was looking straight at him. "So what are you good at?" Clevenger asked him. "Why are you on the planet?"

"I'm very good at getting myself arrested. I can tell you that."

Clevenger kept looking at him. Ten, fifteen seconds. C'mon, he thought to himself, give it up already. Ten more seconds. He was about to give up himself, call it a day, when Kyle finally spoke.

"I'm decent at drawing," he said, all the tough-guy bravado evaporating as he spoke those words, leaving behind someone who looked and sounded shockingly vulnerable. A deer in headlights. "I guess I get that from my mom."

"What kind of drawing?"

"Architectural stuff, like hers. I'm pretty good at that. I mean, I think I am."

"Does she know?"

"No."

"Maybe you should tell her."

"Yeah, maybe I should," he said halfheartedly.

Clevenger knew the trouble Kyle Snow was having with that suggestion. His father's love had been the prize he quietly dreamed of. Actively seeking his mother's affection would mean he had lost his father's, once and for all. "I'm going to tell you something straight out, Kyle," Clevenger said, "because I don't think there's any real chance you're gonna sit down with a shrink a hundred hours or so to figure it out: Your father couldn't love anyone. He worshiped beauty and perfection. He worshiped his own mind. But the whole of him, or anyone else, including your sister, was something he just couldn't embrace. Maybe Grace Baxter could have fixed that, maybe not. It turned out to be too late."

Kyle looked down at the table, shrugged.

"So now you just have to love yourself," Clevenger went on. "There's nowhere else to go. You've got to think of every talent you have, every gift you could give the world around you. And you've got to take the chance of giving it. And if you do that, you'll be too busy to chase Oxycontin. Because you won't be busy hating yourself, anymore."

"Whatever," he said.

Clevenger felt the impulse to step in as Kyle's surrogate father. Was that because Kyle really needed him to? he wondered. Or was it because Clevenger wished someone had done it for him? Either way, he couldn't resist. "Once the investigation is over," he told Kyle, "I'd be happy to take a look at anything you draw up. I've got a few friends who run architecture firms. I'm sure they'd be willing to talk with you about the field."

"As long as you haven't had me arrested for murder, you mean," Kyle said.

Clevenger heard a very direct question bundled inside that seemingly offhand comment, a question about how far Clevenger would go to play Kyle Snow's father. Would he turn him over to the police if it turned out he was guilty? And hearing that made it clear how important it was not to pretend Kyle was his patient, let alone his child. He was in the same danger he had been in with Lindsey Snow—of losing himself inside the emotional dynamics of the Snow family. He looked into Kyle's eyes. "If I have to have you arrested for murder, my friend," he said, "you're gonna have all the time in the world to draw. I'll still be happy to take a look."

North Anderson was waiting for Clevenger in the lobby of the jail when he walked out.

Clevenger walked over to him.

"Coady told me you were headed here," Anderson said. "I found out something you should know."

"What?" Clevenger asked.

"I started checking into the Boards of Directors of military contractors, hoping to find somebody I knew, to help us look into Vortek. No one familiar turned up. That includes Lockheed, Boeing, Grumman. Then I decided to stop in at the State Treasurer's office, pull Snow-Coroway Engineering's corporate filings and check out its own board."

"And?"

"No real surprises. You got Coroway, Snow, a venture capital guy from Merrill Lynch, and a professor from Harvard—this computer genius over there by the name of Russell Frye. The only unusual one was Byron Fitzpatrick, turns out to have been Secretary of State under Ford. But I figure the guy probably sits on a couple hundred boards."

"Maybe," Clevenger said, "but he's also CEO of InterState Commerce, the company Coroway was visiting in D.C. yesterday"

"Then we've got dots to connect. Because my next stop was my buddy at the Mass Department of Revenue. I had him peek at Snow-Coroway's tax returns for the past five years. Guess who bought ten percent of the company in 2002?"

"I'm a psychiatrist, not a psychic."

"The Beacon Street Bank."

The force of that fact made Clevenger take a step back.

"They paid twenty-five million for ten percent of the company."

Clevenger remembered Collin Coroway telling him twenty-five million was the amount of R & D funding originally committed to Vortek. Was that just a coincidence?

"So I figure Reese and Beacon Street had a clear interest in Vortek coming to market," Anderson said.

"Then he'd want Snow alive," Clevenger said.

"At least until Vortek was completed. I think it makes sense for me to head down to D.C. myself, poke around the copyright office. I asked a couple of patent attorneys I know: the actual substance of any missile patent would be classified. But Snow and Coroway would still be on record as having filed one, if they did."

"Be careful. We're obviously stepping on toes here."

"You got that off the pistol-whipping by the Feds, huh?"

Clevenger touched the sore place at the back of his head. "That, and Whitney McCormick flying in to try to get me to cool my heels. She's back with the FBI."

Anderson smiled a very broad smile. "How long were you gonna wait to tell me?"

"She was at Boston P.D. when I went to see Coady."

"Now that's what I call a real development in the case. Your case, anyhow. It was hard enough saying good-bye to her once. She could be back to stay, my friend."

"She's got another agenda."

"Maybe. But I think you're the one who'd better be careful," Anderson said.

"Keep reminding me."

Clevenger called to check in with Kim Moffett at the Boston Forensics offices.

"I went out and rented three computers," she said. "Company check. Hope you don't mind."

"Would it matter if I did?"

"I figure they're going to keep ours a while."

"Good thinking."

"Can I ask you something?"

"I'm all ears."

"Are they gonna look through our personal files and e-mails and everything?"

"If they have a search warrant," Clevenger said. "Maybe even if they don't. Why?"

"No reason."

"C'mon."

"It's just that I have my *Match.com* ad on there with the responses."

"So?"

"It's private. It's embarrassing."

"They'll be discreet. But maybe it's better to take care of that kind of thing on your own time in the future," Clevenger said. "You did ask for a raise last week because you're so busy."

"I don't get many responses to my ad. It takes like two seconds to check."

"I'm sure you're deluged with offers. And I'm kidding about the time."

"I can never tell with you. Your voice doesn't change."

"Psychiatric training. Any messages for me?"

"Just Billy."

"He left me a message at the office?" Clevenger asked.

"He said he tried your cell, couldn't get through."

"What's the message?"

"He left school to scrub in again with Dr. Heller."

"What?"

"I don't think he wanted to tell you in person—I mean, in person over the phone. That's why he called here."

"He say anything else?"

"Just that it's this really big case, so he knew you wouldn't mind. He said it could take all day, half the night."

"Oh, really?"

"I told him it sounded sketchy," Moffett said. "No permission slip from Dad, you know?"

"Did Heller call to ask if it was alright?"

"Nope. Maybe he tried your cell."

"I'll check. What else?"

"John Haggerty has a case for you. An insanity plea. He wants to send over the file."

"Tell him to send it. But it's going to be a while before I can start work."

"I'll let him know."

After Clevenger hung up he checked voice mail on his cell phone. There was one message to call Mike Coady, but none from Heller. He was obviously going to have to set limits on when Billy could visit Mass General.

He dialed Coady, got put through to him. "What's up?" he asked.

"I picked up George Reese a little early."

Clevenger looked at his watch. 1:20 P.M. "Why?"

"He headed over to Logan. I had someone follow him to the International Terminal. He was booked for Madrid."

"A little vacation to get over losing Grace?"

"The ticket was one way."

"Maybe he doesn't like being pinned down to a return flight."

"Well, he's pinned down good and tight now. At least for the moment. He's got Jack LeGrand in his cell with him."

LeGrand was New England's reigning king of criminal law, a defense attorney who fought every case like a gladiator, and won a hell of a lot more than he lost. Clevenger had worked with him on a couple of cases a few years back. "Tell Jack I say 'hello.'"

"I'd like to get you in here sooner, rather than later. I don't know how long I can hold Reese without charging him. And I'm not ready to do that."

"I'll be there in less than an hour," Clevenger said.

"See you then."

Clevenger took the Back Bay exit off Storrow Drive, headed to Mass General. He wanted to make sure Billy was at least telling the truth about why he was skipping school.

He parked in the garage, headed up to the O.R. The receptionist, a rotund woman with ruddy cheeks, about sixty, told him Heller was scrubbed in and confirmed that a young man had scrubbed in with him.

"I'm his father," Clevenger said. "Do you know what the case is?"

"An aneurysm on the basilar artery," she said. "They've been in there three hours. They've got at least five more to go."

The basilar artery ran along the base of the brain. It was part of the Circle of Willis, the major network of vessels feeding the cortex. Clipping an aneurysm there was extremely risky.

"The patient is a nine-year-old girl," the receptionist said.

Clevenger's heart fell. "Nine years old." The tragedy of a little girl going through eight or more hours of neurosurgery brought home how completely impartial and utterly unfair diseases were. He worried how Billy would react if she didn't come through it well.

"She's in great hands," the receptionist said. "Dr. Heller will do anything and everything for a patient. It's always personal for him. He takes it home with him, you know?"

"I've heard that about him," Clevenger said. It was hard to focus on Heller's surgical skills when his social skills seemed to be in grave doubt. He hadn't had the decency to let Clevenger know he was hosting Billy at Mass General again.

He thought of having Billy paged out of the O.R. and taking him home right then and there, just to teach him he couldn't make an independent decision to blow off high school and play doctor. But he didn't want to embarrass him in front of Heller. "Could you tell him I came by to make sure he was alright?" Clevenger asked.

"You're welcome to wait, if you'd like. He's bound to want a break soon."

"I wouldn't bet on that," Clevenger said.

FIFTEEN

Clevenger made it back to Boston Police headquarters just before 2:00 P.M. Coady wanted to meet with him in his office before they took their shot at George Reese.

"Jeremiah Wolfe called," Coady said. "The DNA is back on the baby Grace Baxter was carrying." He took a seat behind his desk. "It was John Snow's. A little boy."

Hearing that fact brought Clevenger back to the idea that Grace Baxter might have been angry enough at Snow for leaving her to want every trace of him gone—including the tainted blood flowing through her body. "All right," he said. "I understand. Anything else?"

Coady shook his head. "You want to question Reese yourself, or watch me do it from behind the one-way mirror? Your call."

"I think we'll get more out of him if we rattle him," Clevenger said. "Either he's really got a head of steam for me, or he'll want to make it look that way. Maybe he'll have trouble keeping his story straight."

"Maybe you ought to think about that private detail I offered you to watch your back. Between the Feds and Reese . . ."

"We'll talk about it."

"When?" Coady asked.

"Later."

"This isn't a joke, Frank."

"You see me laughing?"

Coady shook his head. "Kyle Snow went home. His mother posted bail. A hundred grand. Like breaking sticks for these people."

"What do you make of him?"

"He hated his old man, that's for sure."

"I hated mine. I didn't shoot him."

"Why not?"

"Good question," Clevenger said. He had fantasized more than once about strangling him with the belt he used to mete out beatings. "He didn't have a gun."

Coady barely smiled. "Sometimes opportunity is the mother of invention," he said. "Truth is, you treat a kid the way Snow treated his son, you don't want to keep a firearm in the house."

"I'm not ready to take Kyle off any list," Clevenger said.

"How about Lindsey?"

"She had access to the gun, just like her brother. She knew about the affair, like he did. And her whole world was changing because Snow was changing."

"So she stays," Coady said. "And the wife?"

"Ditto. Snow was like the keystone in the arch of this family. He pulls himself free, the family crumbles. And they all knew it—at least unconsciously."

"Like I said, generating a list of suspects in a case like this is easy. The hard part is whittling it down."

"True," Clevenger said. "But I'm glad we've got Reese here, all the same. He's the only one on the list who was covered in blood when I met him."

Clevenger opened the door to the interview room and walked inside.

Reese, in a gray pinstriped suit, white cuff shirt and shiny burgundy tie, stood up at the long wooden table where he had been sitting with Attorney Jack LeGrand. "What the hell are you doing here?" he asked Clevenger.

"I work with the police, remember?" Clevenger said. "I have a few questions for you."

"*You* have questions for *me*?"

"Sit down," Clevenger said.

Reese stayed on his feet.

LeGrand put a hand on Reese's arm, gently pulled him into his seat. He was about fifty years old, with wavy, rust-colored hair, full lips, longish eyebrows and deep brown, almost black eyes. He looked like a pensive wolf decked out in a two-thousand-dollar Armani suit. "Good to see you, Frank," he said, in a throaty voice that could instantaneously turn thunderous in a courtroom.

Clevenger nodded to him, walked to the table. He pulled out a chair, sat down. "You've been read your rights?" he asked Reese.

"They should be reading you yours," Reese deadpanned.

"He's not under arrest," LeGrand said. "He's here voluntarily."

"Let's get right to it, then," Clevenger said. He looked at Reese. "When did you find out your wife was having an affair with John Snow?"

Reese looked back at him, unfazed.

"He's not going to answer that question," LeGrand said. "I'm sure you understand."

"I'm not sure I do," Clevenger said, even though he knew exactly why LeGrand would instruct his client not to respond. There was nothing for him to gain by going on the record. The only reason LeGrand was allowing the questioning in the first place was to get a sense of what direction the police might be headed in. "You're invoking his Fifth Amendment right against self-incrimination?" Clevenger asked him.

"I don't need to do that," LeGrand said. "He hasn't been charged. You're not a Grand Juror. This isn't a trial. He doesn't choose to respond to you, that's all. Maybe he doesn't like your tone of voice."

Clevenger looked back at Reese. "Were you aware they met at the Four Seasons?"

"Beautiful hotel," Reese said. "I like it myself."

"Where did you find your wife's suicide note?" Clevenger asked.

The muscles in Reese's jaw started working. "You have nerve bringing up my wife's suicide. If it weren't for you, she'd still be alive."

Those words still hit a raw place inside Clevenger. He did what he could to prevent it from showing.

"How many times did she call you for help that day?" Reese asked.

LeGrand touched Reese's arm. "Again," he told Clevenger, "my client has no comment about whether or where he did or did not find any suicide note."

It looked to Clevenger like the discussion might never flow. He wanted to throw Reese off balance, make him wonder how much the police might really have on him. "You met with Kyle Snow, is that right?"

"No comment," LeGrand said.

"Did he give you anything at that meeting?" Clevenger asked.

"Don't answer," LeGrand told Reese.

"Have him take the Fifth," Clevenger said, never looking away from Reese.

"No need," LeGrand said.

Clevenger kept staring at Reese. "Then let him talk. He's got nothing to hide, right?"

"Move on," LeGrand said.

"The night your wife was found dead, you told Officer Coady

you had been to see a divorce attorney," Clevenger said to Reese. "You said that was why the suicide note found at your wife's bedside talked about a break-up. Which attorney did you go to see?"

"No comment," LeGrand said.

"The man says he went to visit a divorce attorney," Clevenger said, glancing at LeGrand. "Let him go on record with who that was—if he went at all."

LeGrand just smiled.

Clevenger needed to push harder. "Did you know your wife was pregnant, Mr. Reese?"

Reese's brow furrowed. A flash of pain registered in his eyes.

LeGrand leaned forward.

"About three months pregnant," Clevenger said.

"Maybe we should shut this down right now," LeGrand said, glancing at Reese.

Clevenger knew he didn't have much time. "When she was in my office, she told me she felt like a prisoner in your marriage."

"You're a goddamn liar," Reese shot back.

That response seemed odd from a man who considered his marriage at the point of dissolution. "The diamond bracelets you gave her? She told me they were no better than handcuffs."

Reese looked at Clevenger like he very much wanted to reach over the table and strangle him.

"We're done," LeGrand said to Reese.

Reese kept staring at Clevenger.

"The child was John Snow's, by the way," Clevenger said. "The genetic testing just came back."

Reese's eyes closed for an instant.

"George, I really think we should leave," LeGrand said.

Clevenger wanted to deliver Reese one more piece of information. "Your bank was a major investor in Snow-Coroway Engineering. We know that. Were you actually foolish enough to introduce your wife to John Snow? The man was an inventor. A genius. Women love that."

Reese glared at Clevenger.

LeGrand stood up. "George," he said. "We're out of here. Now."

Reese didn't move.

"Could you tell right away they would end up lovers? They say that happens sometimes, you know—that it's that obvious, from the beginning. *Lovemaps,* they call them. People meant for one another."

"Back off, Frank," LeGrand said.

Reese's hands closed into fists.

"It's not a pretty picture," Clevenger said. "He took your money and then your wife. Twenty-five million, and Grace. That has to be infuriating. I mean, talk about no return on your investment."

Reese lunged across the table for Clevenger. Clevenger tried to lean back, but Reese caught hold of his jacket collar with his left hand, swung with his right, connecting with Clevenger's lip and chin.

Clevenger tasted blood. He stared at Reese, without trying to pull away. "You have an explosive temper, George. What did Grace say to make you lose it? Did she tell you she loved Snow, that she was pregnant with his child?"

Reese swung again, connected with Clevenger's forehead.

LeGrand was trying to pull Reese away from the table, but could barely keep him on one side of it.

"Did she want to keep the baby?" Clevenger asked. "Was she really the one who wanted to leave?"

Coady ran into the room, helped pull Reese away from the table. He looked back at Clevenger. "You're all done," he told him. "I'll see you in my office."

Clevenger didn't move.

Reese tried to break free to go after him again, but Coady and LeGrand held him back.

Clevenger looked into Reese's eyes.

"What the fuck are you looking at, you piece of garbage?" Reese yelled. His neck and face were beet red. "You know what it is to see your wife bleeding to death? Do you have any fucking idea?"

"Go!" Coady told Clevenger.

Clevenger waited a few seconds, then turned and walked out.

"You're gonna hear from us on this," LeGrand said to Coady. "What you just saw was harrassment, not police work. The doctor wanted this to happen."

Clevenger was sitting in Coady's desk chair when he walked in.

"What the hell was that?" Coady asked.

"He wasn't gonna give me anything," Clevenger said. "I had to take it."

Coady sat down in the metal folding chair in front of his desk. "So what did you get, besides a fat lip?"

"I'm not sure."

"Wonderful. I would have liked to be able to tell the Chief we actually got something for our money when LeGrand sues us for a million bucks."

"I said I'm not sure what we got. I didn't say we got nothing. What did you see from the observation room?"

"Now I'm being quizzed?" Coady asked, shaking his head.

"C'mon. Indulge me."

"I'll tell you what I didn't see. I didn't see him confess. I didn't see him answer a single question. I saw him explode. I saw you ride him until he blew up."

"Yeah, but when?"

"When? When you started in about his wife."

"What about his wife?"

"What do you mean? About her shacking up with Snow."

Clevenger shook his head. "No. That isn't when it happened." He stood up, started pacing.

Coady followed him with his eyes. "Don't play Socrates here, Frank. I'm not your frickin' med student."

Clevenger stopped pacing, looked at him. "He didn't explode when I talked about his wife sleeping with Snow. It was when I talked about her loving him."

"So what?"

"So Kyle Snow told me Reese took the news about the affair—including Grace's suicide note—pretty much in stride. Almost like he knew it was going on."

"Okay . . . Maybe he did. Plenty of guys focus on the love thing when they find out their wives are cheating. 'Do you love him?' Isn't that the cliché?"

"Sure," Clevenger said. "But usually once they get around to asking that, they're sad, not enraged. They're looking to win a woman back, salvage the relationship." He took a deep breath, let it out. "He knew they were together, Mike. What he didn't know was that they were in love. And that part is what made George Reese angry enough to come at me, and maybe angry enough to kill his wife."

"How does that help us right now?"

"It gets me inside his head," Clevenger said. "It gets me thinking like him."

"Great, Frank." Coady rubbed the heels of his hands into his eyes. "Let me give you that private detail, all right? You got a swollen jaw, a fat lip and a welt on the back of your head. Let's quit while you're behind."

"Chances are, if someone wanted me dead, I wouldn't be talking to you right now."

"You really want to play the odds when it comes to your life? I know you got yourself sober. It's a real inspiration to some of the guys around here. Word around the department is you beat the gambling thing, too. But maybe they don't have that quite right."

Clevenger hung his head, tried to think of why the notion of having a bodyguard bothered him so much. And like most of the connections that explain the pain in our hearts, he couldn't bring it to mind. He couldn't see the truth because it was too big and it was right in front of him. It was as big as his father had seemed, towering over him when he was a child. And to recognize it would be to remember how vulnerable and terrified he had felt then, how helpless he had been, how much in need of protection and love, and how neither came his way. "I don't like the idea," he said. "I don't want Billy seeing it." He shook his head. Because he knew he wasn't explaining himself at all. "I just don't want it," he said.

• 3:50 P.M.

Clevenger had left his cell phone in his truck. He pulled out of the Boston P.D. lot, dialed voice mail. Billy had left a message at 3:12 P.M.

"I heard you were looking for me," he said. "I'm headed over to the gym."

That was odd, given that the operation on the nine-year-old girl was scheduled to go into the night. Clevenger wondered whether checking on Billy at the O.R. had somehow ruined the experience for him, infantilized him in front of Heller. He dialed Billy's cell phone, got no answer. He decided to drive over to the gym to see him.

When he walked in, Billy was in the ring, backing his opponent into a corner. The other kid was lanky, but ropy, at least six inches taller than Billy. He fired off a jab that caught Billy on the side of the head, then another that landed squarely on his nose.

Billy kept coming.

Clevenger leaned against the cinder block wall, nodded over at Buddy Donovan, Billy's trainer.

Donovan nodded back.

The other kid's back was against the ropes. He crouched a bit and leaned side-to-side as Billy fired off a series of lefts and rights, most of them wild. When the kid could, he got off his own punches, scoring with a couple quick shots.

Clevenger waited for the inevitable, barely controlled explosion that was Billy's way of finishing a fight.

The other kid threw a right hook that slammed into the side of Billy's neck.

Billy took a step back.

Donovan looked over at Clevenger, shrugged. He stepped closer to the ring. "What are you doing in there, Bishop?" he called out. "You got him where you want him. What are you waiting for?"

Billy threw what looked like a series of halfhearted punches. Two landed, forcing his opponent to cover up again. But neither one seemed to have anything behind it. Then Billy took another step back.

"I miss something?" Donovan asked, looking up at him from the side of the ring. "He throw a phantom punch, or you're just not interested in fighting today? Maybe you figure you're ready to go pro? Bored with us amateurs. That it?"

Billy glanced down at him. Just as he did, he took a hard right to the chin that staggered him.

"Good punch, Jackie," Donovan said to the other fighter. "I

226

think he's all yours. Taking a little break for himself today. But watch yourself."

The kid took two steps toward Billy, the muscles in his arms taut, ready. He leaned right, about to throw a right hook, but just as he did, Billy delivered a single left hook that came out of nowhere and dropped him to one knee.

Donovan looked up at the kid, saw he was struggling not to keel over. "Back off, Billy. He's all done," he yelled.

Billy had already turned around and headed for his corner. He picked up his towel, spread the ropes and climbed out of the ring.

Clevenger walked over to him. "I didn't think you were paying attention there. I guess I was wrong."

Billy shrugged. "Looks like you let your guard down yourself."

Clevenger touched his lip. "A suspect who didn't like my line of questioning. Weren't you supposed to be in the O.R. until tonight?"

"I got bored." He wiped the sweat off his face. "I have something for you in my locker. You want to come out back?"

"Sure. What is it?"

"C'mon."

Clevenger followed him to the locker room.

Billy started dialing numbers into his combination lock.

"We got to talk at some point about you missing classes today," Clevenger said.

Billy stopped dialing for a second, started again.

"I get that you love surgery. I think that's great. I really do. But it can't interfere with school."

"Doesn't matter," Billy said, squinting at the lock. "Like I said, I was bored." He went back to dialing numbers.

Skipping school did matter, and Clevenger didn't like the way Billy seemed to be brushing it off. "Let's just talk when we get home," he said.

Billy shrugged, pulled open his locker.

Being shrugged off didn't sit well with Clevenger, either. "We've also got to talk about you and my computer—going through my files."

Billy shook his head. "You think I'm spying on you?"

"I didn't say that."

Billy turned, looked at him. "Yeah, you did."

"We don't need to get into this right now."

"You don't want me near your stuff. I get that."

"I don't go through your things. I don't expect you to look through mine. That's all."

"Cool," Billy said. "Maybe we should draw a line down the middle of the apartment."

"Where is this coming from?"

Billy reached into his locker, pulled out a sheaf of papers, thrust them toward Clevenger.

Clevenger took the papers. John Snow's journal. "Where did you get this?"

"Off your desk," Billy said. "I grabbed it and stuffed it in my jacket when the Feds came to the loft. But, don't worry. I won't violate your personal space ever again."

Clevenger wasn't sure what to say. Billy did need to respect his space. "Look, I appreciate this," he said. "I really do. It helps me out on the Snow case. But there is the issue of living together and respecting . . ."

"No sweat," Billy said. "Done." He closed his locker. "Let's just go."

They didn't speak on the ride home. When they got to the loft it was after 5:00 P.M. and already dark. Billy went straight to his room, shut the door.

Clevenger figured he'd give him some time to decompress from whatever had him wound so tightly. He walked over to his desk, touched the empty space where his computer had sat. He opened his drawers. All his discs had been confiscated, even the new ones still in shrink wrap. He pulled out his file drawer, saw that papers had been taken out and replaced haphazardly; they'd rifled through those, too.

He checked his phone messages, then called and checked in with Kim Moffett. Nothing urgent.

He grabbed John Snow's journal, some ice for his lip, and sat down on the couch. He flipped to the drawing of Grace Baxter— her face as a collage of numbers, letters and arithmetic symbols. He kept looking at it, thinking how completely Baxter had infiltrated Snow's mind, how entwined her energy had become with his creative spirit. Amazing, he thought, that one person could be entered so completely by another. Amazing, too, that Snow would choose to break free of that embrace, even after Grace had made it clear in her note that she might not survive alone, that she had come to consider the two of them one.

A few minutes later, someone knocked on the door to the loft.

Clevenger got up, walked to the door. "Who is it?" he called out.

"Jet," J. T. Heller said.

Clevenger opened the door.

Heller, dressed in jeans, a black turtleneck sweater and his black alligator cowboy boots, was holding onto the door jam to hold himself up. He was pale and reeked of scotch. "How's he doing?" he asked.

"Fine, I guess. Why?"

"He walked out of the O.R. before I could talk to him."

"He just walked out?"

Heller nodded. "It was already a lost cause, but . . ."

"What was a lost cause?"

"The girl. There was just nothing to that artery. It was like tissue paper for ten millimeters. I tried to save it, save her, but . . ." He closed his eyes.

"She died?"

He opened his eyes, looked directly into Clevenger's. "Fucking nine years old."

"I'm sorry. I didn't . . . Billy didn't tell me." He put a hand on Heller's shoulder. "Come on in."

Heller stood there. "Maybe if I had approached from the palate—going up." He was looking through Clevenger now, to something beyond either of them. "I dissected down." He touched the crown of his head. "Through the sagittal sinus. That makes sense if you're inserting a clip, but it makes it very hard to place a graft. You know?"

"C'mon in," Clevenger said.

Heller let go of the door jam, swayed slightly.

Clevenger grabbed hold of him and walked him inside.

They sat on opposite sides of the couch.

"Billy's in his room," Clevenger said. "I think he's asleep."

"See, I had a chance," Heller said quietly. "God was with me in there today. I could feel Him. I think *I* blew it."

"Didn't you tell me we're human? I'm no neurosurgeon, but I remember enough from med school to know that a ten-millimeter aneurysm on the basilar artery isn't generally curable, no matter who's holding the scalpel."

"I didn't make my name on what happens 'generally,' " Heller said. "Neither did you." He covered his face with his hand, massaged his temples with his thumb and fingers. "I had to tell her mother and father. They were waiting for the good news. I could see it in their faces. I was out early. They figured it had gone better than expected."

"How were they when you told them?"

Heller looked up at him. "How were they? They died with her. That's how it is. They may not even know it yet. But they will. They'll know it once the wake is over, and the funeral, when everyone has gone home, and they're looking at each other and seeing that their lives are nothing."

For some reason, Clevenger had a fleeting thought of Grace Baxter—of her feeling that she wouldn't be able to go on without Snow. "Drinking yourself to death won't solve anything," he told Heller. "There are a lot of other people relying on you."

Heller smiled. "'Jet Heller will go to hell and back to save your life.'" He laughed morosely.

Clevenger said nothing for several seconds. "I'm not sure this is the best time to talk to Billy about what happened," he said.

"I don't look like much of a role model right now, huh?" He nodded. "Agreed." He stood up. "You know, for what it's worth, I think I understand why you do the work you do."

"Maybe you can clue me in," Clevenger said, standing.

"Simple. The disease model. If you can find the pathogen responsible for a murder—i.d. the warped person—you might be able to prevent another good man from dying. And that's all there is for us, Frank. Battling the Grim Reaper. Day in, day out. Today, he won. And he won when John Snow took that bullet from some monster. But if you can find out who killed him, isolate that pathogen, you can wipe it off the face of the earth."

"Or put it in quarantine. Prison."

"That isn't God's view of things, my friend. An eye for an eye. That's the only way the battle is won. You can't be afraid to cut out a malignancy."

Clevenger was certain the good guys had to operate on a higher level than the killers—just for society to keep track of who was who. But he knew it wasn't the time or place to argue social policy. "I don't see it that way," he said, and left it at that.

"I know that about you," Heller said. "Dr. Gandhi." He swayed on his feet, caught himself.

"Why don't you crash here?"

Heller shook his head. "I have a taxi waiting. I'm fine." He held out his hand. "Good night, my friend."

Clevenger squeezed his hand, let it go. "I'll tell Billy about the girl."

"You're lucky," Heller said. "Being his father. What a wonderful thing. I never thought much about having a kid. Billy makes me feel like I should have."

Clevenger knew Heller was drunk, but even alcohol didn't explain what was sounding like an irrational attachment. Heller had only known Billy a few days. "Be careful getting home," Clevenger said.

"Right," Heller said. He turned and headed to the door, opened it. "Tell Billy I apologize. I'll make it up to him."

"I'll make sure he knows there was nothing you could do."

"Thank you," Heller said. He walked out, closed the door behind him.

Clevenger walked to Billy's room. He was about to knock on the door when it opened.

Billy stood just inside the room. His lip was quivering.

"Hey, buddy," Clevenger said. "You hear all that?"

"I didn't get bored," Billy managed, fighting back tears.

"What do you mean?"

"In the O.R. I wasn't bored."

"Okay . . ." Clevenger said. "What were you?"

A tear started down his cheek. "I was . . . I was scared. I was scared for that little girl."

Clevenger felt his skin turn to gooseflesh. What growing up with a sadistic father, living through the death of a sibling, facing countless kids twice his age in street fights and stepping into the ring again and again hadn't done for Billy, a couple of trips to the O.R. with Jet Heller had. Billy was feeling afraid, and not just for himself, but for another person. He was empathizing with another human being. That was a kind of miracle. Maybe God really had scrubbed in with Jet Heller that day. Maybe the little girl on the table just wasn't the one he was able to heal. "Come here," Clevenger said. He held out his arms.

Billy stepped into them, buried his face on Clevenger's shoulder. Clevenger held him close.

"How can something like that happen?" Billy asked through his tears. "She was so little."

Clevenger wanted to come up with an answer, wanted to shield Billy from the fact that death was capricious, that entropy was as great a force as anything in the universe, that the love of the best parent couldn't protect the most innocent child from an aneurysm or cancer or a car crash or murder. He wanted to shield him, but he loved him too much to lie to him. "I don't know," he said. "I wish I did, Billy. But I don't."

SIXTEEN

• 8:37 P.M.

Clevenger left his loft to meet Whitney McCormick at the Four Seasons Hotel. He climbed into his truck, then noticed a piece of paper tucked under his windshield wiper. He got out, grabbed it.

It was a card in an unsealed envelope with his name written on it in purple ink. He pulled it out. The front was a watercolor of a rainbow. He flipped it open, saw a note written in purple, signed by Lindsey Snow:

Dr. Clevenger:

I don't expect anything from you. I won't haunt you. I just want you to know how close I feel to you. I don't think it's a father-daughter thing, or anything weird like that. I don't think it has anything at all to do with losing my dad.

In my heart, I'm so sure we were meant to be close to one another.

People sometimes just know these things, don't they?

Yours,

Lindsey

Lindsey's protests that her feelings for Clevenger had nothing to do with her feelings for her father were classic denial. The connection was so close she needed to disavow it not once, but twice, in the very first paragraph.

Clevenger slipped the card into his jacket pocket and climbed back into the driver's seat. He figured it was time to stop by the Snows' house again in the morning to check whether pressing Lindsey, Kyle and Theresa Snow might yield anything new on the case.

He put the key in the ignition, turned it. He heard a hollow click. He tried it again, then heard what sounded like the crack of a whip under the hood. His gut told him to get the hell out. He threw open the door and dove for the ground.

The truck burst into flames.

One arm of his jacket was on fire. He rolled on the pavement, managed to put it out. Then he looked back at his truck, saw a plume of smoke spewing twenty feet into the air. The hood and cabin were black and smoldering. The windshield was blown out.

Billy came running out the door of the building, raced over and knelt down beside him. He looked panicked. "What the hell . . . ? Are you hurt?"

Clevenger moved each of his legs, each of his arms. He ran his fingertips over his face, looked for blood. None. "No. I'm okay."

"What happened?" Billy said.

"Someone's trying to tell me I'm getting warm," Clevenger said.

"You think someone at John Snow's company did this? They make bombs or whatever, don't they?"

Clevenger couldn't help feeling again that he wanted Billy as far from the investigation as possible. "I have no idea who did it," he said. "I'm just glad the person wasn't any better at it." He thought of the note in his pocket—of Lindsey. He remembered that one of Kyle Snow's arrests had been for a bomb threat at his prep school. But then another memory popped into his mind—J. T. Heller's peculiar statement about wanting a son like Billy. Was there any chance Heller would try to take a shortcut, to take Billy for himself? Or was that thought a paranoid projection of Clevenger's own jealousy and competitiveness?

The thought didn't go away. It spawned others. Why hadn't Clevenger ever asked Heller precisely where he had been minutes before John Snow was rushed to the emergency room at Mass General? Was it just a coincidence that Heller had been so close to the E.R. to begin with? Was it a coincidence that the work he did trying to save Snow destroyed the anatomic landmarks that would have allowed Jeremiah Wolfe to formally rule his death murder or suicide?

Could the brotherhood of medicine have led Clevenger to give Heller the benefit of the doubt when he didn't deserve it?

"You think this has to do with you going to Washington to see Collin Coroway?" Billy asked.

"It could," Clevenger conceded, wishing Billy would stop probing.

Billy pulled him up and out of the road.

They watched the truck smoldering. Sirens began blaring in the distance.

"It was, what, a '98?" Billy asked.

Clevenger felt Billy's hand on his waist, helping him stay on his feet. He put his arm around Billy's shoulders. "They come with leather and navigation now, I think," Clevenger said. "What are you doing this weekend?"

"Buying a truck with my father?"

"Sounds like a plan."

The Chelsea Police Department sent four cruisers of their own to Clevenger's building, along with a bomb squad on loan from Boston. Two members of the team got to work on Clevenger's truck while another three officers searched the elevator, staircase and hallways leading to Clevenger's loft space.

As he watched them work, Clevenger used his cell phone to reschedule with Whitney McCormick for an 11:00 P.M. drink in the Four Seasons' Bristol lounge. He told her he would explain later.

His first instinct had been to cancel altogether, but the idea of yielding a night's work irked him. He was obviously making people nervous.

He called Mike Coady next.

"Hey, Frank," Coady answered.

"I had a little problem with my truck," Clevenger said.

"Where are you? I'll send a cruiser to pick you up."

"Four cruisers from Chelsea are here already," Clevenger said. "It didn't break down. Somebody blew it up."

"Jesus Christ. Are you alright?"

"I got out in time. New truck and new leather jacket, and I'll be as good as new."

"Any idea who did it?"

"None. There was a note on the windshield from Lindsey Snow, but I don't think she knows how to wire a car to explode."

"What did the note say?"

"She's confused. She thinks she has feelings for me. It's really all about her being close with her father and missing him."

"Okay. . . . How long had the truck been parked?"

"Three, three-and-a-half hours."

"I'm sending an officer out to keep tabs on you," Coady said.

"Like I said, I don't do the entourage thing," Clevenger said. "But it would be nice to know someone was looking out for Billy. He's hanging out with me right now, but I have to leave. He'll be up in the loft."

"I'll have a car in front of your place all night, every night, until we wrap this case up."

"Thanks."

"Anything from Anderson's trip to D.C.?"

"Not that I know of." He realized he should alert Anderson to how far someone had gone to stop the investigation. "I'll check in with him right now."

"Let me know if he's turned up anything. I'm gonna check in with Kyle Snow to see if he can account for his whereabouts this evening. It wouldn't be the first time he delivered something for his sister. I'll drop in on Collin Coroway and George Reese, too."

"I'll call you tomorrow morning."

"I'll be here."

Clevenger hung up. He dialed Anderson, got him on his cell and found out he had landed at Logan on the last shuttle, hadn't quite gotten to his home in Nahant. He told him about the explosion.

"Maybe you should lay low a few days," Anderson said. "I can pick up the slack."

"We've got someone running scared. I don't want to let up."

"I don't know if blowing up your truck qualifies for 'running scared,' but I get the general idea."

"Tell me about D.C."

"I got a very cold reception at the patent office today, but I still got some of what we needed."

"Shoot."

"Every patent of Snow-Coroway's is classified. They hold fifty-seven. All that's on record is the date they applied for each and the date each of them was awarded. The content of the applications is kept secret."

"Any recent applications?"

"As recent as the day after Snow died," Anderson said. "The company applied for two patents that afternoon."

"Vortek?"

"I tried every way I know to get the patent office to disclose the general focus of the applications—as in, missile design," Anderson said. "I even had a patent attorney I know from Nantucket take a shot, cite the Freedom of Information Act. They wouldn't budge."

"If Snow gave Collin Coroway and George Reese what they needed, if he created Vortek and turned over the intellectual property, then he was expendable. He was the only thing in the way of a public offering of Snow-Coroway stock. But why kill Grace?"

"Good question."

"It doesn't feel like we've got a lot of time to find the answer."

"That must mean we're gonna win soon."

"I love your optimism," Clevenger said.

"When it starts looking like euphoria, you can put me on meds."

"I'll let you know."

Clevenger took a taxi and got to the Four Seasons at 10:55 P.M., dialed the operator from the lobby and got put through to Whitney McCormick's room.

"Hey," she answered.

"I'm downstairs."

"Give me two minutes."

"I'll be outside The Bristol."

She met him beside the hostess's desk. She was wearing a black skirt and a trim-fitting, cream-color, cashmere cardigan with pearl buttons. She'd obviously taken time with her hair and makeup. She looked elegant and beautiful. Nothing overdone, nothing racy, which made her all the more alluring.

Clevenger felt a key sliding into the lock on his soul. "You look magnificent," he said. He leaned and kissed her cheek, lingered a moment to whisper into her ear. "You always do."

"Likewise, Doctor."

"Thanks," he said, straightening up. "But if you smell burning metal, I can explain."

She smiled. "What are you talking about?"

"Let's sit down."

The hostess escorted them to a set of deep, pillowy armchairs by the window, looking out on the Public Garden, its gracious trees lined with white lights. A waitress magically appeared. Clevenger ordered a coffee. McCormick ordered a merlot.

"I have a good excuse for being late," Clevenger said.

"Try me." She reached and took his hand.

He hadn't expected her touch, but instantly warmed to it. "My truck blew up. I mean, somebody blew it up."

"You're joking."

"Who would joke about something like that?"

She went pale, let go of his hand.

"What?"

"I have to tell you again," she said. "You're in way over your head."

"I always swam better in the deep end," he said. "It helps motivate me, knowing the only alternative is drowning."

"You're over your head in national security issues," she said, in a detached, professional tone. "It isn't wise, and I already told you I think it's unnecessary."

"Are you speaking for yourself, or the FBI?"

"What's the difference?"

Maybe there wasn't a difference anymore. "Talk about job loyalty," Clevenger said. "I hope you get a company car. Just make sure it comes with a remote starter."

"You think this is funny. I don't."

Clevenger heard concern in her voice, not irritation. "I'll watch myself," he said.

"Watch yourself? *Someone blew up your car.*"

"What do you want? I'm not about to let a murderer walk."

"Why don't we see if the case can be turned over to the Bureau?"

That sounded like a power play. "It's my case."

"No, it's Mike Coady's case. He brought you in as a consultant."

"You're interfering."

"I'm trying to help. The way to read the Agency's involvement is simply as a sign that there are forces in play you can't control."

"One thing I learned when I put down the booze: The only thing I can control is myself."

"Maybe you're onto something there," she said. "Maybe the reason you can't back off the case is because you're addicted to it."

"What exactly would I be addicted to? Having my apartment ransacked or my skull fractured?"

"To darkness. To some idealized, uncompromising vision of the truth, which only you can see. Maybe that's why you won't take my advice. Because you can't."

"Possible," Clevenger allowed. "But I have to be honest: I'm never kicking this habit. It's what I do. It's what I am."

The waitress brought their drinks.

Clevenger watched McCormick's lips kiss the edge of her glass. "Since I'm incurable, maybe you'd help me get over a particular craving of mine," Clevenger said.

"Maybe," McCormick said, obviously thinking they were done talking shop. She put down her glass.

"North went down to Washington to see whether Snow-Coroway filed any patents related to Vortek. They filed two, the day after Snow was shot. The content is classified. I don't know if they have to do with Vortek or not. Maybe you can find out."

"You can't be serious. I'm telling you to back off. I wouldn't help you get in deeper, even if I could, which I can't."

"Your father might be able to." He knew her relationship with her ex-senator father was a sore point with them, maybe the reason their relationship had never worked out, but he had to ask the favor.

She smiled. "Let's face it, my father isn't about to use his contacts to help you."

"Why would he have to know he was helping me?"

"Because I don't lie to him."

Clevenger nodded. Within ten minutes of sitting down together they were right back at the psychological dynamic most responsible for them separating—McCormick believing she needed to choose between devotion to her father and romantic love. "I'm sorry," Clevenger said. "Forget I asked. It wasn't appropriate."

She closed her eyes a second, shook her head. Then she looked back at Clevenger. "How about we forget the professional reason I flew up here and focus on the personal one?"

Maybe that was still possible. "Sounds good to me," Clevenger said.

"I miss you."

How did she do it? She could shift gears flawlessly between work and play, probably the reason it had felt so easy to fall more and more deeply in love with her as they tracked the Highway Killer. But, somehow, when they'd finally caught up with him, their relationship had gone from hot to warm. Was that because violence fueled their passion? Did hunting a killer, seeing their own exquisite mortality in the faces of his victims, make love feel like the only antidote to death? Is that why Clevenger felt as drawn to McCormick that very moment as the first time he had laid eyes on her? "I miss you, too," he said. He meant it.

"Coady told me John Snow and Grace Baxter used to meet here to make love," she said.

"In a suite overlooking the Garden." He sat back in his seat. "I thought we weren't going to talk shop, anymore."

"We're not." She opened her left hand and showed him the key to her room.

They made it inside the door, but not to the bed. McCormick backed him against the wall, kissed him deeply.

He didn't let the haze of passion take him completely. He wanted to feel her lips on his, her tongue on his. He ran his hands over her delicate shoulder blades, felt her press even closer to him, then ran his hands down her back.

She kissed his ear, his neck.

He pulled her skirt up and ran his hands under her panties, pulling her against him, telling her without words how much he wanted her, how ready his body was for hers. But there was much more unspoken in that embrace: whole chapters of a life story spent in search of truth, but also of love, running from the sadism of his father and the cold withdrawal of his mother.

She unstrapped his belt, unzipped his pants, ran her hand inside his underwear.

He sighed.

She held him tightly, stroking him gently, again and again.

He moved his hand between her legs. She was warm, wet, for him, which other men might take for granted, but he took for a miracle, as much evidence for the existence of God as he was likely to find in this world.

She pulled him down toward the thick carpet, guided him onto his back, then inside her. And then she moved for both of them, her rhythm a wish that loneliness could be banished, that hope could be eternal, that death could be defeated.

———

They lay naked together, under a single sheet, looking out on a fantasy of lighted trees.

"You think they saw what we're seeing right now?" she asked him.

"Probably," Clevenger said.

"They must have felt very safe."

"Because . . ."

"It's warm in here, cold out there, you know? You have to bundle up, in a couple different ways. It's real life. It isn't about love. It's about getting things done, getting ahead."

Clevenger didn't miss McCormick's go-getter vision of herself in the outside world, or the fact that she had used the word love to describe what she felt inside the room. "I wonder if they were really in love," he said. "I don't understand why Snow would have gone forward with the neurosurgery, if it meant saying good-bye to her."

"It's easy to think you're in love inside these four walls. Everything is pretty and clean. Perfect. Maybe reality intruded."

"In the form of George Reese?"

"Possibly. But Snow couldn't have known Grace Baxter—*really* known her—by meeting her in a luxury suite once or twice a week. She could have fallen short some other way."

Clevenger thought about Snow's love of beauty and perfection. In the same way that Snow had relied on his work to take him away from the realities of family life, including its imperfections, the Four Seasons suite, with its sheer curtains and surreal view, could have helped obscure the real Grace Baxter. Maybe he got a glimpse of something about her that was imperfect—or worse, truly ugly.

He thought again of Baxter sitting in his office, tugging at her diamond bracelets. *I don't want to hurt anyone, ever again,* she had said. *I'm a bad person. A horrible person.* Had she hurt Snow, shattered the illusion that she was perfect? Was that the reason he had come to see a scalpel as his only way out, his only truth?

"What are you thinking about?" McCormick asked him.

He wasn't comfortable sharing his insights on the Snow case, which told him that although he might love McCormick, he didn't trust her completely. He wondered whether that was possible. "I'm thinking whether you can know anyone, ever, whether you're ever safer with another person than you are alone."

She snuggled closer under the sheet. "I think almost everyone gives up before they ever get there," she said. "We should just keep trying."

He looked at her, saw in her eyes that she was being sincere. Maybe two people could join into something greater than either one of them. Or maybe that was a fantasy, too. Folie à deux. A shared insanity. "I'd like that," he said. He ran his hand onto her abdomen. "Maybe that's the whole idea, you know?"

"What?"

"To keep trying. Maybe the trying is the thing. Maybe it doesn't get better than that. Maybe you never quite get there. And maybe that's okay."

"You know what I think?" she asked, sliding her hand over his.

"What do you think?"

"I think you should get back into therapy." She laughed.

He moved his hand lower. "When's my next appointment?"

SEVENTEEN

• JANUARY 15, 2004

Clevenger got back to the loft at 1:10 A.M. He made himself a pot of coffee, picked up his copy of Snow's journal and sat down on the couch to read it. He flipped page after page, stopping here and there to sample Snow's philosophy, but finding his attention drifting again and again to Snow's drawings of Grace. They were where Snow's passion was most obviously engaged. They were where he seemed most human.

He flipped to the last drawing, in which Snow had drawn Grace's face as a collage of numbers, letters and mathematical symbols. He stared at it over a minute. And, for the first time, it occurred to him that Grace might not have been intruding on Snow's creativity, nor merely coexisting with it. She may have been fueling it.

Was Snow using Grace Baxter? Was she the first woman who had tapped his passion or merely a new source of energy he had tapped into? Was he becoming more human, or was he a vampire, siphoning the life blood of a vulnerable woman?

The life blood. The words made Clevenger think again about the possibility Grace had sliced her own carotids. If Snow had drained her emotionally and promptly discarded her, she might have turned his psychological crime into its physical equivalent, making her bloodless corpse the concrete symbol of their aborted affair.

But that scenario just didn't square with the observations of Lindsey and Kyle Snow that their father was indeed transformed. It didn't fit with Jet Heller's assessment that Snow had truly fallen for Baxter.

He put the journal down and closed his eyes, giving in to sleep he had denied too long. But he woke after just fifteen minutes, thinking of something George Reese had said the day before at the police station. He stood up and started to pace. Maybe his memory was playing tricks on him, maybe he was making too much of words spoken in anger, but he couldn't get them out of his head.

He picked up the phone and dialed Mike Coady, got him at home.

"Good morning, almost," Coady said, half asleep.

"When I was interviewing Reese yesterday, he screamed at me about how painful it was to find his wife bleeding to death."

"Yeah."

"Is that what you remember? His exact words?"

"I think so."

"You *think* so?"

"No, no." He let out a long breath, cleared his throat. "I'm sure of it. He said, 'You know what it's like to find your wife bleeding to death? You have any fucking idea?' "

"That's what I remember, too."

"Excellent. You want to tell me why that's important enough to call me in the middle of the night?"

"She wasn't bleeding to death, Mike. She was dead. Her carotids were severed. She couldn't have been alive when he found her, unless he found her within seconds of the act."

"Maybe he didn't realize she was dead until he tried to resuscitate her. Maybe that's what he remembers—thinking she was on her way out."

"But he knew she had tried suicide before. He'd seen her with her wrists slashed. Suicidal gestures. Those were sun showers. This was a goddamn hurricane. I don't see how he would mix up the two. Unless . . ."

"What?"

"You said you found no razor blades stained with blood in the bathroom," Clevenger said.

"None."

"But Jeremiah Wolfe told us her wounds were from two different implements—something like a razor that cut her wrists and something with a slightly thicker, stiffer blade—the carpet knife."

"I'm with you," Coady said, new energy in his voice.

"So where's the razor blade?"

Coady was silent several seconds. "Who knows? Maybe she flushed it. What difference does it make? Cause of death was loss of blood from the carotids."

Clevenger wasn't ready to share his theory. It was one piece of a puzzle. And he wanted the time and space to put the whole thing together. If he told Coady what he was thinking, other cops would get wind of it, then Reese's lawyer, Jack LeGrand. Then there'd be time for LeGrand to generate a convenient explanation—Reese threw the razor blade in the trash downstairs and no one thought to retrieve it. The EMT workers grabbed it and lost it. Clevenger took it himself. He'd start interviewing the responding officers to build a case for sloppy control of the crime scene. "You're probably right," Clevenger told Coady. "Let me think more on it." He wanted to switch topics before Coady got too attached to the one at hand. "Did you find out anything about my truck?"

"Kyle Snow was at home last night. Confirmed by his mother. She seemed believable. I couldn't find Coroway."

"Gettin' to be a habit with him."

"I'm glad you've got the cruiser downstairs. Billy okay with them keeping tabs on him?"

Clevenger walked to Billy's room. The door was slightly ajar.

He wanted to watch him as he slept, the secret joy of every decent parent in the world. He pushed the door open just a few inches more, looked in. And he saw that Billy was gone.

He walked downstairs, then up to the cruiser parked out front in the dark. The officer, a baby-faced man who couldn't have been more than twenty-five, rolled down the window. "Good morning, Dr. Clevenger."

"Morning. Billy's not at home. Did you see him leave?"

The cop glanced nervously out his passenger window, then into the rearview mirror, like he was checking for him right then and there. Not a good sign. "I thought he was upstairs," he said.

Billy knew three different exits from the building, but Clevenger couldn't imagine why he would want to slip out unnoticed. And not knowing made his heart race. "Thanks," he said.

He jogged back up to the loft, dialed Billy's cell phone, got no answer. He walked to his room, flipped on the light. His bed was unmade. He'd been asleep, or at least in bed, before taking off. Maybe he'd gotten a call from a buddy of his with some bright idea to see a late movie. But it was even later now than Billy would stay out when he was taking liberties on a school night.

He called Coady back, told him to put the word out to Chelsea police that they should drive Billy home if they spotted him. Then he tried Billy's cell phone again. Nothing. He walked back downstairs, then over to the Store 24 around the corner. Kahal Ahmad, who worked the night shift, said he hadn't seen Billy at all.

There wasn't much more Clevenger could do. He walked back to the loft and poured himself another cup of coffee. Then he sat down on the couch, sipping it, looking out at the steel skeleton of the Tobin Bridge arching across the blue-black sky into Boston, occasional headlights snaking their way through its steel girders. He let his head fall back, figuring he'd doze a couple minutes.

He woke to the front door opening. He looked at his watch. 2:05 A.M. He stood up.

Billy walked into the room, looking anxious.

"What's wrong?" Clevenger asked him.

He squinted into the distance, the way he always did when he was wrestling with his conscience, like he was trying to figure a way out of a jam or around the truth.

"The police detail is out front for a reason," Clevenger said. "If you need to go somewhere, let them take you. Just until this case is over."

Billy nodded. "I didn't want anyone following me."

"Where? Where were you?"

"With Casey."

Casey Simms, his seventeen-year-old ex-girlfriend from Newburyport. Clevenger felt all the stress leave his muscles. Maybe Billy was back with her. Or maybe they'd decided to call it off for good. Either way, it sounded like a run-of-the-mill adolescent drama. "You want to talk about it?" he asked.

"It's all fucked up," Billy said.

"What? What happened?"

"Everything."

"You think it's over for good this time?"

He shrugged, hung his head.

Something was really weighing on him. "What is it? Did she hurt you? You didn't want it to end? Believe me, I've been there. You can tell me."

"You haven't been here. Not where I'm at. I don't think so, anyhow." He looked away.

Clevenger let that warning register. This wasn't sounding like a simple breakup. "Where's that?" Clevenger asked. "Wherever you find yourself, Billy, you're not alone. You won't be, so long as I'm around."

He took a deep breath, squinted at something far away, again. "She says she's pregnant," he said. "She did a test."

Clevenger tried to conceal his own shock and disappointment, which had to be a fraction of Billy's, the panic of a life story wrenched in an unexpected direction, jumping whatever tracks he thought would carry him into a more certain future. "Do her parents know?"

He shook his head.

"What do you think about it?" he asked.

"I want her to get rid of it," he said, angrily. "But she won't."

Clevenger nodded. "How far along is she?"

"Like a month."

"Okay."

"Okay, what?" Billy said, choked up.

"Just that. Come over here."

Billy walked over to him, stopped a few feet away.

Clevenger laid his hand on Billy's broad shoulder, his fingers touching his powerful neck. "We'll handle it. That's what. Whatever happens, we'll figure it out together. We'll make it work together." He pulled him close, held him a few seconds, but let go when he realized Billy was rigid in his arms.

"I got to get some sleep," Billy said, avoiding eye contact. He walked to his room, closed the door.

Billy turned out his light about 3:00 A.M.

Clevenger lay awake in bed. He pictured Billy's face when Billy told him Casey was pregnant. He looked frightened. Panicked. And Clevenger wanted to make certain he understood his life could go on, even with the intrusion of events over which he felt he had no control, even if one of those events was the birth of a son or daughter in his eighteenth year of life.

Clevenger had known long before ever hearing of John Snow or Grace Baxter that people were most at risk for depression and even suicide when they felt their lives had been hijacked, that they were passengers on a plane going somewhere they very much did not want to go.

Sometimes, when parenting Billy was the toughest, when memories of his own father's brutality were the clearest, when he came to wonder whether that lunatic had obliterated something essential inside him, something inside other people that allowed them to feel comfort in the world and with one another, he felt hijacked himself. And he had fantasized more times than he could remember about boarding one of the giant oil tankers that floated in and out of Chelsea Harbor, signing on for whatever work they could give him, and disappearing.

He thought of John Snow, how he had somehow generated the resolve to actually break free of his wife and children and business partner, but also from a woman he had fallen deeply in love with, a woman carrying his child. The force of that bond was like gravity for most people. It kept men and women circling one another for decades—sometimes with great angst, but round and round, season after season, year after year.

Something explosive had knocked John Snow out of Grace Baxter's orbit, something more powerful than their love. Or at least something that felt more powerful.

Clevenger saw the light in Billy's room turn back on. He wasn't sleeping any better than Clevenger. A minute later he heard his footsteps in the main room, moving to the wall of windows overlooking the Tobin Bridge, stopping there.

Clevenger wanted to get out of bed and stand there with him, but he remembered how Billy had stiffened in his arms. And he had to admit there were some things you couldn't do for your son, like erase his mistakes. You could suffer with him, but not in his place.

Billy was on the move again. But this time his footsteps were coming closer.

He knocked on the door jam.

"Hey, buddy," Clevenger said, propping himself on an elbow, turning on his bedside lamp. "C'mon in."

Billy stayed where he was. He looked worse than he had an hour before—paler, even more frightened.

"Tough night," Clevenger said. "I don't think either of us is gonna get much sleep. Maybe we should just throw on some jeans and grab pancakes at Savino's."

Billy didn't answer.

"Could throw in a DVD," Clevenger tried.

"I have something else to tell you," Billy said.

Clevenger's heart fell. He sat up on the side of the bed. "I'm listening."

"I lied to you."

Clevenger waited.

"I didn't just look at your computer files," Billy said. He looked down at the floor, then back at Clevenger. "I made copies of them."

"The discs? You made copies?"

"The discs and the journal."

Clevenger felt a sense of impending doom. Whatever had brought Billy to his door was troubling him enough to eclipse his panic over getting his girlfriend pregnant. "Why would you make copies of the discs?" he asked.

"For Jet," Billy said.

"Excuse me?"

"I made them for Dr. Heller. I gave them to him."

Clevenger was on his feet. "You gave Heller copies? He asked you to?"

"He asked me to tell him anything I could find out about the Snow case."

"Did he say why he wanted you to do that?"

"He told me he wanted to know who murdered his patient. He wanted to help find the person. He said whoever killed John Snow killed everyone who would have come after him, everybody who would have been able to get the surgery Snow was going to get."

That sounded noble—and difficult to believe. The simpler explanation was that J. T. Heller was worried about being implicated in Snow's murder and wanted to eavesdrop on the investigation. That didn't mean he was guilty, but it rocketed him up the suspect list.

"I'm sorry," Billy said.

He sounded like he meant it, but his feeling sorry didn't fix anything. "Why did you do it?" Clevenger asked him.

"I don't know. Nobody's ever been as good to me as you. Like tonight. I figured you'd throw me out or something. You didn't. So I wanted to tell you the truth about what I did."

The part of Clevenger that was a psychiatrist understood two things about Billy: that he was bound to test Clevenger's love and that he was vulnerable to the agendas of other men who acted fatherly toward him. If Jet Heller had been a bookie, Billy would probably be spending hours and hours taking numbers in a Chelsea bar room instead of holding retractors in the Mass General O.R.

But there was another part of Clevenger, the more vulnerable part, maybe the more human part, that still felt things at a gut level, instead of a cerebral one. And that part of him was enraged at being double-crossed by someone he had bent over backwards to help. "You lied to me," he said. "And you jeopardized a murder investigation."

"You want me to leave?" Billy asked.

Clevenger looked at him, saw that his question wasn't about leaving the room, but leaving the loft, for good. Billy was testing the limits of his love for him, but he was also testing his ability to set limits, to shape Billy's character, to the extent that that was still possible at age eighteen. "I don't want you to leave," Clevenger said. "I love you. Having this not work out for us would be pretty much the worst thing that's ever happened to me." He let that sink in a few seconds. "But if you're going to steal from me and torpedo my work, we won't have a choice." He looked Billy in the eyes. "You just wouldn't be able to stay here anymore."

"It won't happen again. Ever."

Clevenger nodded. "You're not to speak with Jet Heller. Understand? He had no right to use you the way he did. He isn't your friend. And I don't know why he wanted to be so close to the investigation. I don't really know him at all. And neither do you."

"Okay," Billy said.

Clevenger wondered whether Billy was just humoring him. But he was reassured by the fact that Billy had volunteered the information on Heller. He had taken that much responsibility. "Try to get some sleep," he said. "We'll get through this. And we'll figure out how to make things work with Casey."

"I know I don't deserve the help."

"You know what?" Clevenger said. "It's time you stop trying to prove that."

EIGHTEEN

• 8:00 A.M.

Clevenger hadn't done more than doze ten minutes at a time, less than an hour's sleep, total. He'd gotten up for good at 5:00 A.M., called for a rent-a-car from Logan Airport and had them deliver him a Ford Explorer. He knew where he wanted to drive first.

He called Jet Heller's office and got Sascha Monroe.

"It's Frank Clevenger," he said.

"It's good to hear your voice."

"Same here." He let a moment pass to mark the immeasurable connection that clearly existed between them. "I need to come see Jet."

"He isn't in."

"The whole day?"

"He said he'll be here by eleven. He canceled his first case in the O.R. It was set for six."

"I didn't know The Great Heller canceled cases."

"Not once in the five years I've known him."

"Is he alright?"

"You should ask him when you come in."

"You're worried about him."

"He lost that girl. The one with the aneurysm Billy scrubbed in on."

"I know."

"I think it's even more than that, though."

"What do you mean?"

"It started when he lost John Snow." She paused. "I don't know why I'm telling you all this. You're not his psychiatrist. Neither am I."

"You care about him," Clevenger said. "Just like you cared about John Snow."

That helped Monroe say more. "He hasn't been himself. He keeps talking about John being killed, going over and over it. Have I read anything in the newspaper, seen anything on television? He's obsessed."

"Why, do you think?"

"Honestly? I think he saw parts of himself in John."

"Such as . . . ?"

"The idea of overcoming your past, forgetting the people who've hurt you—and the people you've hurt. I think he wanted to cure John of his seizures, but he was even more committed to freeing him from his memories."

"Why would that be so important to him?"

"I think because of what happened to Jet when he was young."

Clevenger remembered the story—Heller being abandoned by his biological parents, truant from school, locked up for assault by the Department of Youth Services. "He told me," he said. "When he found neurosurgery everything changed for him."

"It could have been anything that gave him the chance to save lives. I mean, he didn't mean to shoot that boy. He was only eleven. A screwed-up kid. But, deep down, I don't think he believes that. I don't think he's ever forgiven himself."

Heller hadn't told Clevenger his DYS arrest was for shooting someone. He had said he assaulted someone. "Did the boy survive?" Clevenger asked. "He didn't say."

"No," Monroe said. "That's just it. He died."

Clevenger could barely come up with words to follow that revelation. Heller had killed someone. That certainly didn't prove he had killed again, but it raised that specter. Killers are different from the rest of us—unrestrained by empathy. Maybe Heller had changed, maybe he hadn't.

"It seems like Jet wished he was getting the surgery he was ready to perform on John," Monroe continued. "That's why it mattered so much to him. Even if he saves a thousand lives, I don't think he'll ever forget taking a life. And I think he'd like to live without the guilt for once, start fresh."

"You can join my practice whenever you want," Clevenger said, hoping to end the discussion without showing how taken aback he was.

"Thanks. But I can barely keep my own life on track, never mind figuring out other people."

That was an invitation to go deeper into Monroe's life story. "We should talk about that sometime."

"Sometime," she said. "Shall we expect you at eleven, then?"

"That would be great."

"I'll put you in the book. See you then."

"Take care."

Clevenger hung up. He walked to the wall of windows, looked out at the bridge. Monroe's assessment of Heller could be correct. His thirst to be liberated from his own conscience could have fueled an extraordinary desire to liberate Snow, along with outrage when someone snuffed out his plan.

But there was another way to see Heller. Maybe the excitement of pulling off the surgery of the decade had worn thin as its moral implications became clearer to him. His entire life's work, after all, had been driven by the desire to make amends for the life he had taken. Cleanly severing a man from his past deeds may ultimately have felt like helping a fugitive escape justice.

Heller had told Clevenger over drinks at the Alpine that he would have performed surgery on Snow even if his seizures were not actual epilepsy, but pseudoseizures. But what if that wasn't true? What if Heller had come to see that there was no way to cure Snow of his "fits" with a scalpel, that his only agenda in the O.R. would be destroying Snow's memory? And what if making that kind of medical history would have made Heller feel like a fraud, a traitor to the profession he loved? Then killing Snow may have seemed like the only way out, the only way to defend the purity of what he called his religion—neurosurgery.

Heller had killed once before. Had becoming a doctor, healing people, merely obscured the core darkness inside him—until now? Was his life story—his karma—ultimately as inescapable as John Snow's?

Gravity. Orbits. The relentless pull of the past. Did anyone really break free, ever?

Clevenger heard Billy step out of his room. He turned around.

Billy was dressed in baggy jeans, a gray, long-sleeved sweatshirt, a baseball cap with the logo of a skateboarding company spray-painted across the front. He'd added a few iron beads to the ends of his dreadlocks. "You want me to go get the stuff I gave Jet?" he asked.

Hearing Billy use Heller's first name made Clevenger wonder just how violated Billy really felt, how seriously he was taking the whole thing. And the fact that he would consider going to see him was even more concerning. "I want to be clear," Clevenger told him. "You don't talk to Jet Heller. You don't stop by Jet Heller's office. You don't take Jet Heller's calls. Got it?"

"I just want to make things right."

"I need your word you'll steer clear of him."

Billy shrugged. "I promise," he said. He sighed. "Any hints about what to say to Casey?"

"What do you want to say to her?"

"That she's screwing up both our lives."

Clevenger could have smiled at Billy's plain speaking. He resisted. "If I were you, I wouldn't say anything right now. Let her have some time to herself. She's got a lot to think about."

Billy nodded. "See you when I get home? Say, five?"

"You got it." He watched him leaving. "Hey, Billy," he called out, before the front door closed.

Billy poked his head back inside. "Yeah?"

"You've got a limo today—the cruiser out front. Just let him know where to drop you off."

"Cool." He left.

Clevenger picked up the phone and called North Anderson, filled him in on Heller.

"Maybe I ought to stop in at Mass General again," Anderson said. "Find out whether anyone can confirm Heller was *inside* the hospital when Snow was shot."

"Good idea. What else is up?"

"I'm doing what I can to track George Reese's financials. I've found several brokerage accounts, a half-dozen money market accounts—so far. This guy was loaded, but losing twenty-five million on Vortek might have changed that."

"How much do you think he was worth?"

"So far, unless he's got money offshore, maybe thirty, thirty-five million. And I don't know what other loans the Beacon Street Bank has outstanding. If a few of their bigger borrowers flaked on them, along with Vortek failing, I could see the whole thing imploding."

"Any way to track actual deposits? Coroway told me he returned about half the R & D money dedicated to Vortek. It was that much of a lost cause. I'd like to know if he really did."

"I might need a little help from Vania O'Connor if he isn't scared off. A password or two."

"He doesn't scare easily. Call him up."

"Will do. Where you headed?"

"Heller's office."

"You want backup?"

"No. He's not likely to attack me at the hospital. If he's our man, he'd find me in a dark alley—or blow up my car."

"People do funny things when they're cornered."

"I'll watch myself."

"I've said the same thing a million times, but I don't know how you actually do that."

Clevenger smiled. "I'll be fine. Call me with anything you turn up."

"Will do, buddy."

Clevenger got to Jet Heller's office at 10:50. Half-a-dozen patients were in the waiting area. Sascha Monroe was working on her computer. He walked up to her desk. "Hey," he said.

She looked up. "Hey."

What was it about not knowing a person that allowed you to wonder whether she might be the answer to all your problems? Where did a *lovemap* ultimately lead—ecstasy, contentment; or disappointment, betrayal? If he invited Sascha Monroe into his life, got to know her as a real and complete person, would he still be able to fantasize about her, to worship her? ·

"I'm early," he said.

"He hasn't called in," she said, sounding worried.

"Is that unusual?"

"For Jet? He normally calls five times before he hits the front door. 'Get this file.' 'Call this patient.' 'Print out labs.'"

"But nothing today."

"Not a word. I called his house. No answer. No answer on his cell."

That did sound strange. "Is this typical for him when he loses a patient?" Clevenger asked, keeping his voice down to avoid any of the patients overhearing.

"That doesn't typically happen. When it does, he isn't himself, but he doesn't go missing."

"It isn't quite 11:00 yet."

"I know. But, still."

"Let's wait and see what happens."

Sascha nodded. But she was clearly anxious.

Clevenger took a seat in the waiting area, picked up a copy of *TIME* and glanced through it. Five minutes passed. Ten. Fifteen. Two more patients came in. A man with a shunt emerging from his scalp who had been waiting checked his watch, shook his head in irritation. Clevenger looked over at Sascha, saw she was looking at him, real worry on her face now. He stood up, walked over to her.

"Something's wrong," she said. "I just know it."

"Why don't I drive over to his place, see if I can find him there."

"You'd do that?"

"Sure. Where does he live?"

"Fifteen Chestnut Street. The penthouse. Unit three."

That was on Beacon Hill, just about a mile away. "If he's there I'll have him call you."

Clevenger left his car in the Mass General garage. Chestnut Street was only a ten minute walk, and the air was cold, but not uncomfortable. The sun was bright. No wind. The kind of day that makes people visiting Boston, walking the cobblestones and old brick, decide to pick up and move there.

He got to 15 Chestnut, a towering, three-story, bowfront. He opened the massive oak door to the inner lobby, saw Heller's name engraved on a brass plaque beside a buzzer for unit 3. He pressed it, waited. No answer. He pressed it again. Nothing.

He walked outside, then to the back of the building. There were three parking spaces. The one assigned to unit 3 had an Aston Martin in it. Red. Hundred-and-fifty grand. That had to be Heller's. He looked up, saw the shutters in Heller's apartment were closed.

He walked back out front, into the entryway. He buzzed unit 1.

Several seconds passed, then a woman with a foreign accent answered, "Yes? May I help you?"

"Delivery," Clevenger said.

"For Mrs. Webster?"

"Delivery," Clevenger repeated. When people can do something simple to avoid conflict—say, hit a button or unlock a latch—they'll generally do it. That's why home invaders don't usually have to break down doors. "Delivery," he said again.

"UPS?"

"Delivery."

The buzzer sounded. He pulled open the door, took the stairs to the third floor.

Heller's door was slightly ajar. Clevenger used the large brass knocker, anyhow. No answer. He pushed the door open, walked in.

The windows were all shuttered, keeping the late morning sun down to a filtered, shadowy glow. The place was architecturally stunning, with a towering stone fireplace, fluted columns, gleaming hardwood floors. But it was nearly empty. The only furniture in the great room out front was a black leather couch, a fifty-inch flat panel television mounted to the wall opposite it. A Mark Rothko oil painting, probably worth $500,000 was propped against the chair rail of another wall. A sculpture of twisted stainless steel sat atop the black granite center island in the kitchen.

"Jet?" Clevenger called out.

No answer.

He walked deeper into the apartment, closer to the stone fireplace, and thought he heard movement from down a hallway that looked like it would lead to the bedrooms. "Jet?"

The sounds stopped.

He walked down the hall, passing one closed door, moving toward an open one about twenty feet away. He was almost there when he heard footsteps behind him and swung around.

Heller stood in the hallway, dressed in jeans and a gray, Harvard sweatshirt, torn into a "V" neck. He had a gun in his hand. He looked pale and exhausted. He was unshaven. "Frank?" he asked. "What are you doing here?" He leaned in Clevenger's direction, brow furrowed, eyes bloodshot. "This is my home," he said, sounding a little unsure even of that.

From fifteen feet away, Clevenger could smell the odor of scotch wafting off him. He flexed his calf, felt the pistol strapped there. "Place looks kind of empty," he said, forcing a smile. "Moving out?"

"I just never moved much in," Heller said. "I live at work."

Clevenger knew Heller was telling the truth. He could afford a $5 million dollar penthouse apartment, but had no interest in furnishing it. He lived and breathed neurosurgery. "I went by your office. Sascha's been trying to get ahold of you. She worried when you didn't return her calls. So I came over here."

"She likes you."

"She's a very nice person."

"Very nice? She's an eleven on a scale of one to ten, Frank. You should have been all over that."

Was Heller trying to distract him? And why was he speaking of him in the past tense? "You never know what the future might hold," Clevenger said.

Heller raised his gun.

Clevenger thought of going for his own gun, but Heller never took aim. He held the gun in front of his chest, pointed sideways, staring at it like a wounded bird.

"Snow was shot point-blank in the heart," Heller said. "Imagine the panic." He shook his head, took a deep breath. "I've seen a man shot, Frank. It's a horrible thing. Truly." He looked up at Clevenger. "Have you?"

"Yes, I have."

"I'm sorry for that."

Clevenger wanted to move the discussion away from shooting people. "Why didn't you go into work?" he asked Heller.

"I am at work," Heller said. "Just a different kind of work." He nodded toward the open door beside him. "Want to take a look?"

"Sure," Clevenger said. He walked slowly toward Heller. "Mind putting down the gun? Accidents happen."

"No problem," Heller said. He disappeared out of the corridor, into the room.

Clevenger reached to his calf, pulled his pistol out of its holster and shoved it inside the waistband of his jeans, under his black turtleneck. Then he walked toward the doorway. Part of him wondered why he was still there at all. He could get out, come back with Anderson or Coady. But he didn't think there was any chance he'd get anything out of Heller that way. And there was nothing to arrest him for yet.

He stepped into the doorway of the room, and stopped, transfixed by what he saw. Heller sat at a table made out of a door and two metal construction horses, studying a computer monitor that glowed with numbers and symbols and letters. His gun lay next to the keyboard. Every other square inch of the table, walls and floor were covered with sheets of paper and books.

"Don't worry about stepping on things," Heller said, never looking away from the monitor.

Clevenger looked down, saw that the sheets of paper at his feet were pages of computer code. The books were textbooks on physics and aeronautical engineering. He stepped around those he could. He looked more closely at the walls, saw that pages from John Snow's journal were taped one next to the other. Row after row after row. "What are you doing?" Clevenger asked.

"Bringing my patient back to life," Heller said.

"Okay . . ." Had Heller gone mad? "How long you been at it?"

Heller glanced at the shuttered windows. "I don't know." He turned to Clevenger. "What does a man have left when he dies?"

"What he's done with his life. Whatever he's left behind."

"His legacy," Heller said. "That's all John Snow has left. His work, for one. And the answer to one question: Was he or was he not a coward? Did he or did he not let me down?"

"What's your diagnosis, so far?" Clevenger asked, keeping an eye on how far Heller's hand was from his gun.

"He was no quitter. He was ready to go the distance."

"Why do you say that?"

"Because he was carrying his most treasured idea in that black travel bag they found with his body. A man leaving the planet doesn't take his work with him."

"I'm not sure I understand."

"Take a look."

Heller stood up, picked up his gun, moved aside.

Clevenger didn't like the idea of sitting with his back to Heller. Not with the gun in his hand. "There you go with that gun," he said.

Heller put the gun down on the table, but stayed within arm's reach of it. "I'm not even sure why I took it out of the safe. I hate the thing. I don't know why I bought it, in the first place."

"You must have some idea."

"Maybe to prove I'll never use it. Kind of like an alcoholic keeps a bottle of scotch on the mantel for ten years to prove he can resist, that he's not just sober, he's beyond sober."

"Maybe you should try that trick, too. Seems like you've been drinking around the clock."

"Don't be blinded by your own disorder, Frank. I'm no alcoholic. I'm simply in pain. It's anesthesia to me. Two, three, four days, I'll be alright. Then I won't touch it."

"I'll check in with you on day four," Clevenger said, walking to the table. He sat down in Heller's seat, leaned to look at the monitor. Lines of numbers, letters and mathematical symbols filled the screen. "What I am looking at?" he asked.

"Grace Baxter."

Clevenger looked up at Heller, who smiled a mysterious smile. "Don't speak in riddles," he said. "I'm tired, too, for Christ's sake."

Heller massaged Clevenger's shoulder. "I know you are, brother." He nodded at the screen. "I put together a computer model to analyze Snow's final drawing of Grace in his journal—the one he made out of a collage of numbers and mathematical symbols. I got some help from a friend at Cal Tech. Hit *F1* while you hold down the *Control* and *Delete* buttons."

Clevenger did as Heller asked. And then he sat back as the lines of code on the screen began moving, the numbers and letters and other symbols flowing into and around one another until they gradually reorganized themselves into a luminous version of the portrait Snow had drawn of Grace.

"She was in his head as deep as you can go," Heller said. "Stretched out like a cat across the right and left sides of his brain. Hit *F2, Control, Delete*."

Clevenger did as Heller suggested. The portrait began disassembling itself back into the lines of code Clevenger had seen before.

"The portrait holds the solution to the rest of this," Heller said, waving at the pages taped to his walls. He walked around the room, scanning them, touching some of them. "How do you create a flying object with pure forward momentum, invisible to radar."

Clevenger kept staring at the computer screen, realizing Snow had finished his work on the invention that had eluded him for so long. He reached to the keyboard again, pressed *F1*, *Control*, *Delete*. And as he watched, the numbers, letters and symbols flowed into place again, recreating the portrait of Grace Baxter.

Snow's passion for Grace and his creative genius had merged, yielding what Collin Coroway and George Reese wanted from him: Vortek.

"Why did you really come here?" Heller asked.

Clevenger looked at him.

"You said you were worried about me. That was a lie. What's the real reason?"

"Where did you get the discs and the journal?" Clevenger asked him.

Heller didn't respond for a few seconds. "I know people in the police department," Heller said.

That was an admirable lie, in one respect. Heller wasn't throwing Billy under the bus. Was that because he cared about him, or because he thought he could keep using him? "You're not to contact my son, again. Do you understand?"

"You want to keep him away from what you do. What's the harm if he comes close? He loves you."

"That's none of your business. Stay away from him."

"He needs something to occupy his mind and his heart. He has darkness inside him. I can see it. Because I see it in myself."

"Stay away, or . . ."

"Or you'll kill me?" He chuckled to himself. "Maybe we're more alike than you imagine."

"We're not the same," Clevenger said. "You're lost in this case. I'm working it."

Heller's eyes drifted back to the computer screen. "John Snow was my patient. His life was in my hands."

Clevenger thought of what Sascha Monroe had told him—that Heller fantasized about being reborn himself, without his guilty conscience, that setting Snow free from his past felt like setting himself free. "The tragedy is you could have been a kind of role model for Billy," Clevenger said. "You could have helped him get to a new place in his life—if you hadn't used him."

"All of us get used from time to time, Frank. Even when you're doing God's work, you're just on loan."

Clevenger turned around and walked out.

NINETEEN

Clevenger knew that Whitney McCormick was staying in Boston until the end of the day, then heading back to Washington. He dialed her cell phone.

"How's my favorite patient?" she answered.

"Not cured yet."

"Good."

"Where are you?" he asked her.

"Making calls at the hotel."

"Meet me for coffee?"

"Why don't I just call room service?"

Chestnut Street was one mile from the Four Seasons. "I'm around the corner."

"Hurry up."

He knocked on her door ten minutes later.

She opened it. She was wearing jeans worn to threads at one knee and an oversized white men's-style shirt, and she looked every bit as beautiful as she had the night before.

Clevenger shook his head. "You ever have a bad hair day, an occasional blemish, anything to give a guy a break?

"We don't see each other much. Two good days in a row is unusual for me."

"Why don't I believe that?"

He pulled her close. They kissed. He moved his lips to her neck. She pushed the door shut, pulled him to the bed.

They made love slowly, looking into one another's eyes as Clevenger moved inside her body, each of them reveling in release from their individual existences, in being swept away by a force greater than the simple sum of their energies.

They lay together, spent, enjoying those few minutes when lovers barely know which arm and which leg belongs to whom.

She turned her head toward him, her lips close to his ear. "I like this place. We should do this more often."

"We will." He closed his eyes, took a deep breath, let it out. He thought to himself how strange it was that Whitney and he were meeting at the Four Seasons, that they should plan to keep meeting there. It was almost as if the two of them were lost in some sort of countertransference to the case, acting it out. He opened his eyes. "I have to ask you one more time . . ."

She smiled. "You don't have to ask."

"It's about the case," he said, propping himself on his elbow.

"Okay. What?"

"Those patents."

She looked at him, her eyes slowly losing their warmth, invaded by some terrible mixture of hurt, anger and a cold resignation to the reality of what they did for a living, that they had not met as lovers first, that they might never be that alone. "What about them?" she asked.

He hesitated to say more, felt himself stumbling out of one role, into another. But the pull of what he needed to know was an undertow. "If Snow-Coroway filed patents for Vortek, I'd know for sure that Collin Coroway and George Reese got everything they needed to get from John Snow. They got the invention they needed to take the company public. That would make Snow dispensable."

"But I can't get that information."

He couldn't let it go at that, couldn't let go of his profession, his calling—not even for her, even though he had been on a short road to loving her from the moment he had laid eyes on her. "I don't want to bring up your father again. But as a former senator, having served on the Intelligence Subcommittee, he must still have his contacts . . ." He saw he had gone too far. "I'm not trying to imply in any way that this is some sort of choice between . . ."

"Then why would you feel the need to deny it?" She got up, started gathering her clothes. "I'm a psychiatrist, too, Frank."

He stood up. "What I wanted to say . . ."

"I know what you want."

"Look," he sighed, "I was wrong to bring it up."

"You can't help yourself. Work is your shield. It helps you avoid everything else. It always has. It always will."

"Such as . . . ?"

"A real relationship, for one thing." She pulled on her jeans. "Don't you even get why you took this case in the first place, Frank? Don't you see just a little bit of John Snow when you look in the mirror? Addicted to solving puzzles? Keeping everyone at a distance? Avoiding true intimacy? Sound familiar?"

All he could do now was listen.

She zipped up her jeans, slipped into her shirt. "One thing about my father," she said, buttoning buttons. "He never used me."

He shook his head, thinking how indelicate and how misunderstood he had been at the same time. "I didn't make love with you to get you to do anything," he said.

"I guess it just feels that way." She put on her shoes, grabbed her jacket off the back of the desk chair.

"Whitney, wait."

"For what?" She stormed out.

He walked to the windows and looked outside, saw her cross the street and disappear into the Public Garden, the icy branches of the trees swaying in a light wind.

Kim Moffett held up a short stack of messages when Clevenger walked through the door to Boston Forensics. "John Haggerty called three times about that new case," she said. "Lindsey Snow called twice. And the FBI called four times. But that's because I keep hounding them about my computer."

"You called the FBI?"

"The evidence room at Quantico."

"Kim . . ."

"They need to give it back. It has my stuff on it."

"These things take time. They could hold onto it a year, maybe longer."

"What about my rights? What about a person's privacy? Did all that just go to hell after 9/11?"

She wasn't going to let it drop. "I'll do whatever I can."

"Thank you." She smiled. "North wanted me to tell you he's on his way here. He tried your cell twice."

Clevenger nodded, started to walk into his office.

"Another thing," Moffett said.

He turned around.

"You have a smudge of pink lipstick on your jacket."

He looked down, saw the subtlest hint of Whitney's light pink lipstick on the black leather. "Why would you think that's lipstick?"

She turned and started word processing.

He walked into his office, took off his jacket, wiped the smudge away. He tossed it on a chair, sat down at his desk and called Lindsey Snow's cell phone.

She answered.

"It's Dr. Clevenger."

"Can I come see you? It's about my dad. About him being shot."

Being shot. That was new. Lindsey's theory had been that she had pushed her father into suicide. Did she believe now that he had been murdered? "When can you get here?" Clevenger asked her.

"Less than an hour."

"That works."

"Thanks." She hung up.

He tried to return John Haggerty's calls, got his message machine. "I'm not taking on any new cases until the Snow case is wrapped up," he said. "I'll call you when that happens."

He put his feet up on his desk, leaned back in his chair and closed his eyes. He pictured Whitney McCormick disappearing into the Public Garden. He thought how he might have lost her for good, mixing business with pleasure. And then his eyes flicked open with the answer to one of the questions he had been asking himself: Why would John Snow go through with his surgery and leave his life if he had found the love of his life?

The answer was simple, so simple it had been hard to see until he mimicked the drama with McCormick. Either Snow or Baxter had betrayed the other in some way. Their love was no longer the pristine thing it had been. Something had gone terribly wrong.

"Hey, stranger," Anderson said from the doorway.

Clevenger pulled his feet off the desk, turned to him. "What's up?"

"I'll be reading George Reese's personal banking and brokerage account statements by the end of the day. Vania's making good progress."

"He still working out of his house? I worry about him."

Anderson shook his head. "He's at my place. No one's going to find him there, unless they spot the coffee cups piling up in my garbage. I keep him supplied every couple hours. Large, cream . . ."

"Four sugars."

"He's got everyone trained."

"Anything else up?"

"I haven't found anyone at MGH able to put Heller inside the hospital when Snow was shot. Not yet, anyhow. Not that that proves anything."

"Not that it does."

"How's Billy doing, by the way?"

Clevenger looked at his watch. 2:15 P.M.. Billy was still in school—or should be. "He's working out a couple problems right now," he said, and left it at that.

"Anything I can do?"

"I'm not sure how much anyone can do, myself included. But I'll let you know."

"Fair enough."

"Lindsey Snow's on her way over here."

"And the beat goes on."

Lindsey sat in the chair she had sat in the last time she visited Clevenger's office. She was wearing a short, lime green skirt and a ribbed, off-white turtleneck sweater. When she crossed her legs, Clevenger could see she was wearing tiny, black satin panties. "If I tell you something," she said. "You have to promise me you'll never say you heard it from me."

"I can keep a secret," Clevenger said, deliberately keeping his eyes focused on hers.

"I'm telling you because I feel close to you."

If she did feel close to him, he knew it had nothing to do with him and everything to do with missing John Snow. Lindsey was like an atom of oxygen, exquisitely unstable, desperately trying to bond. And part of Clevenger wanted to tell her so, to explain that her attraction to him was only due to the sudden loss of balance she felt losing her father. But she wasn't his patient. She was a suspect. He didn't owe her a psychotherapeutic relationship, or anything else. He was free to trade on her needs, seduce her into opening up. That's what it could take to break open a murder case. White lies of the heart, in service to the truth. It wasn't a fragrant business, but it was his business. He dropped his eyes to her thighs, just long enough for her to notice his gaze. "Go ahead," he said. "I want you to tell me." He knew she would hear only the first three words: *I want you.*

She blushed, caught her lower lip between her teeth. "The last week or so my dad was alive, he was pretty down. It was like all the energy that had flowed into him was leaving him. He stopped talking to everyone. Even me."

Clevenger nodded. He wondered whether Lindsey was still stuck on her suicide theory.

"So Kyle decided to take Dad's gun. So he wouldn't hurt himself. At least, that's what he said."

Clevenger tried not to show any emotion, even though he felt like the case might be taking a final turn on its long, twisted path. "How did he get the gun?"

"Dad always kept it in the same place—the top shelf of the shirt rack in his closet. We've both seen him take it from there when he was going to work and put it back there when he got home. He hid the bullets somewhere else."

"Didn't your father wonder what happened to his gun?"

"Kyle told him. He told him he'd taken it—and why."

"And your mother knew?"

Lindsey nodded.

That might explain Theresa Snow's attempt to block Clevenger from talking with Kyle. "How does Kyle explain your father being shot with that gun?"

"He says he only kept it until the night before. He told me Dad wanted it back, that he threatened to turn him in for violating his probation. So he got pissed and gave it to him." Her eyes filled up. "He says he told him to go ahead and shoot himself, if that's what he wanted."

"Do you believe him? Do you think he gave the gun back?"

She uncrossed, then recrossed her legs in a way that drew Clevenger's gaze, again. "All I know is he's been happier over the past few days than I've ever seen him," she said. "And he says he can't go to Dad's funeral. He says it wouldn't be 'honest.' "

Was Lindsey telling the truth, or was she trying to finish off her brother, punish him for siphoning off her father's adoration? If Clevenger was just a stand-in for Snow, Lindsey might want him to jail Kyle, the equivalent of banishing him to another state the way Snow had. "Do you think your brother shot your father?" Clevenger asked her.

"I don't want to, but . . ." She looked away.

He let a few moments pass. "Thank you for telling me, Lindsey," he said.

She looked back at him, tilted her head, bringing her silky hair cascading down over half her face. "So, is that it?"

"I'll follow up with your brother and see where we go from here."

"Where do *we* go from here?" she asked plaintively.

Clevenger wanted to avoid injuring her. That didn't need to be part of the job. "As pretty as you are, Lindsey," he said, as gently as he could, "and as much as I might want to spend time with you outside the office, I can't do that."

"Ever?"

That question made it clear Lindsey was willing to wait a long, long time for him. Maybe even forever. And that helped Clevenger see again that her drug wasn't sex with her father, but the *potential* for sexual union with him. Snow had kept her tethered to him by adoring her beyond all others, without ever actually touching her. She was looking for her next supplier of that adoration, not her next lover. "You're much too beautiful for me to say never," he told her.

She glowed. "You're not with . . ." She nodded in the direction Kim Moffett's desk.

He shook his head.

She took a deep breath, let it out. "Cool. So, just give you time?"

"Give me some time."

"I understand." She stood, started to put on her jacket.

He stood up, watched her. She was a beautiful young woman. There wasn't even a white lie in that. "You're extraordinary, you know," he told her.

For the first time, she looked taken aback.

"And not just because your father thought so, or because I think so."

"What do you mean?"

"I mean . . ." He realized he was speaking a language she couldn't understand. Telling her that other men would not only find her desirable, but act on it, that they would be *honest* with her in every way, wouldn't register with her. Her self-worth had always come from her reflection in John Snow's eyes. "It's not important right now," he said.

She seemed happy to let it go at that. "See you."

"Take care."

She walked out.

Kim Moffett walked in ten seconds later. "Whitney McCormick's holding for you," she said.

Hearing her name was enough to make Clevenger smell her perfume, imagine her fingers moving through his hair. Amorous hallucinations. "Thanks." He waited for Moffett to leave, picked up the phone. "Whitney."

"I talked to my dad," McCormick said.

He stayed silent.

"Two patents were filed for a flight stabilization system, registered jointly to Snow-Coroway, InterState Commerce and Lockheed Martin."

"Coroway lied to me in D.C," Clevenger said. "He and Reese got Vortek. Snow delivered. They didn't need him anymore."

"I know the feeling. Must be going around."

"Listen," Clevenger said, "I was wrong bringing up the case the way I did earlier. I . . ."

"You could just say 'nice doing business,'" she said, coldly.

"When can I see you?"

She hung up.

THE FOUR SEASONS

• JUST TWENTY DAYS BEFORE.

1:45 P.M.

He could hardly wait to see her, to tell her. He was wearing a light blue Armani shirt and deep blue Armani suit he had bought on Newbury Street the prior day. A black crocodile belt. Shiny, black slip-ons. He was freshly shaven, his hair neatly trimmed. He stood at the window overlooking the Public Garden and watched her step out of a cab at the curb, her auburn hair caught by the cold wind.

She walked toward the hotel entrance.

Two weeks had changed everything. Two weeks ago he had told her they needed to stop seeing one another, that the magic she had worked on him months before, holding him after his seizure, was for naught. He had been at the bottom of his existence, unable to take the final step to create the invention that had alluded him for so long. Vortek really was an illusion. He was a fraud.

His daughter had learned of his affair and shunned him.

His son had withdrawn from him.

Even his own imagination had forsaken him.

He had never felt more alone, more unworthy of love.

But then Grace had told him that she would rather die than live without him, that she was carrying their child.

She loved him. More than life itself. And that made the difference. Her love turned a key inside him—again.

The ice began to melt. The gears of his mind began to catch.

Wheels turned. He had dreams in which whole equations worked themselves out, bringing together more and more pieces of the puzzle he was solving.

There was a knock at the door to the suite.

He walked to it, opened it.

At first she looked exhausted and worried. But her face lit up at the sight of him. "You look brand new," she said.

"I feel brand new."

She walked into the suite, turned to face him.

He shut the door, held out his journal, open to a portrait of her he had drawn out of numbers and letters and mathematical symbols.

"What's this?" she asked with a smile. She took it from him.

"Vortek," he said.

She looked up at him for an explanation.

"Whenever I ran into a roadblock, I thought of you. I pictured your face." He reached out, lightly touched her cheek. "That worked, every time. So when it came time to take the final step and write out the complete solution I decided to keep you at the very front of my mind. And all the dominos fell." He nodded at the drawing. "Straighten out the curves, separate the lines, and you have twenty-nine equations, the blueprint for flying through radar undetected—like a ghost."

"You did it," she said, with amazement.

"We did it."

"No." She shook her head.

"This was a joint venture."

She looked worried, again.

"What?" he asked. "There's nothing in our way now."

She stepped into his arms, buried her face against his neck. "I love you," she whispered. "I'm proud of you. But there shouldn't have been anything in our way to begin with."

TWENTY

Mike Coady picked Kyle Snow up at the house on Brattle Street and delivered him to Clevenger at Boston P.D. headquarters. He came voluntarily, no doubt to avoid another drug test that would have landed him in jail again for violating probation.

Clevenger and he sat across from one another, this time in the same interview room where Clevenger had met with George Reese. Coady watched from behind the one-way mirror.

"Tell me about your dad's gun," Clevenger said.

"What about it?"

Clevenger stayed silent. He noticed Kyle's pupils were pinpoints, even though the light in the room was dim. He was high, probably on Percocet or Oxycontin.

"I don't know what you're talking about," Kyle said. "I don't know anything about . . ."

"He kept it in his closet, right? On the top shelf of his shirt rack."

Kyle shrugged.

"I understand what happened, Kyle. He paid attention to you for the first time in your life, and then he pulled away, again. He reopened the wound. A very deep wound."

"Like I said before, he couldn't hurt me. I never expected anything from him."

"You don't chase opiates unless you feel raw and empty inside.

And you saw the chance to be relieved of that pain. You couldn't resist it. Not at sixteen."

Kyle flipped his black hair off his forehead, leaned toward Clevenger. "You don't know shit about me."

"So you took his gun—from the closet."

"Says who?"

"You said you gave it back to him the night before he was shot." Clevenger watched Kyle's face, saw his eyes thin, his jaw set. "But you didn't."

"My sister tell you this?"

"It doesn't matter."

Kyle looked very angry now. "What a bitch."

"Your dad's prints weren't on the gun," Clevenger said. "If you gave it back to him, and he shot himself, they would have been. Somebody wiped that gun clean. I don't see your dad doing that." He raised his voice slightly. "Why would your father wipe his own gun clean before shooting himself?"

Kyle's jaw muscles were churning.

"We've got you as the last person with your father's pistol. We've got you down the street from Mass General the morning he was shot. We know you hated him. It all adds up. That's why when I asked your mother about interviewing you, she told me no."

"I didn't murder him," Kyle said, his eyes filling up.

"No?" Clevenger pressed. "You told me you wanted him dead. You wanted to watch him killed. Now I'm supposed to believe you took the gun and didn't . . ."

"I took it so he wouldn't kill himself. But I couldn't keep it."

"Why not?"

"Because I wanted to use it."

"Help me understand this. You're all worried he might kill himself, but you can't keep the gun for fear *you'll* kill him?" Having said it, Clevenger realized it might very well be true. Kyle was simultaneously that much in need of his father and that enraged at him. But he pressed ahead, feeling the truth was about to surface. "No," he said. "You wanted to use and you did use it. You killed him. You killed your father."

"No," Kyle shouted. Tears began streaming down his face. "I wanted to, so I gave it away."

"You gave it away," Clevenger repeated, feigning anger. "What did you do, just walk down to Harvard Square and hand it off to some undergrad? Who the hell would take it from you?"

"Collin," he blurted out. He covered his face with his hands. "I gave it to Collin."

"You gave it to Collin." He paused. "Why?" he asked quietly. "Why Collin?"

"I don't know." Kyle was heaving with sobs now. "Why can't you just leave us alone? Just leave us alone."

Clevenger nodded. He stared at Kyle as he wept, his face shielded from view, his plea still echoing in Clevenger's mind. *Why can't you just leave us alone? Us.* And everything became clear. That's how the truth breaks sometimes. Like a submarine surfacing, or a missile appearing on a radar screen. The roots of destruction, the method to a particular madness, emerging into the light, of a sudden. "I understand," he said.

"You believe him?" Coady asked as Clevenger walked into the observation room.

He glanced through the one-way at Kyle. "I don't think he's our shooter."

"I don't get that off him, either. Which brings us right back to Coroway. If Kyle's willing to testify, and if he's credible to a jury, we've got Coroway at Mass General, with John Snow's gun. We've got motive: Coroway's suddenly got carte blanche to market

Vortek and take Snow-Coroway public—which Snow would have resisted. He happens to register Vortek with the Patent Office one day after Snow is shot. The only thing we don't have is an eyewitness. We can't put him in that alleyway. I checked Snow's cell phone records. He didn't take any call from Coroway the morning he was killed. And there's another problem: We have no motive for Coroway killing Grace Baxter."

"Let's bring him in anyway," Clevenger said.

"You think you can get a confession?"

"I think I can get what we need."

Coady looked at him askance.

Clevenger looked through the one-way, again. "I've got a hunch I'd like to play. But I need everybody in one room. The Snows, Coroway, Reese—and Jet Heller."

"Listen. I pick up Reese, Jack LeGrand comes with him. Realistically, Reese isn't saying a thing with his attorney by his side. And we're already on thin ice with the Commissioner."

"He said plenty last time. LeGrand was there then, too."

"I'm telling you: This is gonna be your last shot at him. You sure you want to take it now?"

"I'm sure."

"What are you planning? A little group therapy?"

"Exactly. And you'll be able to watch the whole thing through the one-way mirror."

Coady didn't respond right away. "This better be good," he said, finally.

Clevenger was at his desk in his office, rereading his copy of Snow's journal, waiting for Billy to come by after boxing practice. He had decided to invite him to watch the interrogation, to finally take him fully into his confidence.

The phone rang. He picked it up.

"I've got North for you," Kim Moffett said.

"Put him through." He waited a second. "What's up?"

"I'm not sure what to make of it," Anderson said, "but we've got a very large, very peculiar transaction in George Reese's money market account about two weeks ago. And it isn't a deposit that would square with him getting his investment in Vortek back. It's a wire out of his account."

"How much?"

"Five million dollars."

"To who?"

"Grace Baxter."

Clevenger literally shivered. He closed his eyes, pictured Baxter tugging at her diamond bracelets. Her handcuffs. *I'm a bad person. A horrible, horrible person.*

"What do you think?" Anderson asked. "Some sort of settlement, in advance of splitting?"

Clevenger opened his eyes. He felt a great weight of sadness in his gut—for Baxter, for Snow, for the countless others who try to break free of what they are, only to find themselves sinking into the quicksand of the lives they so desperately want to leave behind. "Every piece of the puzzle fits now," he told Anderson.

TWENTY-ONE

George Reese, Attorney Jack LeGrand, Theresa, Lindsey and Kyle Snow, Collin Coroway, and Jet Heller sat around the long table in the interview room.

Clevenger, North Anderson, Mike Coady, and Billy Bishop watched them from the observation room.

No one in the interview room would look at anyone else for the first minute or so. Kyle finally snuck a glance at Coroway, who nodded toward him in a fatherly way that turned Clevenger's stomach.

LeGrand looked at his watch.

Heller, his eyes bloodshot, his long hair wild, stared down at the table.

Theresa Snow brushed Lindsey's hair out of her face.

Reese and Coroway made eye contact, held it a few moments.

Clevenger watched Billy checking out the scene through the one-way mirror. And rather than feeling self-conscious about him invading his space, rather than worrying that exposing him to crime would turn him into a criminal, he simply felt grateful Billy was there—that he *wanted* to be there.

"All set?" Coady asked Clevenger.

He'd told Coady his plan. "All set," Clevenger said.

"Good luck," Coady said. "If this works, it's one for the record books."

Clevenger left the observation room, walked into the interview room. He took a seat at the head of the table, opposite George Reese and Jack LeGrand. Collin Coroway sat on one side, next to Jet Heller. The Snow family was seated across from them.

Clevenger looked around the table. "Anyone care to start?" he asked.

Silence. A few glances exchanged. Lindsey staring at him.

Reese shifted in his seat.

"I don't know what kind of game you're playing, Doctor," LeGrand said. "But if you have no specific questions, my client would like to get back to work at the bank."

"The bank," Clevenger said. "That's as good a place to start as any." He looked at Coroway. "Mr. Reese and the Beacon Street Bank invested in Snow-Coroway Engineering. Is that right?"

"That's right," Coroway said, without emotion.

"A substantial investment," Clevenger said, looking at Reese. "Is that correct?"

Reese didn't respond.

"Twenty-five million dollars," Clevenger said. "And the Beacon Street Bank isn't exactly built on granite. You're swimming against a tide of delinquent loans. A twenty-five-million-dollar loss could land you in bankruptcy court."

"My client doesn't run a public company," LeGrand said. "His assets are his own affair. And I'd ask you to refrain from implying his business is insolvent."

"I apologize," Clevenger said. He turned to Theresa Snow. "Your husband was very close to coming up with an invention that would have solved Mr. Reese's financial problems many times over," he said. "Not to mention making Mr. Coroway here even richer than he was. Far richer. But then everything went wrong. There was something in your husband's way. Call it a mental block. And when he tried to push through it . . . Well, we all know," Clevenger continued, looking around the table, "that John Snow had a seizure disorder. Too much stress, a problem he couldn't solve, and his mind would short-circuit. Now, maybe those seizures were real, maybe they weren't. But they plagued him. We know that much for sure. And that's one of the reasons he was going forward with neurosurgery. He was tired of his limitations." He focused on Theresa Snow, again. "You knew that."

She barely nodded.

"You all knew that," Clevenger said, scanning the group. He let his gaze linger a few seconds on Heller, to make sure he was holding together. "So the question was how to help John Snow clear that final creative hurdle. How do you inspire a genius whose brain—or mind—can't go the last mile?" He shrugged. "Anyone want to take a shot?" He waited. No takers. "Well . . ." He looked down the table at George Reese. "What if he were to fall in love?"

Reese turned slightly in his seat, averted his gaze.

Jack LeGrand seemed to be wondering why Reese looked so uncomfortable.

"It goes something like this," Clevenger said, keeping his eyes on Reese. "Your wife comes home one day and tells you she's made a nice sale at her art gallery. Two hundred thousand dollars. A single painting. And it happens to be a painting of her." He paused, glanced at Theresa Snow, who looked away. "She's proud of herself," Clevenger continued, "because she knows things have been pretty bleak, financially. What she's always cared about—which happens to be money—is running out."

"According to you," LeGrand said.

Clevenger didn't break stride. "So you inquire, Mr. Reese, as any husband would, who the buyer is. After all, someone must be very taken with your wife."

Reese looked up at him.

"And she tells you the man's name is John Snow," Clevenger

went on. "He's an aeronautical engineer, owns his own company. Very, very smart, but, socially, rather inept. Odd. He seems captivated by her—almost bewitched. She feels like she could sell him anything. She finds it almost funny. And the wheels in your mind start turning." He looked into Reese's eyes. "Want to take it from there?"

"Screw yourself," Reese said.

Clevenger saw Coroway raise his fingers off the table, signaling Reese to stay in control. He looked over at him. "Mr. Reese has a front-row seat to John Snow falling for his wife, because Snow has the bad habit of confiding in his business partner. And you had never seen him so energized, Mr. Coroway—from the very first day he met Grace Baxter. You'd never seen him so alive." He paused. "So you and Mr. Reese came up with a little plan. Why not let Grace Baxter be John Snow's muse? If he's already got the information you need, maybe he'll divulge it to her. If he's really blocked, maybe she can motivate him to go the final mile, make that last creative leap. After all, he wouldn't be the first great artist or intellect inspired by a beautiful woman." Clevenger shrugged, looked back at Reese. "He's already half in love with her. And it's not like she's gonna fall in love with him herself. The man can hardly dress himself."

Clevenger thought of Billy in the observation room, primed for what he was about to see and hear. He worked to keep himself focused on the group at the table. "No one, in fact, would ever think of Grace Baxter and John Snow getting together for real." He turned to Theresa Snow. "Certainly not you. That's why you didn't object to the scheme when Collin Coroway let you in on it. You knew your husband's passion was limited to his science. He was hardly a romantic, hardly about to steal away a glamorous young woman from her multimillionaire husband. So when he hung a portrait of Grace in your home, you kept your eye on the prize. On the invention—and the money that would come from Snow-Coroway Engineering going public. You did what you felt you had to do to get him through that mental block. If his muse needed a little wall space over your mantel, so be it."

Lindsey Snow looked at her mother in horror. "You knew? From the beginning?"

Her mother didn't answer her.

Clevenger waited several seconds. "Of course she knew," he said.

Theresa Snow's face hardened into something very ugly, her eyes steely, her teeth slightly bared. For the first time she looked like what she was—a woman thrice scorned, first by her husband's love of inventing, then by his adoration of his daughter, then by his passion for another woman.

Clevenger turned to Coroway. "And you knew something else about John Snow. Because he told you that, too. You knew chances were he would be a very different man after his surgery, that he was starting over. A blank slate."

"I don't need to sit here and listen to this nonsense," Coroway said.

"You do," Clevenger said. "You do because Theresa isn't going to be charged with anything. She knew Grace Baxter was seducing her husband. She knew the whole thing was staged. But that's not a crime. You're the one who shot him."

Heller sat up, glared at Coroway. "You fucking, sonofa- . . ."

Clevenger put a hand on Heller's arm.

Coroway stayed silent.

"See, everyone here may be guilty of something, Collin, but you go to jail alone. Because you acted alone."

"I gave him the gun," Kyle Snow said, his voice shaky.

Clevenger looked at him, then looked back at Coroway. "Kyle

293

gave you his father's gun. And he feels very guilty about that. Because deep down he knew exactly what you would do with it. He had been thinking very seriously of doing it himself."

Coroway glanced at Kyle.

"Killers know one another," Clevenger said to Coroway. "You took the bait. He used you."

"You could never prove any of this," Coroway said.

"We can and we will," Clevenger said.

"I don't see any legal peril for my client," Jack LeGrand said, a hint of anxiety in his voice. "We'll be on our way, if that's all right with you."

"I'd wait on that," Clevenger said. He pointed at Lindsey and Kyle. "See, these kids had been through a great deal with their dad. And they weren't about to lose him to Grace Baxter. So Lindsey had her brother deliver Baxter's suicide note to the Beacon Street Bank—to make Mr. Reese read how his wife didn't want to live without her lover, John Snow. They figured that would end the affair." He looked straight at Reese. "That would be the note you put at the bedside after you killed your wife. You took the bait, too."

"We're done," LeGrand said, standing.

Reese stayed put. Deep down, everyone wants the truth.

LeGrand slowly took his seat again.

"See, the plan had worked well," Clevenger went on. "John Snow met Grace Baxter again and again in a suite at the Four Seasons Hotel. You learned quickly that Snow wasn't holding out on you. He really couldn't come up with the final solution to Vortek. But Grace brought him energy he never knew he had. And his mind literally used that energy to break through the creative barrier that had kept Vortek from becoming a reality. He used it to go further intellectually than he had ever gone. He blew right past his seizure threshold. Because she held him steady. She was so entwined with his intellect and intuition that when he finally solved the problem he had wrestled with for so long, he wrote out the solution as a portrait of her in his journal. He actually drew her hair and her eyes, her nose, her lips out of a collage of numbers and mathematical symbols—equations that added up to the invention that had eluded him for so long."

"I'm not aware the journal is in evidence any longer," LeGrand said.

"I happen to have a photocopy my son made before the FBI intervened," Clevenger said. "It's in evidence. So is the record of Mr. Reese transferring five million dollars to his wife's account to pay her for seducing John Snow. She got the money the day after Vortek was patented."

"Very interesting," LeGrand said. "But all your theory really proves is that my client and his wife were completely committed to one another. She would do anything for him, and vice versa. The only one with a real motive to kill Grace is Mrs. Snow, John's wife. She's the only one he betrayed."

Theresa Snow didn't respond.

"That might be true if the scheme had worked about as well as your client thought it would," Clevenger said. "But it worked a little too well. Not only did John Snow fall in love with Grace Baxter. She fell in love with him. She was pregnant with his child. And she wanted to have that child."

Lindsey Snow winced.

Theresa Snow literally turned away.

Reese jumped to his feet. "That's a lie!"

LeGrand grabbed him, pulled him back into his seat.

Clevenger watched Reese trying to control himself. "The trouble was that no one, including you, Mr. Reese, had taken into account the fact that John Snow was a remarkable individual. He wasn't a fashion plate. He was no athlete. He would be lost at the fancy parties you throw. But his mind was a miraculous thing. He was a genius. An inventor. His imagination was so powerful his brain could hardly contain it. And that was very seductive to your wife. Because, in truth, money never satisfied her. It held the best parts of her hostage. She ran much deeper than you knew. Deeper than she knew. Even you delivering the five million you had promised her didn't make her forget John Snow." He watched that fact burrow its way into Reese's psyche. "You came home when your wife didn't show up for that cocktail party at the bank," he said. "You had already read the terrible truth in her suicide note. She loved Snow. She didn't want to live without him. And when you found her on the bed with her wrists cut that evening, one day after he was shot, you couldn't take it, anymore. She wasn't going to die from those wounds. You knew that. She'd played at suicide before. But there was a difference this time. This time, you had really lost her—to another man. A dead man. So you picked up the carpet knife and you cut her throat."

"You better have evidence to back up . . ." LeGrand started.

"Her wounds were made by two different blades," Clevenger interrupted. "The carpet knife your client used to sever his wife's carotids, and something finer, like a razor blade, that she used to lacerate her own wrists."

LeGrand lost his game face.

"The police never found any bloodied razor blade. That's because Mr. Reese got rid of it before they arrived." He paused. "It all makes perfect sense to me. And it will to a jury."

"He killed both of them," Coroway blurted out, pointing at Reese. "Kyle delivered Grace's suicide note and John's gun to the same person. George Reese. He killed John. And then he killed his own wife. Because they fell in love when they weren't supposed to. I didn't do anything more than Theresa did. I just helped keep the fantasy alive between them. I'm not guilty of any crime."

Clevenger looked at him. He shook his head. "You're the keystone in this arch. Because once you'd gotten what you wanted from your partner—Vortek—you told him the truth. You told him he'd been set up. He'd fallen in love with an actress. Because underneath it all, you hated him, Collin. You hated his intellect. You hated the fact that he was a genius and you kept the books. And to think he would end up with Grace Baxter on top of it all? No. You couldn't stand that. You told him what he thought was love was just a ruse. You destroyed him. And that's when he said good-bye. That's when he told you he was leaving everyone, that his surgery would do more than stop his seizures. It would take away all his pain. Because he wouldn't remember any of you."

Heller was gripping the side of the table, his knuckles white.

"I don't know what you're talking about," Coroway said.

"You couldn't very well have a man with John Snow's knowledge of weapons systems floating free in the world. He might share your trade secrets. He might start his own company, put you right out of business. It all came down to the money. So you went to Mass General that morning and arranged to meet him in that alleyway," Clevenger went on. "You shot him point-blank in the heart. You killed him before he ever got his chance to be reborn."

Heller flew out of his seat, rushed Coroway and threw him up against the wall. He started to strangle him.

Lindsey Snow screamed.

"Who were you to take my patient from me?" Heller shouted. "Are you God?"

Clevenger and Kyle Snow rushed over, tried to pull Heller away.

Heller's hands only tightened around Coroway's neck. "We were about to make history," he seethed.

The door to the room swung open.

Out of the corner of his eye, Clevenger saw Mike Coady and Billy step into the doorway. Coady's gun was drawn.

"Doctor Heller," Billy said. "Don't."

Heller glanced at him, then at his own hands.

"Please," Billy said.

Heller slowly let go.

Coroway fell to the ground, gasping for air.

Coady lowered his gun. "I happen to have two sets of cuffs with me," he said, looking over at George Reese, and holding them up. "No diamonds on either one of 'em. You'll just have to make do."

TWENTY-TWO

Theresa Snow walked into Clevenger's office at Boston Forensics a little over an hour later. Clevenger had reached her just as she got home, told her he needed to meet with her right away.

He pulled a chair closer to his desk, motioned for her to take it. He sat in his desk chair.

"What is it you'd like to talk about?" she asked.

"The truth."

She met his gaze, held it. "The truth about what?"

"About John."

"Tell me what you mean."

"I know what really happened, Theresa. And I know why." He looked away. "I'm not proud of what I did in that interview room. But I would do it again."

She stayed silent.

He looked back at her, lowered his voice. "I know why you killed John. And I don't blame you for it."

"You're insane," she said, tentatively.

"Your mind was in love with John's mind. But the rest of you was dead all the years you were married to him."

No response.

"You stood by him when anyone else would have left. You stayed even though he was cruel to your son. You stayed while he

299

lavished all his affection on your daughter. You put yourself last. Him, first. Because he was extraordinary."

"Marriages are about different things," she said. "Ours was about John's work."

"Which is why you went along with Coroway and Reese. You let them stage a romance for John. Because you knew how badly John suffered when he was blocked, when he couldn't invent. Vortek was torturing him. And then he stumbled on someone who gave him a new kind of energy, energy the two of you never had together, energy that had the potential to jump-start his creativity. So you sacrificed your feelings—again. For him."

"She wasn't supposed to actually . . . You know."

"Sleep with him."

She looked wounded by those words. "She was supposed to tell him how much she cared for him, but that she needed to figure out her own marriage first. She was supposed to channel his energy back into his work."

"Until he was finished with Vortek. Then it would be over between them."

She nodded.

"But it wasn't over. Not for her. Not for him. All those years you stood by him, all Kyle's suffering, didn't seem to count for anything. John didn't want to live without Grace Baxter any more than she wanted to live without him. So you—not Collin—told John that Grace had been put up to seducing him. You shattered his belief in her. And that's when he told you he was leaving—everyone. He told you the surgery would make you and him strangers."

"He wouldn't even remember what he had done to me."

"You wouldn't exist for him," Clevenger said. "He was the one threatening you with annihilation. No one could expect you to let that happen." He slid his hand a few inches toward her.

She gazed longingly at it.

Clevenger saw the hunger in her eyes, hunger for the kind of connection her husband had found with another woman. "There's a reason nothing turned out the way Coroway and Reese told you it would," he said. "Sometimes when people meet, they feel something they've never felt before. It's a lock and key fit. An old professor of mine used to say it was like finding your *lovemap*. Grace Baxter was John's. And vice versa."

"Will I ever . . . ?" She looked into his eyes.

"Tell me how it felt," Clevenger said.

"What?"

"Shooting him."

She hesitated.

"You can tell me anything. It's over now. Reese will be convicted of Grace's murder. Coroway will be convicted of John's." He paused. "Did it feel good?"

She closed her eyes, opened them, like a cat. "I felt like a person for the first time."

"For once, you put your feelings before his."

"I honestly didn't think I could pull the trigger. But then he had the gall to tell me to get over the past, to reinvent myself. After I had given him my whole life." She moved her hand so that it was nearly touching Clevenger's. "The strange thing is that, by shooting him, I think I did reinvent myself. I think I changed the whole architecture of my life."

"Do you think that's why Kyle gave you John's gun? So you could escape?"

"We both needed to."

Clevenger took a deep breath, shook his head. "Coroway gets life in prison. I don't know if he deserves that."

"Collin, George and I all knew we were playing with fire," Theresa said. "Any of us could have been burned at any time."

"That's true," Clevenger said. "You just never know when or how it's gonna happen." He swiveled his chair toward the large, ornately framed mirror that hung on the opposite wall.

Theresa turned and looked into the mirror, too. She smiled at their reflection.

Clevenger reached back to a button built into the underside of his desk.

Their reflection gradually receded as the lights in the office dimmed, turning the mirror transparent, revealing Collin Coroway, Mike Coady, Billy Bishop and Jet Heller standing behind it.

"Frank?" Theresa asked, confused and panicked.

"Forgive me for staging another drama at your expense."

"No one can testify to anything I told you," she protested. "You're a psychiatrist. This is your office."

"But I'm not your psychiatrist. And this isn't therapy. It's a murder investigation."

Her eyes filled up. "Was it Kyle? Did he tell you?"

"He would never betray you. You were all he had all those years," Clevenger said. "It just didn't make sense to me that he would give John's gun to Collin. Your son is much too perceptive for that. He wanted your husband dead. Collin's only real motive for murder would be money, and he was worth a fortune, already. But, you—you would kill out of passion, out of jealousy, out of rage. You would kill for the same reasons as George Reese killed Grace. Because you couldn't stand the thought of your partner being reborn. Not when you had lived so long in a marriage that was dead."

The door to the office opened. Coady walked in, cuffs in hand.

"I thought you understood me," Theresa said, sounding exquisitely vulnerable. "I thought . . . You don't feel anything for me?"

"I do," Clevenger said. "I feel badly we didn't actually meet as doctor and patient, before any of this ever happened. Maybe then you would have had a chance at real freedom, instead of life behind bars."

Billy Bishop sat on the window seat, catty-corner to Clevenger's desk. He had known in advance how the drama would unfold at Boston Police Headquarters.

"So who do you think blew up your truck?" he asked Clevenger.

"Ten-to-one, Kyle Snow," Clevenger said. "He had motive. He knows a little bit about explosives. But I can't prove it."

"That's the way I figure it, too," Billy said. "He helped get Grace Baxter and his father killed—and he nearly killed you. All because he hates himself. I can see it in his eyes. He's gonna need more Oxycontin than ever."

"You're getting good at this."

"Dr. Heller was pretty convincing in there. He can act."

"He has no plans to quit his day job. He told me he's taking a week off, then he's got a very big case scheduled. Another little girl—this one with a tumor."

Billy winced. "You think he'll be steady enough?"

"He'll pull himself together," Clevenger said. "John Snow's case is closed, partly due to him—and you."

Billy looked like he had something important to say that he couldn't quite put into words.

"I'm sure you could scrub in with him, if you want," Clevenger said. "He loves having you in the O.R. I certainly don't mind."

"I wasn't thinking about Dr. Heller."

Clevenger waited.

"I talked to Casey about the baby," Billy said. "Late last night."

Talk about no transition. Clevenger wanted to help him keep perspective. "Like I told you, it's still too early to know whether she's really going to want to have it," he said.

"I know that," Billy said. "But I told her it was all right if she did."

Clevenger couldn't think of any quick response.

"I mean, it's a person, right?" Billy went on. "Or it has the potential to be. So if she loves it already, I'm not gonna be the one to force her to do something she doesn't want to, something she might regret the rest of her life."

That sounded admirable. It also sounded like the first step on a very long, very tough road. "Sounds like you love this girl," Clevenger said.

Billy actually blushed, looked at his feet a second, then back at Clevenger. "Did you call Whitney?"

"Not yet."

Billy nodded. "I'll see you at the loft." He stood up.

Clevenger stood up, too.

They hugged, holding on a few seconds longer than the mannish touch-and-go that was their habit.

Billy left.

Clevenger sat back down. He stared at the phone ten, fifteen seconds before picking up the receiver. He dialed Whitney McCormick in D.C. And he listened to her phone ring once, twice, three times.

"Hello?" she answered.

"It's Frank."

Silence.

He looked out his window at Chelsea Harbor, deep blue and frothy from a steady winter wind. "I don't want to let it—to let us—end." He could hear her breathing, but she didn't answer him. "I think we should try to spend more time together, not less. Because when you meet someone who makes you feel like you could be more than what you are, it's a rare thing. I really believe that now. It's one-in-a-million. And I think we have that." Still no response. He sighed. "Or we did."

"We do," she said.

Clevenger closed his eyes. "I want to see you."

"Give me a little while?"

"Of course I will." He opened his eyes.

"And I think we better try The Ritz," she said. "Start our own tradition."